In the Absence of Iles

IN THE ABSENCE
OF ILES

Bill James

London

Constable & Robinson Ltd
3 The Lanchesters
162 Fulham Palace Road
London W6 9ER
www.constablerobinson.com

First published in the UK by Constable,
an imprint of Constable & Robinson 2008

A copy of the British Library Cataloguing in Publication
Data is available from the British Library.

UK ISBN: 978-1-84529-705-3

Printed and bound in the EU

PEFC

PEFC/16-33-111
CATG-PEFC-052
www.pefc.org

Chapter One

Yes, on the whole she liked it best when conferences took place at one of these long-windowed, narrow-gabled, stone-built, converted Victorian country mansions in fine grounds. Well, think of the alternative: some state-of-the-art urban cop shop – the kind she spent most of her life in – all glare-lit corridors and phoney wood doors, except for the cell block. The theme of the conference frightened her. Anything to do with running undercover police operations frightened Esther. The sedate setting might solace her a little. Might. A little.

Most of the renovated old properties were reached along artfully curving drives, tarmacked or gravelled, so the building could not be seen from the gates because of good tree clumps, mostly conifer, oak, larch. The houses had a separateness, had been built purposely to get separateness. Esther fancied a bit of separateness, more or less always did, but rarely got much of it, what with the Assistant Chief job, and Gerald. Of course, there'd been a time when she'd delighted in togetherness with Gerald. She had no trouble remembering those days and nights, but they couldn't be brought back, although she had tried for a while, and might have another go if things ever got to look more promising. Despite the violence, he definitely still had some good aspects. She worked at encouraging these and never treated Gerald as having become totally fatuous or irrecoverably on the skids.

For now, anyway, she could enjoy the sight and setting of Fieldfare House, this secluded, gracious, secretive rendezvous. About a hundred and fifty years ago, the first, jumped-up creators of estates like this financed the land purchase and construction with magnificent profits from their new factories in hurriedly industrialized towns; or from their coal mines; or from laying railways. They wanted distance between these work sites and their homes, so they could flit from the innovative, cash-flow ugliness to somewhere green and tranquil and private and, of course, with status: the big, solid residences in landscaped, parkland acreage had been pretentious boltholes. A successful labour master would look out on lawns and minor lakes and rhododendron clumps and stables and a paddock, perhaps even on deer, not on the splendid, unsightly enterprises that bought them. Where there was muck there was brass, yes, but the brass would buy a spread where he could forget the muck at weekends. He'd hope, and might believe, his family would be here for centuries, or for ever, the same as dukes at Chatsworth and popes at Rome.

As a matter of fact, no such luck. But Esther Davidson, turning up today at Fieldfare, could sense and enjoy for a moment that former sureness and optimism, and the comfy impression of being apart from the routine tangles of existence. Naturally, she knew the feeling was irrelevant and stupid, brought on only by a classy setting. The feeling came just the same, though, and lingered briefly. And, in the circumstances, there was a bit to be said for this boost to her morale, never mind how temporary and false. What circumstances? Well, during the next three days, Assistant Chief Constable Davidson would be involved in life-and-death presentations and discussions of what an agenda sheet called 'The Efficient and Secure Management of Out-located Personnel'. In the cause of security, that slab of jargon was very deliberately a slab of jargon, and very deliberately unintelligible.

Decoded, it said: How to place an undercover detective in a targeted gang, cell, clan, crew and make certain (by – see above – due Management) he/she (a) comes up with enough stuff usable at trial to convict on (i.e. – see above – is Efficient) ; and, above all, (b) stays undiscovered, untortured, and unsunk in a concrete bodysock (i.e. – see above – is Secure).

'Out-located' meant one very precise thing, and, also, its very precise opposite. True, the officer would be Out-located from family, from normal duties, from usual colleagues and, crucially, from standard life-lines and protective back-up. But this was in order that he/she could penetrate a crooked team – could, in fact, be deeply and secretly *In*-located: that is, become part of, or seem to, the targeted gang, cell, clan, crew. It would usually be a gang, cell, clan, crew, that had shown itself unbeatable, unsmashable, unjailable, over at least months, and more likely years, by any other police method. Standard investigative ploys will have done nothing. Because of the hellish, continuous perils, you tried every alternative before deciding to install a spy. And if you got that far you prayed the secrecy would last, and had a unit ready to go in and recover the officer in time, if it didn't. Or *try* to recover the officer in time. Esther knew that very soon she might have to smuggle one of her people into the biggest, most savage, enduring, prospering and expanding criminal firm back on her own ground. She hated the notion, but maybe at Fieldfare she'd learn something handy and extra and reassuring, to go with what she'd learned already from other undercover gambles.

The original got-rich-quick occupant of Fieldfare House could never have visualized what actually would happen to his grand, deserved, dignified property. So, what did? Time happened. It wasn't unique. Those who came after the mighty industrialist would eventually, or sooner, have found the place too costly to run and maintain. They'd begin to think about the comforts of suburbia, and soon the removal vans would roll. Servants for a place like this, and central heating and damp courses and tonnes of re-roofing slates, could grow unacceptably expensive. The Home Office – the *Home* Office – intelligently interested itself in such homes or ex-homes and bought Fieldfare and its surrounds at not much above peanuts. Then, after thorough repairs and decent refurbishment, turned it into a venue for the kind of sometimes dark, sometimes unnerving get-togethers Esther and colleagues from the Association of Chief Police Officers nationwide had been invited to now.

Chapter Two

Thursday 22nd June 2006, 1400 hours, Simpkins Suite
Out-Located Operations: Two Personal Narratives
Officer A: 1400–1500 hours
1500–1530 hours, Questions
Officer B: 1530–1630 hours
1630–1700 hours, Questions

Esther tried to recall from school history lessons whether any of the great Industrial Revolution contractors had been called Simpkins; possibly not quite as renowned as Watt or Arkwright, but important. To christen one of the rooms after Fieldfare's original owner would be a nod to scholarship which might appeal to some knowledgeable Home Office dignitary, and there were a few of those. Did Alfred or Samuel or Bertram Simpkins invent an early version of the fork-lift truck? Should she have heard of 'The Simpkins Hercules Hoist'?

There were civilian staff at Fieldfare, of course, all excluded from the Simpkins Suite and other Suites while sessions about Out-location took place. Just the same, there might be leaks. And so, the two featured officers who had been undercover, and who might go undercover again, appeared merely as A and B when they gave their 'personal narratives': that is, described and analysed their Out-located experiences for this gathering of brass; no names and no indication of which part of the country they worked in. A and B's ranks, as well as their names, remained undisclosed. But, almost certainly, they'd be detective

9

constables only, or, at the highest, detective sergeants. Years ago, as a detective constable, Esther herself did some Out-location, slangily known then, though, simply as 'leeching'.

She wondered whether A and B found it daunting to take the platform and instruct a roomful of Association of Chief Police Officer members. But was that crazy? After all, A and B had lived for weeks, even months, in situations needing a stack more bravery than confronting an ACPO collection. Nobody at Fieldfare would put a knife to their throats, a daily and nightly chance for Out-located detectives. Esther had never known more fear than when undercover.

Officer A: Meet Mr Adjustable

He'd be about twenty-eight or -nine and before saying anything catwalked back and forth like a model on the small, temporary platform at the end of the room. Occasionally, he pirouetted, so they could take in the all-round glory of his three-piece, double-breasted, grey suit, which was all-round glorious. Unquestionably, it had been custom-made. The cloth held to his shoulders in the affec-tionate, unruffled, congratulatory way a midwife might present a just-born baby to its mother. The lapels were mid-width and timeless, no ludicrously sharp, wool spear points at the top. Not much of the waistcoat showed under his buttoned-up jacket, but Esther could tell it fitted right, and the pockets contained nothing bulky to destroy the general line. His striped blue, white and aubergine silk tie had impact without luridness. She thought A's black lace-up shoes would be from Fellowes, or Mason and Caltrop, and possibly also custom-made. He'd had his hair done in a moderately up-tuft style, but, again, nothing coarse, nothing farcical. You could see men with haircuts like this presenting unextreme television programmes or running charity shops.

He came to the edge of the platform and gazed at them: 'You might have to shell out on this kind of tailoring and so on,' he said. 'It's all paid for by the police. I've got three outfits of similar quality, two K a throw, and a stack more shoes. Upper grade villains dress upper grade. And conventional. You've got to match it on your boy – on your girl, too, if you decide to pick female, though gangs tend to be male and sexist, and the rules for what women wear are different.' Esther couldn't pinpoint any accent. He grinned. 'So, you have to wonder, could you afford me?'

He assumed instant charge of the Simpkins Suite. A Simpkins descendant couldn't have been more at home. For God's sake, Esther had madly imagined he might be nervy and hesitant in front of them! She realized he reminded her of someone, not the actual looks but his radiant cockiness. In a moment, she pinpointed who: Joel Grey, as the singer and club master of ceremonies, in that Liza Minnelli film, *Cabaret*, on DVD. She saw the same mixture of lavish insolence and impishness in Officer A. His voice, the glare of his eyes and the aggressive, challenging tilt of his modish head said he didn't recognize much of any real worth in this puffed-up audience and thought they might as well push off right away, back to their snug, well-pensioned, desk-bound sinecures. *He* had lived in, survived in, a rough, non-stop dangerous scene, and might have to again. They needn't expect any kowtowing from him. He couldn't know that Esther, and perhaps others in the room, had also entered that dangerous scene in the past. He shot the cuffs of his stupendously white shirt. Gold links flashed, like 'Fuck the lot of you' in Morse.

But then he turned his back for a moment and when he slowly spun and faced them once more seemed suddenly . . . seemed suddenly what she'd originally expected: nervy and hesitant. In small, arse-licking, sing-song tones he said: 'Ladies, gentlemen, this is a privilege and an important responsibility to address so many chief officers.' His body signalled prodigious cringe now. The suit had somehow abruptly lost its oomph and might have been an entirely

11

ordinary, reach-me-down, sixty-quid job. You could suspect him of having pinched at least the cuff-links, and possibly the shoes. 'I speak for my colleague, B, and myself,' he went on, 'in saying that we are, indeed, surpassingly grateful for the interest shown in our work by high representatives from so many British police forces. I – we – are honoured by such interest, which will encourage, nay, inspire us, when next we are required to take on infiltration assignments. It is especially appropriate that this valuable endorsement of our special duties should occur in the magnificent Simpkins Suite of the renowned Fieldfare House, a symbol of success in another era through boldness, vision and effort. These are characteristics which B and myself will seek to emulate, in this twenty-first century, deeply heartened by your presence here today.'

He smiled a minion's greasy smile, and passed the tip of his tongue gingerly along his upper lip, like playing the word 'lickspittle' in Charades. Now, when he flashed his cuffs and the links, the gesture seemed pathetically boastful – a desperate ploy by someone frantically struggling to come over as significant.

Esther realized they were watching a performer who could have made it big in the theatre. He did roles, inhabited them instantly, no matter how different from one another. During her days at Fieldfare, Esther would several times run across the word 'protean', meaning able to change appearance and character at will. And A seemed to have decided to give a demonstration of this flair, or had been instructed to, so Esther and the rest of the audience would know the kind of talents they must demand in their undercover people. Next for A, King Lear. Or Bottom. Just tell him what you wanted. He brought out crummy words like 'nay' and 'indeed' without a tremor. He was made for Out-location, In-location. That is if, as well as his acting range, he knew what to look for, and remembered it, and brought it back in a form fit to prop a prosecution.

He might never appear on the witness stand himself, or that could be the end of him in secret operations. Might be the end of him altogether: relatives and friends of those he helped send down would want a reckoning if they saw plainly and painfully at trial how they'd been gulled. But A, and those in his game, must be able to guide and brief and cue the colleagues who *could* do the arrests and give the evidence in court. He, personally, would stay out of sight, watching his back, counting his suits, cooking up insults and smarm for his next appearance at Fieldfare.

Judges sometimes turned nosy and obstructive in cases based on undercover evidence. Of course, judges would never be *told* the prosecution rested on undercover evidence. Those words – 'undercover', 'Out-located' – had to be kept from the wise; the allegedly wise. But some of them tactlessly sensed or sniffed out gaps in material as it came before the jury. A detective in the box might say that, 'acting on information received', he turned up at the right place and at the right time to witness the accused doing what he was accused of, and to arrest him. 'On information received from where and how?' some intellectually unkempt judge might ask. Because the source had to stay confidential, no proper answer could be given, and there were judges who regarded this as either an affront to themselves and therefore to the whole edifice of British justice, and/or cool defiance of themselves and therefore of the whole edifice of British justice. They regarded spying as a sneaky, obnoxious trade, unless done years ago by Alec Guinness in *Smiley's People* on BBC television. The prosecution case might get thrown out. Undercover people accepted this as customary, high-minded, wig-powered, Inns of Court absolutism and idiocy, and waited for the next casting, or promotion into Traffic.

Subsequently today, Officer A turned philosopher and theologian for a while. For this, he put a real whack of solemnity into his voice and manner. 'Think the movie, *Reservoir Dogs*,' he said. 'Think ethics, think acute and inevitable spiritual confusion. Consider how your man or woman undercover must in the interests of his/her disguise temporarily become a villain, going enthusiastically along with all kinds of gang crimes, including possible murders. Will that be acceptable to you? If not, perhaps you should forget undercover capers. Do it some other way. For credibility, and to see offences at first hand, your planted officer might have to take part in the actual lawlessness he/she has gone undercover to expose and thwart. His/Her Honour, concerned to guard his/her honour and the court's, will possibly disapprove of such *dis*honourable behaviour, if Her/His Honour should get sight of it. He/she might find it hard to believe the supposed good end justifies the dirty means, and QCs climbed to be QCs by highlighting the dirty means so judges *did* notice them; unless the QCs were hired by the Prosecution, in which case they'd downplay the dirty means, naturally, and try to blank off the judge from them.

'And, then, yes, think *Reservoir Dogs*. You'll remember, Tim Roth, the cop spy playing gang member, "Mr Orange", has to join in the very self-same diamond robbery he has already tipped off his chiefs about, and gets fatally gut-shot by the actual ambush police answering his whisper. Could you face that kind of agonizing irony? Again I say, you possibly shouldn't mess with undercover if not, because undercover can be very messy.'

Esther chewed on that lot. Of course, she'd known already that undercover presented deeply troublesome, hellishly slippery issues of right and wrong. And, also of course, she'd heard the tale and the rumours about an Assistant Chief Constable, Desmond Iles, whose ground lay not all that far from Fieldfare. Apparently, Iles had very reluctantly authorized the placement of an undercover detective in a local criminal band.* Soon, though, this officer's real identity got known to the gang, and he was garrotted. Police arrested two men for the murder and prepared what they considered an irresistible case. The court acquitted both. But not long afterwards the pair were found dead, also garrotted. These killings remained a

* See *Halo Parade*

mystery. Some described them as 'rough justice'. But, surely, police dealt in justice as plain justice, not justice with fancy adjectives stuck on. Esther tried to believe no Assistant Chief would carry out such tit-for-tat attacks, regardless of how racked he might have felt for sending a man undercover, so causing his death. And regardless of how enraged he might reasonably have felt at the perverse failure of the court to convict. She found herself confused by the issues involved here. Did the two villains deserve what came their way, though from no court? Should a senior police officer think like that? '"Vengeance is *mine*," saith the Lord,' in the Bible, really emphasizing that 'mine'. There's no mention of Assistant Chief Constables.

She liked to think the Fieldfare sessions might bring clarity to these debates she had with herself. And maybe Officer A did offer a kind of clarity, though not a soothing kind. He slapped the problems in front of you squarely, brutally, almost insubordinately, and more or less told you to get lost if such insoluble moral conundrums deeply niggled your pious, prissy soul making you not much more use than a judge. The conundrums deeply niggled Esther's soul. She'd stay for the full Fieldfare course, though. It was such a treat to get away from Gerald and his little rages. She gathered Desmond Iles totally forbade undercover in his Force since those rough events on his patch, so he probably wouldn't be at this conference. No nominal roll of those attending had been issued, of course; further security.

Esther hoped Officer A would eventually reach something that could truly be called a personal narrative, as described in the advertisement for this session, i.e. his own story, rather than displays of disdain, tailoring, bumsucking servility, brilliant footwear and toughness. He did. Soon, he described his selection for undercover duties via psychometric assessment at another of these huge, adapted, Home Office Victorian houses, Hilston Manor. Esther had naturally heard of it and of the magic art, psychometrics – mind and brain measuring. She'd never

15

been to Hilston, though. It and psychometrics were an advance since her own undercover spells.

Now, Officer A grew very heavily technical. Jargon galloped back. Esther made some notes, though she didn't understand everything she wrote. At the Manor, he said, they used a specially adapted character test based on the findings of the famous psychologist, Carl Jung. This had been originally designed to assess the ability of candidates for high posts in business to read and interpret information, then act on it. It had an obvious bearing on undercover work. A talked of 'scale scores', and the 'high and non-negotiable requirement' to reach a good, specified level at these skills before qualifying for Out-location. He told of 'interaction complexities', 'profile dimensions' and 'fakeometers', designed to expose those who gave false answers, to conceal unsuitable personality quirks. He mentioned what was dubbed at Hilston 'the unconfined, or protean, persona', meaning, apparently, the flair of A and others at becoming something one moment, and then its opposite the moment after, and then a modification of both, or of one, or neither, as thought necessary. 'I'm sure you'll all be familiar with Proteus, that classical sea god who could switch shape whenever he fancied.'

From here he went into accounts of his own undercover work in several settings, some requiring the status suits and shoes, some less formal. All these penetrations of villain firms had clearly been deeply dangerous, several successful, a few not, though he told of each absolutely deadpan: another from his stock of ready-made, adaptable, suitable faces.

But Esther realized she had come to think of him not as a face at all, more as a suit, shoes, a stance. The impact of the suit could certainly vary, depending on his stance, and the changeability somehow made it memorable. Although his face had massive changeability, too, this didn't seem to register on Esther with the same vividness. His shoes, of course, kept their constant, gentle and gentlemanly splendour. And, yes, the suit, also, could at times look for ever

16

just right, and mutedly but undeniably superior, like something worn by Sir Cedric Hardwicke in old films. Or, because of the way A hunched up his body or sidled or twitched, it could look entirely cheap-jack cut and sewn, probably from somewhere poky abroad where the Department of Health and Safety's writ did not run, and where they'd never heard of the minimum wage; serviceable for a month or two until wear and tear set in; not quite the right size, though nearish; and very, very deniably superior. Sir Cedric would not have been seen dead in it, or even poorly.

His face, then, and physique? He was about six feet and 185 pounds, light on his feet, so necessary for the fashion pirouettes. He had full, reddish cheeks which, at some stages in his array of identities, could make him appear almost genial. His mouth seemed unusually wide and very ready to open up in a good grin of decently looked-after teeth, if the occasion could take it. Esther felt she would have trouble believing what a mouth like that said. But, then, she didn't know many people whose every word she'd take as true. Who did? After all, lying had its treasured place in serious life. She was at Fieldfare to learn lying as a supreme and useful skill, an accomplishment, a necessary weapon, a revered instrument of good.

At Fieldfare, though, she felt manipulated. Of course she did. If you came on a management course you should expect to be managed. The Fieldfare programme aimed to show how to run 'Out-located personnel'. At the same time, it had to persuade people like Esther into believing that Out-located work worked. Gravely bad tales about these operations flourished. Think of ACC Desmond Iles. Think of *Reservoir Dogs*. At Fieldfare they did not attempt to hide the dark aspects. In fact, Officer A foregrounded them. Perhaps Officer B would, too. It was Officer A who brought *Reservoir Dogs* and the undercover man's ultimately fatal wounds into the reckoning. Those organizing the Fieldfare session, and scheduling Officer A as an early speaker, must know they had an informed, worried, hard-nosed, sceptical audience who would reject any attempt to present undercover as pushover or routine. And so, Officer A with his harsh warnings and, possibly, Officer B, 1530–1630 hours, with more. The Fieldfare sessions resorted to frankness and honesty, because they couldn't get away with less.

But, massively on the positive side for those in charge of the meetings must be the fact that Esther, and the rest of the ACPO audience, had signed up and travelled to them. It proved they wanted to run Out-location schemes; had, perhaps, been forced into wanting Out-location schemes because all other ploys hopelessly nose-dived. They *needed* Out-location. And they'd opted to get along to Fieldfare and hear the latest on how to do it, jargonized or not. Esther would probably have come, even without the bonus of getting shot of Gerald for a while.

All right, Desmond Iles might have decided he did *not* need Out-location, or found its possible price too great to contemplate – too great to contemplate *again*. That could be understandable. But Esther had never suffered such a catastrophe, and she, personally, had survived a stint Out-located. She thought Officer A's warning that undercover might be too morally messy for some of his audience came over as a challenge, not really a warning at all, and probably a challenge by intent. Who at the top of a police force wanted to be labelled dainty and/or prudish? Officers of their various high ranks were accustomed to finding more or less tolerable routes through tricky problems of conscience. Not many of them would be turned off by such apparent discouragement as A offered – or pretended to offer.

His lecture had obviously been choreographed to dispel those problems eventually, anyway, or at least to counter them. This was his object in describing the harsh, sophisticated selection methods of Hilston Manor. Such skilful shaping of his talk was what made Esther feel manipulated. But perhaps manipulated in a worthwhile cause? Officer A abandoned the theorizing now and went for

18

practicalities: OK, OK, yes, he'd admit difficulties existed. So, he'd describe how to deal with them, diminish them. He stressed that only people who came certifiably through the intrusive, gruelling, psychometric tests at Hilston could be considered for undercover duties. This must cut risk. The tests would reveal hazardous, unacceptable weaknesses. And they would identify protective, inbuilt aptitudes. Watching A vary his personality, even his appearance, at the start of today's show, she decided he must have been born to spy. That was obviously the impression he wanted to get across, and had been chosen by the organizers to get across. And the fact that he appeared here at all – had survived so many of these secret intrusions – proved, didn't it, that Out-location really could be managed efficiently and securely, given correct selection? He wouldn't be the only officer with an 'unconfined, or protean, persona'.

Some formidable teasers did remain. She acknowledged this. Could it be right for any police officer, including an incognito police officer who, above all else, had to *stay* incognito – could it be right for him/her to witness serious crimes and do nothing, or even, for the sake of her/his play-acting, physically to take part in serious crimes? But this was the kind of footling, purist, unworldly objection judges might raise. Esther's main job was, in fact, to get major villains in front of a judge – purist, footling, unwordly or not, as it chanced – and then hope for the best. She found when listening to and watching Officer A, that (a) yes, she could believe undercover might help, and (b) another yes, the risk to the spy you chose to commit was possibly justified; chosen from volunteers only, of course. And if your Out-located officer did have to take part in a crime, she'd heard one could seek on his/her behalf what was lumpily termed 'participation authority' from the Crown Prosecution Service. She wondered how often the CPS said OK, though.

Chapter Three

Back on her own ground after Fieldfare, Esther found it was Officer B's talk she remembered best. That might be because B dealt *only* with the practical: no theorizing, no theology, no hearty kicking around of bouncy moral questions. Instead, B was good on organizations and their structure, a subject Esther liked more than ethical jigsaw puzzles. For instance, months before she went to Fieldfare, Esther and a couple of her most senior CID people had tried to draw a structure plan of the so-called Cormax Turton Guild, the most successful, long-lasting, rich and ruthless crime corpus on their patch. Yes, they had the plan and thought it eighty-five per cent accurate, with Cornelius Max Turton still influential and so far untouchable at the top, despite his retina trouble and arthritic knees and knuckles. Immediately beneath him, and actually responsible for the running of the firm, including all waterfront activities since, at the latest, the famous carnage on 17 November 2004, came Ambrose Tutte Turton, aged forty-one, a nephew, and thirty-seven-year-old Nathan Garnet Ivan Crabtree, nicknamed Palliative, one of Cornelius Max's grandchildren, second son of his daughter, Annette Veronica Crabtree, and her first husband, Brent Holywell Crabtree.

Brent, of course, became better known after death than when alive and busy, because his obituary in *The Times* caused noisy protests, not on account of what was said but because it appeared at all, though down the page with a very small photograph, beneath an American woman jazz singer's and a Classics professor's. Some readers, MPs, other papers and bishops thought *The Times* should not allow even this limited publicity to a renowned ex-crook. But, in a hit-back article by one of the editors later, *The Times* argued that it was actually the scale of Brent Crabtree's dark renown that made his obituary necessary, in the same way as Hitler's, Stalin's and Pol Pot's deaths had been registered in the paper's graveyard. The test was not the virtue of the deceased but his/her influence on, and her/his fame or notoriety in, society locally, nationally and possibly abroad. By this standard, Brent Holywell Crabtree had probably earned his broadsheet obit. And the *way* he died, of course, as well as that Moroccan episode, added the sort of fizz journalists liked. Below Cornelius, Ambrose and Palliative in the Guild structure diagram prepared for Esther, there were occasional uncertainties and alterations, as there might be in any company's chart, but the general picture remained pretty well correct.

Yes. Yet, although they had the shape of the Guild reasonably right, they still couldn't stop it operating and winning and growing. And it was this agonizing, humiliating failure that ultimately sent Esther to Fieldfare. She had decided Cormax Turton would have to be quietly, very quietly, intruded upon. Given large luck, resolution and professionalism, in that order, the Guild might be picked to pieces from within.

At Fieldfare, Officer B spoke for about half her time on crooked hierarchies and their systems. As B said, undercover presumed a powerful, aggressive villain empire. Undercover was no use in freelance, private lawlessness. There had to be some complicated, thriving outfit to enter, stay with, get approved of by, trusted by, promoted in, depended on. And to observe, document and parcel up for jail.

Officer B: Meet Ms Vamoose

She was what Esther thought of at first as a 'hearty piece' – open-faced, cheery-looking, hair mousy-to-blonde and

21

worn in a shallow fringe to just over the ears, slightly above middle height, not too thin, big-voiced, apparently a bit offhand – though that could be put on – a couple of years younger than A, and nowhere near his league for clothes. She wore a blue and white striped shirt, perhaps a man's, run-of-the-mill jeans and trainers – the trainers not new – no jewellery, except a big square wristlet watch; eyes blue-black that methodically went left–right, right–left three times over every member of the audience and maybe stored a print of each. Afterwards, she could probably have done a seating scheme with a precise description of all her listeners in their proper spots. This comforted Esther. She felt B might be a fan of elementary method and order and would apply these to the frighteningly shifty and shifting practice of undercover work. True, Officer A had eventually become businesslike and basic in his talk, too, but Esther's early impression, based only on the look of B, was she would treat almost nothing *but* the businesslike and basic, and Esther approved of this. She wanted to feel assured that undercover and its strengths and infinite, perilous snags could be nicely tabulated, and regulated. She liked tabulating.

And B knew plenty about the perilous snags. She began with them: 'You might want to pull your rumbled undercover officer out of the villain stockade in a hurry and with no farewell party or leaving present,' she said, 'just, vamoose. Especially no leaving present. Me: I had to come out in a hurry last time. Why I'm talking to you. *How* I'm talking to you. Me, I'm your vamoose paradigm, ladies and gentlemen. Yes, *such* a hurry. Now they see me, now no way. But, look, this was not defeat. In fact, a plus. The getaway procedures worked. As I said, why I'm talking to you, *how* I'm talking to you. Me, I'm here and OK. And I'm ready to go back. Not into the same firm, of course, nor even in the same bit of the country. The word will be around and my description. Hair dye and specs, plus handlebar moustache and bumper bra won't make me safe there or thereabouts. But in principle, the withdrawal was

fine. See it as like using the escape chamber from a sub-
marine stuck on the sea bottom. Big crisis at the time and
scary, but, afterwards, just a handy experience extra. And
a comfort – one has shown it can be done and one has done
it. Why I'm talking to you. *How* I'm talking to you. The
Song Of The Man/Woman Who Has Come Through.' Her
cheery face grew a few degrees more cheery. She had tidily
proved, at least to herself, that risk, properly dealt with,
brought brilliant rewards. When they charted her morale
at Hilston the graph line must have speared through the
frame top. She'd have led a 1940 advance on Berlin from
Dunkirk beach.

B said: 'Well then, what is the typical shape of the kind
of firm you'll send someone to infiltrate? But, hang on,
hang on . . . you'll ask is it possible – sane – to generalize?
I think so, I think so. However, let's start with a negative,
shall we? When we talk about an organized criminal gang,
this doesn't mean like, say, the way an army regiment is
organized, or an aircraft carrier, with clear lines of command, or ICI, or the C of E, or even a police force. It's going
to be more ad hoc and loose than those. If there's a family
element – very often the case – think of the Krays, and the
Corleones, and some of the eternal south-east London
crook teams – yes, when there's a family side, this may give
a kind of natural shape – perhaps, dad at the top, as long
as he's still got his marbles and balls, and the offspring in
middle-management spots, or below. So, Vito Corleone, the
godfather; then his sons and adopted son running lesser
jobs, until the eldest boy is tommy-gunned to shreds on the
toll bridge; the next son, Fredo, turns out weak; Vito gets
doddery; Michael, the youngest, takes over and kicks out
Tom the adopted lad. Fiction, but not far from possible
reality. We see that, even where there's a sort of stability to
things, based on powerful, wicked, holy kinship, it may be
shaky, and therefore vulnerable to penetration.

'The shakiness can be more so when the firm has no
bonds of family to give at least a steady base, but this isn't
necessarily to your advantage. The reason? Well, such

23

teams are likely to be villains who will join together – will agree to cooperate – for occasional major tasks needing a lot of manpower: e.g, the Great Train Robbers. What I meant by ad hoc. If it goes well, there'll be a share-out afterwards of the particular loot from that particular job. But, when there's no large project around, people waiting for the call will do their own crooked things and pocket their own crooked gains. In other words, the firm is not like a straight commercial company where all members at all times are supposed to be contributing by their work to a central accounts book. We can't compare these criminals with what used to be called "organization men" in legit businesses – people devoted to and looked after by the company – because this organization might only last months, or even weeks. The one-off quality of such outfits makes them difficult from our point of view: they may not be in existence for long enough, first, to identify, and then bluff a way into.'

She shrugged, as though to say undercover was much less than an all-purpose weapon. Most of her audience would know that. Esther did. Hadn't she come to Fieldfare to find which purpose, purposes, undercover *did* suit? B said: 'However, then there's another kind of firm, altogether – not focused on the occasional massive heist – a bullion raid, for instance, or the Great Train frolic – but running a continuous trade, such as cargo-takes or illegal drugs supply. Here, there'll be a need for minor people on the edges, say to watch for one certain super-valuable container from a ship's hold and get it to a pre-arranged spot on the quay; or pushing at street corner level or at clubs, and couriering stuff from bulk suppliers. Lowlife doing that kind of very prole, small-time assignment will come and go, and will probably be doing their own bits of unrelated law-breaking at the same time.

'It's obviously through one of these marginal jobs that implanting a spy will be easiest – not easy, but easiest, though some are gender-specific, of course: you can't put in a lady as dockside labour. But with drug mongers things are different: it's bisexual, and if your woman or man can offer long-term reliability by sticking around, being efficient, not skimming either cash or substances, there'll be a chance of moving up. Vital. You won't want to risk sticking someone undercover to catch two shop doorway dealers and a user. He/she must be able to finger the leadership. We expect, don't we, the prospect of at least ten years' lock-up? We have to hack the heads off firms, not just tread on their toes.' She paused and did another eye-inventory of her listeners. This time, though, it might not be simply to memorize: no, not just memorize, but to check they were mesmerized by her spiel. Esther felt mesmerized.

B began again: 'Now, let's return to the toughest challenge – to firms that are family controlled: dodgy but possible. Several methods exist for getting aboard, but the main and historically most successful is to identify which of the family might feel discriminated against, undervalued, bypassed, and instal our man/woman close to him, on the pretext that she/he admires the runt figure regardless, sees hidden pluses, and can offer help to lessen or end this disrespect. I'll give you a couple of examples.' B had come on to the stage holding a Waitrose carrier bag and set this at her feet. Now, she bent down and brought a red ring binder from it and began to read of tricky but ultimately triumphant infiltrations. Naturally, she wouldn't be mentioning tricky and ultimately disastrous infiltrations.

Esther's mind went back, went back to all that while ago, when first half thinking about an attempt to smuggle someone into the Turton Guild – yes, Esther had wondered then, in fact, whether there might be rivalry, and therefore useful hatred, affecting Ambrose Tutte Turton and Nathan Garnet Ivan Palliative Crabtree. One tale around said that during the sudden rolling warfare spat between the Guild and other firms on 17 November 2004 Palliative had deliberately left Ambrose exposed in the Preston Park battle sector, apparently hoping to simplify the succession for himself to Cornelius Max Turton's supremo post, eventually. Deliberately? This might be the kind of charge difficult for Ambrose or anyone else definitely to prove. And the rumour of a savage enmity looked very dubious, because he and Palliative seemed to have worked all right together since Cornelius went more and more emeritus, as he aged. For instance, Ambrose and Crabtree had almost certainly put together the campaign against Claud Seraph Bayfield as joint commanders. This would have been no pushover. It suggested very effective collaboration. Maybe, if differences had once existed between them, they'd been ditched now, both recognizing that their combined strengths kept the Guild up there, paramount in the city, and acknowledged nationwide, perhaps even beyond.

Or . . . or, it could be that the comradeliness amounted to nothing more than a truce, and the old loathings still lurked, still waited. Esther had realized that, if this were so, her undercover plant might create an alliance with one of them and provoke him into an attack on the other, or at least on the other's woman/women and/or children. That, on its own, could increase splits and damage the Guild. Any prosecutions would be extra. She had never reached a point in her planning, her half-planning, where she decided which of them – Ambrose or Palliative – would be the most promising to fix on. Some said a general, suppressed hostility had always existed between the Turton and Crabtree sides of the family, anyway, and that this was notably sharpened by the *Times* obituary of Brent, because Cornelius could not be sure he, also, would get one, even down the page.

Cornelius apparently put it about that Brent would never have qualified for that kind of post-mortem treatment if it hadn't been for the showy, horrifying way he got himself killed; and Cornelius would undoubtedly not want to go like that. They said Cornelius had heard of the obituary on the morning of publication and sent people to every newsagent within a couple of miles' radius to buy all copies of *The Times* and secretly burn them. Several of

Cornelius's men wanted to break up the shops as penalty for even putting *The Times* on sale that day. Cornelius forbade this, perhaps afraid *The Times* would hold it against him and then certainly refuse him an obit. Apparently, Cornelius liked the way *The Times* did obituaries: just the name in full across the top and then, possibly, a single head and shoulders shot, unless it was an obit of a goalkeeper, when there might be a picture of him crouched in front of the woodwork and netting; or a famous gardener with some kind of decent hedge behind him. People said Cornelius understood the principle that, if you had done genuine great work in life, all you needed as memorial would be an unadorned statement of that work, not some glaring projection of it. Cornelius's hatred of gaudiness was famous. Of course, he would probably have recognized that some sensationalism in the obituary of Brent Holywell Crabtree had been necessary because of the terrible death, and that filthy or comical episode in Morocco, depending on where you were coming from.

B finished describing her examples and said: 'As we see, then, to slip into a family firm via a disaffected member can be one way to reach the pinnacle people. Clearly, though, there are special dangers. Family enmities are generally more vicious than any others. Think of the punch-ups and knifings at typical weddings, christening parties and funerals. Think of Cain and Abel. If you put in undercover to achieve special contact with one brother or cousin or grandson or uncle or grandfather, some of the others are likely to resent this alliance, suspect this alliance. They might see it as an insult to blood, as well as a grubby bit of deviousness.' She nodded hard a couple of times. 'Almost inevitably,' she said. 'I've witnessed that more than once. It can be very hairy.' She went silent, reminiscing, then having a mind-change forced on her by whatever it was she thought of. 'Yes. Very. Forgive me, I'm jumping about rather today, but, look, I think that at this point I must switch from a plod job of categorizing crook firms and revert to the crucial, more urgent question of

27

what the planted officer should do if things turn bad, and what *you* should do, and should have done before planting her/him, in case they turn bad.' She paused again, passed a hand over her face, as though checking for tears. Although she wouldn't talk much about failures, it seemed she couldn't altogether ignore or forget them.

In a while she said: 'Above everything, you'll need to make sure your Out-located man/woman within a targeted firm gets briefed on how to read the signs that her cover – I'll talk female throughout because I am one, but take it as for both sexes – yes, she must, *must*, be taught how to spot that her cover has been suddenly blown.' She frowned, wagged the same hand, to indicate second thoughts. ' I say "suddenly", because that's dramatic and I want to keep you awake, but, really, it's more likely to be a gradual thing. If the cover collapses all at once it will be because of some glaring mistake or bit of diabolically poor luck. Obviously, these should not occur, as long as the preparation has been efficient. The one good factor about such a crisis is that the undercover officer will be instantly aware it has happened and she should leave everything and sprint down the fire escape.

'But when the cover breakdown is bit by bit, things can be difficult and much more dangerous. Why? Well, the officer might not feel totally sure it's taking place. She'll be non-stop tense in any case – you can't be undercover and *not* tense – and so she'll possibly tell herself that, because of the stress, she's *imagining* symptoms of suspicion in the colleague villains around her when, in fact, none exist. Is she getting scared of shadows? She'll *want* to believe everything is fine. This is *her* show. Undercover has almost always to be solo. It can become an ego thing. She'd be ashamed to cave in to simple jitters. And so she stays too long, leaves it too late to alert the on-call rescue party. In a mo I'll list some of the symptoms to be watched for. And, of course, I'll detail now the kind of exit and aid structure you must – again *must* – must have in place before any officer is committed to an undercover spell. Perhaps we all know of cases that have brought tragedy.' Again she touched her face just below the eyes. 'Right then, you will, please, always provide:

1. A posse on continuous readiness to go in and get the officer out, by force if necessary.
2. A communications system that is negation sensitive. That is, there will be set times for the undercover officer to get in touch with base and if one of these fails by more than an agreed duration the posse moves to recover.
3. Gun carriers in the rescue unit.
4. First aiders in the rescue unit.
5. Fat cash with the aid unit in case our officer has been freighted away for execution somewhere and a bribe is crucial to locate her in time. At least a thousand and in old bills no higher than twenties. Preferably tens. Definitely not fucking fifties – *excusez-moi*. People in the firms don't like fifties. They're conspicuous when spent, and might, in any case, include forgeries. Twenties OKish, but producing a lot of them in the shop can be noticeable, too. Rubber-band the wad with no doubling over of the notes, repeat, no doubling over of the notes, so the recipient can flip-check at once to see it's real right through not just a token bit of currency on top and the rest blank paper, sometimes a jolly trick used by villains and us. The speed of the deal could be crucial.'

A West Country accent? Maybe, but so slight as to be from anywhere between Gloucester and Land's End. Put on? Definitely not Hull or Liverpool or Cockneydom. Yes, B liked lists and getting things ordered. Esther had that correct. She was surprised, though, by B's abrupt move from high confidence to a calamity script, and felt disturbed. When B spoke of tragedy, she would almost certainly mean the Iles tale. Did he neglect the exit structure for his implanted detective?

'Somehow, you have to devise emergency support that is always on hand and close but never obvious – the eternal, agonizing undercover quandary, ' B said. 'You are all of Chief Police Officer level, and will no doubt delegate the actual management of any undercover operation to one of your senior staff. But the overall strategy and respons-ibility has to be yours, which is why the Fieldfare invita-tions for this conference are confined to ACPO ranks.'

Certainly, Esther would delegate. As B said, Assistant Chiefs *did* delegate. They'd climbed above the nitty-gritty and into what B called the strategic. Delegation was not a simple game. At that discussion with her two top detec-tives about the Cormax Turton Guild, a long time before Fieldfare, Esther wondered which of the pair she'd tell to control the undercover job, if she did decide to give it a whirl. She'd failed to make the selection then, and still couldn't get her brain to settle who'd do it best. Perhaps the Fieldfare contributions from A and/or B, and/or whoever else took part over the couple of days, would eventually help.

B said: 'A name. I'm going to talk to you about a name. *My* name. I don't mean my real name, obviously. I mean the name I might take to go undercover. As you're all aware, my *real* name is . . . well, is B. That's to say, B con-ceals my real name because my *real* real name is a protected species known only to my mother, the armoury and the Pay Office. But, when I'm doing my crooked role in a firm, I need a working name, and I must become totally the per-son represented by that name. So, let's say I pick the name Dawn. It's got to be a name that sounds as though it could be right. I'm among people who have begun to let me in, but they're still suspicious. They're suspicious of everyone they haven't seen around for at least months, and they're suspicious of them, too. Incidentally, when you select your officer for Out-location it has to be someone with no vivid background of past detective work or he/she is likely to be already familiar to the firms. This proviso can mean that the officer must be young and fairly inexperienced – which may add to risk. And it can mean, too, that he/she is likely to have worked in an outlying police station, not somewhere central and major: distance helps with disguise. Preferably, the officer will have no dependants, though some elasticity might be permitted on that.

'But about names: personally, I wouldn't pick one that sounds like I'm trying hard to come across as through-and-through naffdom and therefore suited to small jobs, such as being called after her parents' honeymoon spot, Bude, or a soccer team – Villa. "Dawn" has good, middle-ground credibility. Yes, it's workable. But then, what I noticed one day was people in the firm started using this name too damn much. Eerie. Chilling. It was, "Dawn, there's a rave at Colly's Palace Friday through Saturday, Dawn. We must have representation there, Dawn. You'll need a tonne of stock, Dawn." I was pushing all sorts for them as my role at the time, and, I thought, getting general recognition as an extremely OK dogsbody. And then, "We'll have Sandy and Mick there as well, Dawn, to see off any competition, so you should get just peaceful selling, Dawn, a real sweet location." That repetition, like a tic – what's going on? Then I work it out. I know I *have* to work it out, fast. It's as if they want to tell me they *really* believe my name's *really* Dawn and are so *really* comfy with it and *really* convinced by it that they'll bring it out *really* matily at every chance now. And, of course, the reason they want to tell me they *really* believe my name's *really* Dawn is because they don't *really* believe it at all. Or they're starting to doubt it, I don't understand why. They're going to do some digging around. Maybe they've *already* done some digging around, testing the CV I come with. Meanwhile, they'll lull me, help me feel absolutely part of the outfit by Dawning me here, there, inside, outside and around the corner. They wouldn't call Sandy or Mick Sandy or Mick every few words because they're *really* certain Sandy and Mick are Sandy's and Mick's *real* names. Maybe there's a touch of mockery as well to all the "Dawns". It's "Dawn", "Dawn", "Dawn", because they've got an idea it's not. They'd like to say it, "Dawn? Dawn??? Dawn!!!! Who ever fucking knew a rat called Dawn?" Minor indicators, yes. What just now I called shadows. But I grow very alert. I'd been watchful before, even though I'd imagined I was winning. Now I'm max watchful. And I might spot some of the bigger signs I promised to give you.

1. The occasional question about my supposed background. This will be nothing too rough – not interrogation, only conversational. And then another question next day, and one the day after. They'll be weighing the answers for consistency, and maybe doing some checks around where I've been claiming I come from. A probably referred to *Reservoir Dogs*. You'll recall how members of the gang chat sweetly and amiably with Mr Orange, who's actually a cop spy, going over tales from his alleged past, looking for flaws. Incidentally, that's an instance where a one-off operation, the jewel robbery, is penetrated. But, it has taken a long time to set up, so maybe for Mr Orange to get himself into the team is just about believable.
2. I might notice someone snooping me from a vehicle while I work. The aim is to see that I trade and nothing else – no chats with someone playing a punter but actually my contact from headquarters.
3. I'll get told well ahead about some operation – say a cash-in-transit project – but, somehow, it doesn't happen. They've been testing, fictionalizing. They want to see whether a police brigade turns up at the spot on my tip-off.
4. If a police brigade doesn't – because I'm cute enough to guess it's a trap – they'll try some other cover-peeling ploy, and then another, until they're satisfied, or not.

'Because of "Dawn, Dawn, Dawn," I knew it was time to leave. Oh, yes, debatable, almost always debatable – but, me, I left. I said to myself, "I'm half sick of shadows."

Self-eject. And the majority view of the chiefs back in my territory was I judged it right: no panic on my part, just good, subtle observation. Not a large majority said so, but a majority. Any undercover type would be content with that. It's like, "Sod brass approval, I'm safe, undisfigured, unmaimed, undead." If there's *some* brass approval, that's all right, too. OK, it's not canonization, but not a stoning, either.'

Chapter Four

When it came to the push and they had someone more or less settled and safe and due to be productive within the Cormax Turton Guild, Esther found it weird to load the inspector heading the on-call aid unit with £1000 in old notes, no fucking fifties. The money bulked him out, put pounds on him, you might say. Obviously, the unit must also handle other emergency situations: it would be preposterously expensive to have a stand-by team only for possible undercover rescue. But possible undercover rescue was the main job and everyone taking part knew it.

All the unit wore dark blue bullet-proof vests, which added inches to their chest measurements, anyway. And then the inspector – or, in fact, the inspectors, because, obviously, they would change every shift of this non-stop duty – the inspectors had to get a thick, rubber-banded wodge of mixed fives, tens, twenties and no fucking fifties into one of their pockets, and a pocket reached easily and fast if they stormed Guild nests and failed to find at once the undercover detective they had come to save and bring out. The money could not be split up and spread around several pockets in more manageable chunks: to avoid delay, the size of the bribe must be plain instantly, and its healthy concentration of fives, tens and twenties, and the inspired, savvy freedom from fucking fifties. This money would be offered only if things had come to look more or less hopeless. In the early stages, the purpose of the raid could not be disclosed and certainly not the name of the officer – not his/her real or any adopted name. The point was, he/she could still be somewhere within the firms with his/her cover intact: the raid might have been triggered in error. To start chucking the money about and asking for his/her whereabouts must expose him/her, and condemn him/her.

Inspectors would already be festooned with gear – pistol, flashlight, cuffs, baton, walkie-talkie, laser gun, maybe: no good at all going streamlined on this kind of job. The thing about the money, though, was, yes, it made whoever carried it that little bit fatter, that little bit bigger as a side-on target, suppose the Guild expected a rescue onslaught, and hit back. The Guild had a reputation for hitting back – also for hitting first – generally at other, competing guilds, syndicates, firms, gangs like Claud Seraph Bayfield's. But a police attack might also get blasted. The Guild looked after itself, had lasted and meant to keep on lasting. If the Cormax Turton had gone in for official notepaper, it could have included under its mastheaded name the impressive boast, 'Established 1986'.

Ultimately, Esther and the inspectors found that the best place for a currency bundle was the inside breast pocket of their combat jacket. The plump money mound lifted one side of the bullet-proof vest a couple of inches and got the inspectors the title, 'One-tit-team-boss', except for a woman inspector, of course. A little ritual occurred three times a twenty-four-hour day when the inspector standing down passed the special cash-wad to his/her replacement. Esther watched occasionally. It made her think of Swiss Guard troops after sentry duty ceremonially handing the keys of the Vatican to their relief unit. One possible gain: there must be a fine chance that, if an inspector were hit in the chest by a bullet, the body armour plus the lumpy plug of utterly non-fifties cash would stop it.

To get the thousand from police funds, Esther had been obliged to do some smart, prolonged and earnest talking. Not everyone could be told what the sum might be needed for. Eventually, Esther did land it from the float used to pay informants their secret salaries and fees, which she could argue was the same shady ballpark. Even some of those who did understand how the cash might be spent thought the idea far-fetched. They couldn't accept that during a frantic, all-out attack on the Guild there'd be any chance to do a late, desperate, swift, dab-in-the-hand, confidential deal with some nonentity member of the firm for pointers to the undercover officer's whereabouts: obviously none of the family, Turton or Crabtree, themselves would be buyable. Oh, God, possibly nobody in the Guild would be. After all, who'd want to save a filthy spy, even for a thousand? Or, to word it another way, for *only* a thousand, taking into account the vast risk of vengeance on the bribee later, and not *much* later. Naturally, one or two of Esther's colleagues considered any kind of bung to a villain as bad, but especially one openly, brazenly provided for in an attack plan. She saw the sense of such objections, yet continued hard seeking the finance. And she realized why – could analyse herself well enough. The process went this way:

(a) At Fieldfare she'd slowly grown convinced that to use undercover against the so-called Guild was right and necessary, even, perhaps, a duty. How else to smash a crooked network established 1986 and to date invincible? This decision came very hesitantly, painfully. The non-attendance of Desmond Iles and the reason for it affected her almost as much as what she heard from the platform; but only *almost* as much. She guessed – was sure – Iles declined because after that appalling loss of one of his people he now considered undercover work stupidly hazardous. He'd know he would not be persuaded by anything offered at Fieldfare. As for Esther, she finally *had* been persuaded, just about, persuaded despite that strong message from Desmond Iles: particularly strong, because done by his silence, his absence, his refusal to recognize even the possibility of effective undercover. Yes, she got the message, but still caved in to the positive side.

(b) Just the same, her uncertainties and fears hung on in the back of her head. And to quieten them, kill them off, she found she needed to stick absolutely and slavishly to everything constructive she heard at Fieldfare. She became unwilling to depart in even minor detail from advice offered there. Those suggestions and recommendations she transformed into iron edicts. They bound her. Pathetic? She was an Assistant Chief but found herself taking orders from Officers A and B who would be sergeants at the highest. Sometimes Esther felt she had fallen into a sort of voodoo superstition, as if scared that to flout any part of the instructions from A and B and the rest of the Fieldfare performers would bring big punishment – big punishment signifying loss of the Out-located officer and failure of the operation . . .

(c) She felt ashamed of such mental cowering, but could not escape it. In some ways this was mad, as well as pathetic, and she realized it. After all, B had said 'at least a thousand' in reserve cash for the possible rescue. This clearly meant it could be more, perhaps *should* be. But, because B quoted a thousand, the figure took on a sacred quality for Esther and she would not vary it, up or down. The same with timing. The retrieve crew should be sent in after a six-hour unexplained communications break because . . . because, hadn't B stipulated six hours? Some would probably regard this as too soon, perhaps panicky: the undercover officer might be in no danger but simply hadn't found a free, unobserved moment to make a call. Could it be wise on account of nothing more than a glitch to destroy a scheme so tricky to set up? Esther would have replied that an Out-located officer was *always* in danger and an unscheduled six-hour failure to make contact amounted to more than a glitch. In any case, some glitches killed. At Fieldfare, B had spoken about the *Godfather* film. Esther recalled a line or two from it now. Marlon Brando, as Vito Corleone, retiring head of the family, is tutoring his son, Michael, the new Don. In his macho way, Vito says: 'I've spent all my life trying not to be careless. Women and children can be careless. Men, no.' Well, Esther would also try *not* to be careless, and she had come to associate carelessness with any failure, even trivial, to observe the rules and rubric laid down by B.

By A, too. He didn't do only the theology and theory of Out-location. He would talk the practicalities if forced. And he was forced when taking questions. He had the full, preposterous jargon stored about him and could retaliate with real clunking zing. Esther had already heard some of it when he spoke about Hilston Manor. Then, later:

Officer A: on 'the necessarily restrictive methodology of under-cover'

God! He'd been asked from the floor whether the returns from Out-locating were 'quantifiable – quantifiable in the normal sense of quantifiable'. Did any data exist to demonstrate that the gains from such tactics justified, 'in the normal sense of justified', the expensive manpower/womanpower commitment? This commitment could be listed as:

1. the Out-located officer him/herself;
2. any stand-by help party at constant readiness, admittedly for other responses besides Out-location rescue, but chiefly for that, and involving, presumably, at least six officers, some gun-trained;
3. the Out-located detective's upper-rank contact handling selection, briefing and debriefing. Selection, particularly, might swallow huge amounts of time: a widespread search for possible talent would be needed, a shortlist, a final choice.

'Quantifiable?' A said.
'In the normal sense of quantifiable.'
'What *is* that?'
'To put it crudely, A, profit and loss.'
'Yes, that's crudely enough,' A said.
'The bottom line.'

'I've heard of it,' A replied.

'We are accountable to our Police Committees.'

'Yes, I understand that, sir,' A said.

'Important budgetary aspects. I recognize that in some ways Out-locating is a special, perhaps mysterious, carry-on, and we can never disclose full details to lay people. Yet, we have to convince our respective Committees – and rightly have to convince them – we have to convince these Committees we are providing value for money, and value for money in all aspects of policing. As far as scrutiny is concerned, there can be no no-go areas. No, no no-go areas.'

'No, no, I don't think any such study has been done,' A said. 'I can't think how it would be. This kind of work doesn't fit into an account book.'

'I'm not sure we could get away with that excuse.'

'It would be worth a try,' A said.

'And then, another point, does this type of activity fit into everyone's work scheme?'

'Sir?'

'I notice that Assistant Chief Constable Desmond Iles is not present at our conference.'

'I don't have a nominal roll of those attending,' A said. 'It's not available for general inspection.'

'There was a bad business on his ground involving an Out-located officer, wasn't there?'

'Things can go awry, sir. It would be absurd to say otherwise.'

'Is that why he's not present? Has he measured profit against loss and found loss wins?'

'I can't answer for him, sir. I wouldn't pretend to know the mind of an ACC, and particularly not the mind of ACC Iles, who is, I understand, rarely easy to read. This isn't to slander him behind his back. I've been told Mr Iles would never claim to be unduly predictable. Obviously, you'll know the Latin tag *sui generis*, sir. Latin. Meaning one-off. I gather Mr Iles couldn't be more *sui*. If he has a nickname it might be that.'

39

'All right, all right, but listen, A: you looked hostile . . . yes, totally hostile . . . others must have noticed it, too . . . yes, you looked damn hostile, possibly vindictive, when I used the word "quantifiable". I could almost hear you mutter to yourself, "Here comes a load of standard management-speak." The fact is, though, A, that we *are* managers and have to meet management criteria, tiresome as they might seem to someone of your . . . to someone at your place in the service. For instance, I would love to see a case study and evaluation of the number of crimes revealed and prosecuted or prevented by a typical Out-located officer over a measured period. In the normal sense of evaluation. Perhaps, after his experience, Mr Iles would, too. Might we be given that during our stay at Fieldfare? An exemplar. This would be a very persuasive piece of research.'

A said: 'It's quite possible there'd only be one.'

'One crime?'

'Oh, yes,' A said. 'Likely.'

'This, you see, is what I mean.'

'Which, sir?' A replied.

'The considerable cost, as against what's accomplished. There's a black hole aspect here.'

'In the normal sense of black hole?'

'The expense open-ended, not subject to scrutiny or control.'

'Out-location is generally aimed at identifying a single, major planned episode of villainy,' A said. 'This is central to what is labelled, I'm afraid, "the necessarily restrictive methodology of undercover". Any embedded officer is focused on one crime, one potential crime. Usually, she/he cannot deal in plurals. That's where "necessarily restrictive" comes in. If he/she passes on good information about other projects and these are ambushed by police, members of the firm will soon sense they have a whispering alien aboard. Every recent addition to the payroll will be watched, and that's sure to include our officer. His/her background will have already been checked, yes. But now

40

it will get a *real* going over. And she/he might be put under serious interrogation, with no solicitor or tapes present to ensure humane treatment. No first aid present, either. In general, a planted officer will need time to secure his/her position within a firm, and should not be asked to supply tip-offs too early, because such tip-offs might betray and kill her/him, as well as the Out-location project.'

This had brought A back to the grey-area philosophizing he seemed to enjoy most. 'And so we have the situation already outlined where an undercover officer must do nothing about crimes he/she is aware of, and might even have to take part in, for the sake of preserving his/her role and achieving a big prosecution later. It is a situation that can be exploited by defence lawyers, and one not at all condoned by some judges. The technical name for it when described in confidential Out-location manuals is "Posed Participation as Accessory", or the "PPA Syndrome". Naturally, we, the police service, would wish to stress the "posed" – i.e. the display only aspect – the seeming, concocted, rather than true, nature of the behaviour as accessory to crimes. But the courts don't always go along with this. They want everything honest and clear. They'll see a crime as a crime.'

'Perhaps that is understandable.'

'Perhaps, sir,' A said. 'It's like Oscar Wilde, isn't it?'

'It is? The play's *The Importance of Being Earnest*, not *The Importance of Being Honest*.'

'Wilde gets a note from Lord Alfred Douglas's father, the Marquess of Queensberry, addressed to "Oscar Wilde posing as a sodomite". *Posing*. Wilde chooses to take this as meaning he *is* a sodomite, which, in Queensberry's view, he is, of course, and disastrously sues, the silly sod.'

'Well, Oscar Wilde is something else. But the procedure you outline means, doesn't it, that a police officer – the officer about to go undercover – has actually to be ordered by his/her superiors to ignore or even assist in any criminal activities of the firm where she/he is embedded, except for the specific, targeted offence? In turn, this would imply that senior officers of the police service, officers of ACPO rank and above, might be proactive parties to the . . . what do you call the Syndrome?'

'Posed Participation as Accessory – PPA, sir.'

'In other words, via this PPA, Assistant Chief level officers themselves become complicit with gang crimes, at one remove. Disturbing?'

'*Posed* complicity and probably at two removes, sir,' A said.

'Why two?'

'ACPO level officers would not normally instruct under-cover detectives direct in PPA, sir. The ACPO level officer will instruct, say, the Detective Chief Superintendent, head of CID and handler of the undercover officer, to instruct the undercover officer in PPA, sir.'

'Are judges likely to accept this distinction, A?'

'Which, sir?'

'*Posed* accessory as against accessory.'

'Some wigs do find it hard to see,' A said. 'Hard-liners. Brainy simpletons.'

'Might they feel the Out-located officer has gone over to the criminal firm for personal gain? This could colour a judge's attitude and, crucially, his/her summing-up to the jury.'

'That is a danger, yes, sir,' A said.

'For myself, speaking entirely personally, I acknowledge as much – and I don't say it with the least pride – possibly the opposite – perhaps I am even conscious of a certain naivety in myself – but I don't believe I would ever be able to suspend, virtually obliterate, my, as it were, drift towards maintenance of the lawful, a drift accelerated, of course, by nurture. My resultant mind-set demands, pretty well irresistibly, by instinct and by . . . by habit, I suppose . . . habit and choice . . . my mind-set demands *my* complicity with the good.'

'You are programmed for virtue, sir, like George Washington, who could not tell a lie.'

'There are boundaries.'

'But you probably won't have to make this kind of difficult choice, sir, because I wouldn't think many ACCs go undercover. '

'A complicity of that other, supervisory, kind might be expected of me, though.'

'Distant.'

'Frankly, A, I hardly understand how any police officer can make the switch from law enforcer to lawbreaker.'

'*Posed* lawbreaker,' A replied.

'Even so, I wouldn't be able to do it, not the actual undercover role.'

'Between those who can act and those who can't there is a great gulf fixed,' A replied.

'And then, how do we know which of our officers has this flair? Do we talent-spot at the headquarters panto?'

'Not headquarters. Detectives stationed there are likely to be known to any vigilant crooked crew, and most of them are very watchful.'

'Rural station pantos, then?'

A seemed to decide big-heartedly to take these questions as serious, not ACPO-level, feeble wind-ups. 'Many detectives will have done a bit of impersonation in small cases, or at least disguised their own nature for a while when investigating. In a uniformed service, plain clothes themselves are a kind of masquerade. You have to check around to locate – locate! – these possible Out-location candidates and then try to assess which of them would do the undercover job best on a larger scale and, probably, for a longer period. This is a matter of personnel selection, a skill routinely exercised by ACCs and senior CID officers. Not magic, not a mystery carry-on, sir. Nous.'

'And then I believe I've heard of another Syndrome, beside PPA.'

'Ah?'

'Is it to do with Stockholm? Something like that?'

'The Stockholm Syndrome, yes, sir,' A said.

'Where the planted officer or a hostage grows so close to the criminals in mind as well as daily routine that eventually he/she actually, not pretendedly, becomes one of them, in some cases seduced by the prospect of wealth, but sometimes simply won over mentally by the captors. For the undercover officer it becomes no longer a pose.'

'That is another danger, yes, sir,' A said. 'This Syndrome takes its name from a siege situation after a bank raid in Stockholm. And it's similar to the turn-around by the American heiress, Patty Hearst, abducted by a political gang but who then adopted their cause and became one of them.'

'Have you seen anything like it happen to an undercover officer, A?'

'The handling senior officer must always be alert to this possibility, sir,' A replied.

'A double treachery.'

A smiled – a smile of sparkling, extensive, sweet, *de bas en haut* contempt, not a face Esther had seen him use previously, but he had a lot. He was on the right side of the great gulf fixed between those who could act and those who couldn't. 'No, sir. If I may differ – we do not regard an officer who goes undercover to expose criminality as treacherous. Villain firms deserve no loyalty from us. We exist to wipe them out. Undercover is a means. It is true policing. It is basic detection. It is protection of the community and of the realm. What we are here for, exist for, I think you'll agree.'

'The officer, if discovered, is regarded as a rat by the criminals.'

'Oh, we don't let their twisted values and language define us, do we, sir?' A replied with a grand, dismissive chuckle. 'After all, what's their term for police in general, including Assistant Chiefs? Pigs. Pigs! Do we go along with that? It would surely be inappropriate to regard an ACC in his/her fine quality dress uniform as a porker. Should we all start grunting and sniffing for truffles? In the corrupted view of villains, some pigs are also rats. It's a merry animal pageant, but we aren't compelled to join in.'

The questions abruptly switched topic: 'You've said

undercover is not treachery, but tell me, A, is it treachery if the officer succumbs to the Stockholm Syndrome and joins the opposition, *really* joins it?'

'Certainly.'

'I see.'

'No question.'

'And what should be the police response?'

'We hunt him/her down, sir, with the rest of the gang, and seek to arrest, charge and convict her/him and the others.'

'I see.'

'Oh, yes.'

'And might we charge him/her then with the offences we would have blindeyed – and would have hoped the court might blindeye – if he/she had not gone over?'

'Certainly,' A said. 'His/her right to unofficial immunity in the interests of a culminating great cause is finished. The court would be with us entirely on this.'

'You think, then, that sometimes judges, the brainy simpletons, can be right?'

'Admittedly, it's a tough one, but this we *have* to believe, sir, don't we, or chaos has come? A judicial system, pre-programmed to muck up? Pandemonium. Although it does look like this sometimes, we try not to despair, I think. After all, there is a rigorous selection process for judges. Several of them may well have *some* little aptitudes. I've been told that the sorting-out tests are even more rigorous than for Chief and Assistant Chief, and we all know that few bad choices are made in those areas. Few.'

Esther liked A, liked the whole spectacle of someone of middling or low rank teaching and outmanoeuvring the brass. She loved the way he used the word 'we' – 'We don't let their twisted language define us.' 'Should we all start grunting?' 'We exist to wipe them out.' – as if A felt he had to coach this magnifico of the police service into a correct view of what essentially 'we', the police service, should be. Esther was a magnifico herself, part of the brass. That did not stop her siding with A, though, in the search for triumph rather than pure purity. Esther thought it would be around about the time of this exchange from the floor with A that she decided she'd try undercover against the Guild. Immediately ahead of her in the Simpkins Suite a chair stood empty and she let herself imagine Iles might have been sitting there, had he come. No question, that did give Esther a message, but A and B, and especially A, gave a message, too, and for now she liked it better.

What Esther learned at Fieldfare, · from the platform, from the questions, from the absence of Iles, was that a very genuine and chilling case against all Out-location work existed, but that it could be more or less defeated. More? Or less? She did waver even now. But it must be significant that one didn't say 'less or more'. 'More or less' surely gave 'more' the precedent, didn't it – more or less? She decided to ask Richard Channing, deputy head of CID, to run the undercover operation. His first job would be to build a shortlist and select from it a detective who might have a reasonable chance of (a) penetrating the Guild; (b) then remaining alive; and (c) being able to bring out information which in some form or another would stand up as evidence.

Esther herself meant to stay close and influential at this selection stage and apply what she had absorbed at Fieldfare. She chose Channing to manage the Out-location because he had the most qualms about it – wise, persistent, treatable qualms. She didn't want someone over-positive and glib, like Channing's CID boss, Simon Tesler. Channing saw the dangers and the drawbacks big and clear and, when landed with the handling job, would struggle and struggle hard to counter them. Esther needed sharp objections she could answer these with what she had picked up in the Simpkins Suite and other rooms at Fieldfare; and to find whether he could come back at her and show that what she had picked up in the Simpkins Suite and other rooms at Fieldfare did not necessarily wash. As to what she had picked up in the Simpkins Suite, her feeling was that Mullins, the ACC who had quizzed A

46

so hard and long, would, in fact, adopt Out-location, most of his objections having been dismissed by A. Mullins had tested his doubts and seen them torched. He had come to Fieldfare for the same sort of reasons as Esther. They wanted their caution dismantled. It had happened.

Richard Channing said: 'Do you know, ma'am, I find I hate the notion of asking some young, novice detective to turn himself/herself into a rat.'

'If you're going to collapse into the language and standpoint of villains, she/he has already opted to become a pig, hasn't he/she? That's how we're known to them,' Esther said. 'Should we start grunting and sniffing for truffles? Pig, rat, it's all much of a muchness, isn't it? In the corrupted view of crooks, some pigs are also rats. It's a merry animal pageant, but we needn't join.'

'Maybe, maybe. I've never thought of it like that.'

'I've always kept this at the front of my mind, Richard.'

'But some very senior people will not countenance undercover in any circumstances, I gather,' Channing said. 'There's an ACC Iles who, as I hear it, forbids Out-location, after the murder of an undercover man there. He's a very experienced officer. Has he decided that the possible advantages of Out-location on his ground can't justify the risk to the undercover detective? I would find that disturbing. There appears to be little quantifying data available on the effectiveness or not of Out-location.'

'I can't answer for him,' Esther said. 'I won't pretend to know the mind of another ACC, and particularly Desmond Iles's mind, rarely easy to read. I'm not slandering him behind his back. I don't think Iles would ever claim to be unduly predictable. You ask for quantifiable returns on undercover operations. I don't see how that would be possible. This is not the kind of work that can be measured in a profit and loss account book.'

'I'm still not totally sure what I'm looking for,' he said.

'Many detectives will have carried out small-scale impersonations for the sake of an inquiry, or at least disguised their own nature. After all, Richard, in a uniformed service plain clothes are a kind of masquerade. You have to trawl around to find these officers and assess which of them might do the Out-location job best on a larger scale and over a longer period, most likely. This is personnel selection, the kind of thing you and I are doing all the time, but in this instance concerned with undercover talent. It's not magic. No mystery carry-on. One needs nous. But you will know that between those who can act and those who can't there is a great gulf fixed.'

Trotting out the Fieldfare formulae Esther felt passably assured and only moderately fraudulent. She thought she had probably settled Channing's entirely reasonable anxieties. And if she could settle his, perhaps her own would shrink a bit more. Her own started from memories of a very scary time undercover herself, and then took in tales of disaster elsewhere, and especially the disaster that could shake someone like Iles so irreparably. A and B and others from the Fieldfare alphabet had undermined these thumbs-down influences pretty well. Yes, pretty well. Was it so strange that she should re-spiel their comforting phrases at near verbatim? Churchgoers got similar comfort repeating the litany.

Her ploys worked. They consoled Esther and helped her persuade Richard Channing that the effort needed to find and install someone in the Guild would pay off. Three weeks ago they Out-located an officer who, so far, seemed safe, even happy, and who kept contact when due. Esther did her regular, around the clock visits to the on-call rescue parties, though, to check their readiness and watch the formal transfer of the vital bribe cash. She must not get careless, or even confident.

Chapter Five

When Desmond Iles arrived unannounced at Esther's office she naturally assumed at first he was there to crow. Although he had not turned up at Fieldfare, she'd met him several times at ACPO conferences previously, and perhaps with that coxcomb profile and dandy gear he always looked like someone who would crow if he had something to crow about, or not. Today, he might think he had. She couldn't really argue.

He must have driven for hours from his own ground to see her, yet his clothes looked in no way tired or roughed up. In fact, his suit exulted. The three-piece, grey job he wore sweetly signalled custom-made, and custom-made by an expensive talent for someone very knowing and very set on getting trousers that did absolutely right by his legs. Iles's legs were not especially long, but slim and immaculately tapering from thigh to ankle, the calf bulge certainly present and suggesting power reserves, yet in no way lumpy and harmful to line. His tailoring took hold of this lean shapeliness with pricey skill. Looking at the trousers, Esther found it impossible to imagine any legs covered by them suffering the usual degrading trouble with legs – gouty knees, sciatica or varicose veins. Iles had a way of walking that would conscript attention to the trousers from all in the vicinity, and therefore to his legs. Although Esther wouldn't call it a sashay or strut, she thought this would be how Field Marshal Montgomery might have stepped into his tent to receive the surrender of the Germans at Lüneberg Heath in May 1945. Even during the very few paces Iles took across Esther's room to shake hands before sitting down, she felt the stoked, conquistador glory of his stride. This was what made her think he had come to tell her how cruelly and predictably wrong she had been to Out-locate one of her people; and condemn her fiercely for a failure to consult him before deciding.

He wanted her to take him to what he called 'the scene, please, as a personal necessity, I know you'll understand'. By now, of course, that's all it was, a scene, a bit of scenery, a bit of coastal geography, nothing exceptional, nothing tragic, washed and clue-cleansed by a lot of tides. 'Someone I think you knew as A phoned me,' Iles said.

'Fieldfare A?'

'He'd heard about the death, of course.'

'Why would he phone *you*?'

'He was distressed.'

'But why call *you*?'

'It wasn't entirely friendly,' Iles said.

'You take calls just like that out of nowhere from people of A's rank?'

'Not often.'

'What's the thinking? A decided, did he, an undercover man is killed by the gang he infiltrated, so I'll ring Assistant Chief Iles? Does it make sense?'

'I believe I have to listen to all who for their own reasons seek me out, Esther,' Iles replied. 'It's one of my facets.'

'Yes, but –'

'At Staff College I was known as Approachable Desmond. Facets are one of the things people notice in me.'

'I'm sure, but –'

'A had a double motive for ringing. One, he wanted me to do something. And, two, he wished to reproach, blame me. You'll immediately ask, one, wanted me to do what? And, two, why reproach, blame me? And I perfectly see why you should wish to quiz me on those aspects.'

'Does A know you – on "Think I'll give Ilesy a bell" terms?' Esther replied. 'But he's not from your domain.'

'Knew *of* me. One of my maxims is, "More folk know

Tom Fool than Tom Fool knows." Many have heard of Desmond Iles. It used to surprise me, but I've come to realize there is an inevitability to it. I accept this. I hope I do not seek or strive for repute, but repute arrives in my case willy-nilly and inescapable.'

Esther drove him out to the bit of beach near Pastel Head. 'You'll ask, one, what A wanted me to do; and, two, why he wished to reproach me,' he said.

'Did he call on the mobile? Or you mean he came through to your switchboard and said, "Let me speak to Assistant Chief Constable Des Iles. Tell him it's A."?'

'I have a direct, secure land line at the nick, as you have, I'm sure.'

'Yes, and the point about secure numbers is that they're secure – and private.'

'A is a detective. He discovers things,' Iles said. 'He used that line.'

'He's obviously determined to reach you, personally.'

'He was weeping,' Iles replied.

'Oh, he dodges in and out of roles. It's referred to as protean. He could be imitating Benny Hill or The Laughing Policeman a minute later.' She would strive not to slip into obvious grief. She still feared Iles had driven here to tell her how insanely wrong she had been – part of his campaign against undercover. She must keep up a tough front.

'Yes, he was weeping,' Iles said.

She parked the car on the cliff and they walked down a slippery path to the pebble beach. Not long ago she'd watched as they carefully carried the body bag *up* that path to an undertaker's van. It was low tide now. She pointed to a spot about halfway to the water. 'There,' she said. Iles walked ahead and stared for a while at the mix of mud and stones, then out at the sea. He would probably judge the sea as almost his equal in Creation. After a couple of minutes, she walked after him, careless of interrupting any communion he and it might be busy on. He turned his head to give her some profile. 'A's first words when he came through were, "Mr Iles, we failed her,"' he said.

51

'Did you understand what he meant?'

'I remained silent,' Iles replied. 'But I stress, it was a permissive silence, not indifference. He would have sensed this. It's a knack I have. I'd even call it an inspiring, liberating knack. This type of silence invited him to continue, to explain. Ironically, my silences cause people to talk.'

'No introduction of himself?'

'Not at that point.'

'So, you'd be baffled?'

'Plainly, I knew it was someone suffering.'

'Did you ask his name?'

'In due course. If someone is suffering you let them control the pace of things. In the presence of human pain, identity doesn't matter all that much pro tem. Pain dominates.'

'But ultimately you said, "Who's speaking?", did you, and he replied, "A, here, Mr Iles." But you weren't at Fieldfare, so you wouldn't understand what A signified. You'd reply, "A what?"'

'Yes, you'll want to ask on what grounds he blamed me. And, clearly, that is the answer,' Iles replied.

'What is clearly the answer?'

'My absence from Fieldfare.'

'But I remember he said he didn't know whether you were there, because people of his rank had no sight of the list.'

'He knew. That glossy, stunted jerk, Mullins, referred to me in Questions, didn't he? Or to the void where I might have been had I turned up? I heard of this.'

'So, this detective sergeant, maybe only a detective constable, reaches you on your personal phone and says, "Mr Iles, you had absolutely no right to skip Fieldfare, you negligent sod"?'

'"Fatally remiss" was the term used. 'We were "fatally remiss, Mr Iles". A added, "B concurs and perhaps others." I said, "I've no means of knowing who B is." He replied: "You have no means of knowing who I, A, am, either." I agreed at once with this and said: "Therefore, you wish me to accept a hearsay report about B, whom I don't know, from yourself, A, whom I have spoken to but also don't know. That is cryptic by any standards." He said: "Much police work of this kind *is* cryptic." I replied: "Surely, my absence from Fieldfare itself spoke."'

'It did to me,' Esther said.

'It did?'

'Certainly.'

'But not enough?'

'Not enough, no.'

'You make his case, I suppose.'

'In what way?' Esther replied.

'You interpreted what you *should* interpret – what all present were intended to interpret from my refusal to attend – yet went ahead with Out-location, regardless. A said, "Fucking sophistry," when I referred to the emphatic, implied, non-clarion but definite message in my non-appearance. "Fucking senior cop's fucking cop-out," he added. He'd begun to recover by then. He said I *owed* you help now, in view of my refusal to be present at Fieldfare and deter you from an undercover operation. This certainly seemed odd coming from him – someone who'd helped persuade you to go with it.'

'Do you see anything here?' she said, nodding towards pebbles and then the sea. '*You* were a detective, weren't you?' Far out, a piled-high container vessel lay at anchor maybe waiting for the tide so she could dock. Cormax Turton did a lot of business with shipped freight, some of it legal. Small, muddy waves broke almost silently a hundred metres away as if exhausted by getting in and out of lock gates.

'"See anything"? In what sense?' Iles said.

'Anything that might help us take the investigation forward and get the sods who did him.'

'I didn't tell A to for God's sake pull himself together when he broke down,' Iles replied. 'It would have been a customary reaction from someone in my rank hearing someone in *his* helplessly grizzle and sob – perhaps

53

self-indulgently. That's not my style, though. I believe people should let their emotions run, rank immaterial. Several
times I waited for him to recover. It seemed only decent. If
he was on pay-as-you-talk, this would be costing him.'

'You mentioned B. We had the rescue unit in within
minutes of his six-hour failure to make contact. Minutes.
She stipulated that. I didn't go with them. It wasn't a job
for an ACC. Later, I did visit one of the sites under search.
Just watched from outside, though. As a matter of fact, the
head of the firm, the prime, uncrackable villain, Cornelius
Turton, came out and spoke to me, claimed not to know
what we were looking for, of course.' Esther felt her voice
grow defensive, plaintive, frantic. She'd done everything
she'd been told, but disaster still arrived.

'A said that during one of his presentations that chatty,
venerable ponce, Mullins, put up some standard, ancient
objections to undercover – stuff about turning officers into
rats, plus all the usual legalistic quibbles, such as, This cop
has become a crook allegedly so as to catch crooks and is
it permissible? Arguments so feeble they only strengthened
the positive,' Iles replied.

'Well, yes.'

'You'll ask what A meant when he spoke of my helping
you in the aftermath situation. It would be more than just
viewing the scene as now,' Iles said.

'Did he have Mullins' name? He wasn't supposed to
know our names.'

'He's a detective.'

'We didn't and still don't have his.'

'Their dainty little secrecy procedures,' Iles said.

'Although they might irritate you, it comforted me not
to know his name.'

'Well, it was *meant* to comfort you, wasn't it?
Salesmanship. Spin. A trick. It aimed to make you think
full concealment is achievable and sustainable. Fieldfare
pretends secrecy can be constructed like any other product
– a car or TV set. It fancies itself as the disguise factory for
undercover. I expect some sessions were in the Simpkins

Suite. As you'll know, of course, Walter Barker Simpkins *circa* 1795 virtually invented one version of what ultimately came to be called the "conveyor belt" – in its day, "the Simpkins Endless Carrier Commodity Link", abbreviated in histories of the Industrial Revolution to "Simpkins' Link", almost up there with "Crompton's Mule". And, in harmony with old Walter B., Fieldfare wishes to think the requirements of all Out-located operations can be efficiently assembled in its workshops and then distributed en masse. Sometimes they're successful. Less often than not? I think so.'

'A wanted you there at the Fieldfare course to say that?' she said. 'To undermine him and to put the rest of us off sponsoring undercover? This is crazy, isn't it?'

'*Now* he would like me to have been there. Today. Flashback. It's guilt. He believes he conned you, pressured you, and he could be right. He considers I might have stopped this. So, I'm "fatally remiss". Fatally. If I *had* been there, of course, he'd have tried to destroy me and my arguments, as he did the comical relic, Mullins. It's the death that brings A the regret and tears and hindsight wisdom.'

They returned up the beach and path towards Esther's car.

'A wanted me to come and apologize to you and to the family,' Iles said. 'He claimed he couldn't face that himself.'

'He can face anything because he's got a sheaf of them – faces.'

'He thought I would understand how you feel. I lost an undercover man myself, you know.'

'Yes.'

'Raymond Street. This is a memory that sticks.'

'It will.'

'My advice is to act impeccably.'

'In what respect?'

'That's my instinct.'

'I'd always try to.'

55

'Get the people who did it, certainly. But get them with straight, incontestable, legit evidence.'

'You didn't do that, did you?'

'The courts and defence QCs will be on supreme alert for any sign of framing people for the death of your man,' Iles replied.

'They saw through your case, didn't they?'

'Lawyers and the court know well how enraged, and sorrow-laden, and determined on a conviction police become if one of their undercover people is abused and executed,' Iles said.

'You and a sidekick tried to tart up the evidence when it happened to your man, didn't you? And, of course, it was spotted and the villains got off on a technicality.'

'Lawyers live by technicalities, the way whores live by blow-jobs. Truth is what the jury believes. That's another of my maxims. Inns of Court jargon dubs technicalities "due process", the vowel sounds stretched out in judicial voices for solemnity. You've an idea who slaughtered your lad, have you?'

'We're trying to get a prosecution together.'

'Vengeance – not a wholesome impulse, but godlike. "Vengeance is mine. I will repay, saith the Lord."'

'"*Mine*". "*I* will repay". I thought that meant leave vengeance to Him. Don't try it yourself.'

'It's from the Epistle to the Romans. They did have a lot of vengeance and violence there, so you could be right and Paul wanted them to calm down, and quoted that Old Testament bit saying God would handle things.'

'I don't think of what we're doing as vengeance, rather as –'

'And then judges – they have their own way of looking at things,' Iles said.

'A told us that.'

'That's what they're there for.'

'What?' Esther said.

'However, to be fair, some judges incontestably come up very nearly to average intelligence. I heard the names of

56

several only the other day. With any luck you might get one of those.'

'You didn't for your case, did you?'

'Sometimes they'll slip in quite relevant questions. I've known it, personally been in court when it happened. I don't deal in gossip. Your witnesses should be warned in advance that a judge might suddenly ask something totally damn sane, to all intents and purposes. It's not just the cross-examination they have to prepare for.'

'One story around was that you actually garrotted the two who got off because you were sure *they'd* previously garrotted your officer,' Esther answered. 'I mean, you did it individually, no hired heavies. Like tit-for-tat. They could never fix it on you – you being smart and brazen – but the tale persists. Why you've never gone beyond Assistant Chief? The pair *were* found garrotted, weren't they?'

'My wish to come out here and see the spot where *your* officer was found might seem to you of no purpose,' Iles replied. 'And it's true I can't altogether explain the desire adequately even to myself. I suppose I'd call it completeness. Yes, completeness. If an Out-located officer's body is washed up on a beach, I have to see that beach. It's something I felt required to do before meeting the family. If I refer to the pebbles they'll know I've been thorough.'

'They're not fond of us, in the circumstances. They see me as responsible.'

'Luckily, empathy is another core facet of mine. I find I can reach people, even people afflicted and perhaps hostile, as these may be.'

'Look, Desmond, it might be best not to talk to them about the similar situation you went through, and the outcome there – the subsequent double garrotting. I don't want them thinking I've sent for you to do the job on suspects in the Cormax Turton Guild, like a hit-man. This might look bad for me.'

They climbed into the car. Iles said: 'Empathy is not an attribute you'll see on the usual schedule of career requirements for an ACC, but in my view it's a nice extra. A mentioned it with gratitude after I'd listened to him and – I think I can claim – consoled him, on the telephone. He said: "Do you know the word that comes to me about your attitude during this conversation, Mr Iles?" Well, do rabbits fuck like crazy – certainly I knew.' Esther drove. 'But I didn't say it. I affected ignorance because, one, for me to reply, "Oh, I expect you mean 'empathy', A," would have sounded like uncharacteristic vanity; plus, two, it might have seemed I'd simply laid it on, the empathy, as if I were used to dealing with his kind of unfortunate collapse – I am, but didn't want A to suspect and feel patronized; and, three, I considered he should have the satisfaction of producing the word himself: it seemed only proper. "Empathy," he said. "Empathy?" I replied, apparently startled and wholly unused to the term. Then I repeated it, more ruminatively, like getting a slice of education from him in vocab: "Empathy. Hm, empathy. Well, you said it, A, not I." "This you radiate," he commented. "That's very kind of you," I remarked. "Yes, empathy, empathy, empathy," he declared, with excellent rising volume, clarity and intensity, as he rang off.'

'Like a curtain line in the theatre,' Esther said. 'A can always put on a brilliant show.'

'Yes, they *are* inclined to be like that, shifty-by-nature undercover people, aren't they? Changeability is a constant. But I've decided, after all, that I don't need to get a different direct phone number at this stage.'

'*I* did undercover once.'

'Absolutely,' Iles said.

Chapter Six

'Please describe to Her Honour and the jury the special duties of Detective Sergeant Dean Martlew in the period immediately before his death.'

Richard Channing said: 'He had successfully infiltrated a group of companies in order to carry out certain inquiries.'

'"Infiltrated", Superintendent,' Longmuir QC said. 'Would you explain what that means here?'

Esther found she could not keep away from the trial, but didn't get there for every session. That would have signalled nervousness about the case. In fact, she was awash with nervousness about the case – the possibility of blame on Channing and therefore on her, the foul possibility, too, of an acquittal and the unpredictable aftermath this might bring. She must not show her anxiety, though. Juries had to be helped into wisdom and cooperation, i.e. into thinking the police considered the case open and shut and that, therefore, it might *be* open and shut and possibly worth a conviction. 'Truth is what the jury believes,' as Iles would say – unless, of course, it believed something he didn't.

Instead of continuous attendance at court, Esther turned up for a morning or afternoon now and then, with no real system, and sat in the public gallery. She wore civilian clothes, and tried not to look jinxed by fret. So far today, she felt reasonably at ease. But it was only the prosecution case and the lawyer a wonderfully committed ally, his wonderful commitment costing an arm and a leg, with refreshers. He simply led Channing into describing the spy game, as far as Channing knew it. To date, the judge seemed tolerable, her interventions egomaniac, wet, but undestructive. Esther feared the cross-examination to come from the Defence, perhaps tomorrow. In a crazy but obsessive way she found herself thinking that if this murderous, torturing sod in the dock somehow got off – and trials had a lot of damn somehows – if this unholy sod got off, the blame torrent for Dean Martlew's death would, and should, drop on her.

After almost endless, picky, and possibly biased, deliberations, she had put him where he was and then failed to get him out from where he was when it was so necessary to get him out from where he was if he wasn't to turn up corpsed on a beach with his face and neck much carved possibly for hours before death. Nominally, Channing ran things, but she'd wilfully chosen Channing above his boss and oversaw Channing – meaning she directed him, told him policy. And she'd chosen him because he hated the risks of undercover which, in her view, then, would keep him super-careful and vigilant, and therefore make Dean Martlew safer. Such reasoning she'd found fell pathetically short – smart-arse perversity. Maybe she understood the brutal tales about Desmond Iles in his terrain more fully now. Had he felt such shame at what happened to his Out-loc man that he decided the swiftest way to redemption and renewed peace of mind was to slaughter the pair of villains himself; the lunatic jury there having, in fact, come up with a different truth from his, despite rigorously assisted evidence? Yes, perhaps. Only perhaps. Nothing had been proved.

This simplistic, abattoir solution would not be available to Esther, though. She knew she'd never have the spirit and/or wrist strength to garrotte. To her, garrotting looked a sinister, damnable skill; in fact a kind of art, a kind of *filthy* art, and Iles had about him much of the good third/fourth-rate artist: arrogance, contempt for usual social and possibly legal standards, some flair, some posturing, some taste, some vision, and the irresistible impulse to create, or its complementary and sometimes necessary opposite, to wipe out.

'"Infiltrated", Superintendent,' Longmuir QC said. 'Would you explain what that means here?'

'He had been able to get himself accepted as a genuine, participating member of the companies.'

'Nobody in the companies suspected he was a police officer?'

'Not for several months, while he was providing us with information. I don't know about later.'

Iles had said he might do another long drive and look in on the trial when he could. He had no strictly professional interest here, though. The trip would be personal, a Desmond Iles odyssey, like the previous one. As far as she could make out, most of his life was a personal Iles odyssey, with police duties tacked on when necessary. Yes, she did think she could sort him out more capably now: he seemed, in his guarded, evasive style, drawn by the similarities of this grim Out-loc case to the earlier one on his own ground. Perhaps until lately Iles thought he had resolved that pain. Did the parallel Dean Martlew death reactivate Iles's old suffering? He didn't name any day for his visit. If he arrived and she missed him that's how it would have to be.

'Is it accurate to say Detective Sergeant Martlew was playing a part?' the QC said.

'Yes.'

'And might his role be known in police language as "undercover"?'

'"Undercover" or "Out-located".'

The judge paused from handwriting her account of the exchange between Channing and Bruno Longmuir QC. 'Out-located?'

'Yes, Your Honour. Or familiarly, Out-loc.'

'Out-located or Out-loc in what sense?' the judge said.

'Such duties are, by their nature, Your Honour, performed separate from, and, apparently, disconnected from, all police colleagues, all police contact – though, of course, there *is* clandestine contact with the managing officer for the passing of information. Very clandestine: the implanted detective must not be seen as associated in any way with his or her usual work conditions and is therefore termed Out-located. It is a kind of code, devised for security purposes. Less revealing than "undercover".'

'But from another point of view,' the judge said, 'an undercover officer could be described as "In-located", couldn't he or she? He or she is *inside* the organization you wish to penetrate and is therefore In-located.' She kept her face pretty deadpan, but clearly felt witty and fleet.

Channing said: 'Well, yes.' He gave it a nice dose of surprise, even astonishment, as if he had never come across this monumental slab of obviousness before. Esther's choice of Channing hadn't worked as she'd hoped, but she still thought he showed big talents. No particular censure could be directed at him for Dean Martlew's death. He handled the operation as well as it could be handled for four months. It might still turn out a part success, though at hellish cost. The verdict here could do big, even fatal damage to the Cormax Turton Guild. Or, then again, to her.

Longmuir said: 'Does this type of police work carry some risk, Superintendent?'

'Often very considerable risk.'

'Why is that so?'

'There is always a danger that his real identity will be exposed. Even if that identity is only suspected, the officer is at serious hazard, if the company or companies he has penetrated is criminal. He's certain to be outnumbered by the people he was sent to watch and will often be in totally cut-off, private surroundings and unable to summon aid. Although when installed in certain organizations he might be armed, as a natural feature of the gangster role he has to play, it's likely he would be overwhelmed before he could protect himself. He could be attacked when asleep or otherwise off-guard.'

'You say "at serious hazard". This might entail his death?'

'Certainly.'

'Torture?'

'Certainly.'

'Can you say why the reactions against the officer might be so extreme?'

'There are two possible reasons,' Channing said, 'one practical, one deeper. The two may act in unison. The Out-located officer will have been embedded to collect information not otherwise obtainable. If he is killed, he plainly cannot pass on any further information. It is an obvious and infallible way to silence him. But, in addition to this, there is a traditional, intense loathing among criminals and criminal gangs of anyone smuggled into their organization to betray it. That would be *their* term, "betray". This could lead to a violent attack – you could say a punishment attack. Because they were deceived, fooled, they may in retaliation behave as though the officer had actually been a proper member of the firm, not a detective playing a role. He is seen as a traitor – a turncoat who gives away gang secrets. This they would treat as the most contemptible and unforgivable act.'

'Finking,' the judge said.

'Exactly, Your Honour,' Channing said.

'And in both cases – the practical, and shall we call it the philosophical? – in both cases the violence might lead to torture and murder?' Longmuir said.

'Yes.'

The judge stirred again. Longmuir's strutting, woozy word, 'philosophical', may have irritated. 'These questions are very general, Mr Longmuir. Shall we return soon to the case before us?'

'Your Honour, we shall. I wanted to establish a context,' Longmuir said.

'Context is very well, I suppose – the, as it were, hinterland. But I'd rather not get bogged down in it – would like to press on and into essentials, please.'

'I will demonstrate, Your Honour, that the accused was motivated in both ways cited by the witness, the practical and the philosophical.'

'Well, we shall be listening, Mr Longmuir,' she said, 'or, as I believe the Americans say, "listening up". They're ever ready to improve our language.'

'Finking', 'listening up': she must want to show she could do slang – especially US, gangs-of-New York slang – and wasn't liable like Longmuir to the ponciness of 'philosophical' and such flab. Dean Martlew's father sat not far from Esther in the public seats, square-faced, square-bodied, grey hair in a pony-tail, around sixty, with rimless glasses. He owned a couple of landscaping firms and was clearly able to take time off when he wanted. As a courtesy, she'd been to see him and the rest of the family soon after discovery of Dean's body at Pastel Head beach, and instantly sensed the hostility and blame. Although at that time the family could only have been guessing at the nature of Dean's special duties, this was enough. In their view, Esther had put him into extreme risk. Well, in her view, too. She'd met no open accusation, no rudeness, but no friendliness either.

Perhaps the father attended all day every day: always when she came he was here. And, although the judge might consider some of Longmuir QC's questions far out, Martlew obviously didn't. He sat forward, jaw tight, eyes hard, very focused on every answer. He, at least, could see the link between Dean's death and the lawyer's court strategy. Perhaps this was the first time the father had heard in detail about Dean's assignment, and the dangers: 'the context', as Longmuir called it. Dean Martlew would have been repeatedly instructed by Channing, and at Hilston, to tell nobody, including kin, that he had volunteered for Out-loc. Esther wondered how Iles and his empathy store had got on with the family. In the court room, Martlew would give her a slight, civil, smile and nod, and nothing beyond, no words.

'I would like now, Superintendent Channing, to take you to what in Her Honour's word would be one of the "essentials" – the discovery of Dean Martlew's body.

You were present shortly after the discovery, were you not?'

'I received a message that the body of a young man, at that stage not officially identified, had been found by early morning fishermen on the beach below Pastel Head. I went there at once.'

'Would the call come to you because you had been managing the undercover officer?'

'Surely not, surely not,' the judge said. 'As I understand it, this was a secret operation.'

'That's correct, Your Honour,' Channing said.

'Thank you, Your Honour,' Longmuir said.

'There had been no positive identification at that stage,' Channing said, 'and, in any case, it would not be known to any officers other than my immediate superiors that I was running the Out-location programme, or, in fact, that the programme existed. I received the call as deputy head of CID. All major incidents of this kind are routinely reported to me in the first instance. If they are serious enough I would then, of course, inform the head of CID, Mr Tesler, and the Assistant Chief Constable, Operations, Mrs Davidson.'

'And will you tell the court what you found on the beach?'

Dean's mother never came to the trial, or not when Esther was present. Perhaps Mrs Martlew didn't want to be told in public how her son had willingly let himself in for blatant peril, and so for disfigurement and death. Esther knew Dean's family circumstances well: father, mother, a married sister, a younger brother. No wife. No partner. Esther felt glad Mrs Martlew was not here today. She might read the proceedings in the Press, but that would lack at least a little of the terrible immediacy and thoroughness in Channing's words.

He said: 'I saw the body of a man on the pebbles just below high water mark, fully dressed in a dark double-breasted suit, collar and tie, black shoes.'

'Did you know at once that he was Dean Martlew?'

'Almost at once. The formal clothes gave an indication. Members of some organizations tend to dress in that style and I knew he had adopted it as part of his role.'

'And, of course, you would recognize him as one of your departmental men and from the selection procedures and subsequent contact?'

'Yes, but there were initial difficulties.' Channing hesitated, then continued slowly. 'He had been shot in the head from the front, twice. And he had a number of wounds to his face and neck, seemingly made by a knife or knives. His appearance had been altered to a degree by these injuries and by possible buffeting in the sea and against rocks along the shore.'

Esther thought that to be as considerately put as it could be. Channing spoke with a kind of fatalistic plod, as if he had always expected something like this must end any Out-loc project, and now, here on the beach below Pastel Head, it had happened. She would agree with Channing's description. Of course, he had called her as soon as he knew this to be Dean Martlew on the beach and she followed him out there. No, Dean was not easy to recognize that morning. Both the fishermen who found him needed counselling for weeks afterwards. As Esther recalled, in life he had been strong-featured and alert-looking, very nearly handsome. In fact, at selection time, she had found it hard to accept that someone so presentable was not into a relationship. Recalling the Fieldfare recommendation, she'd hoped to recruit someone free of involvement. Although she never made it an absolute condition, she had let Channing know she would much prefer this if possible.

Channing had carried out his scour of the domain looking for suitable people and, as he slowly built a shortlist, put the full, personal records of each in front of Esther. She had read them over so often and with such concentration before making her choice that she could have recited the background facts of each of the five even now. Fieldfare hadn't given definite advice to exclude married or partnered officers from undercover duties, though there'd been those big hints. Esther considered this a bad lapse. She had wanted orders, not pointers; rules, not mere guidance. But she did see this might be unfeasible. Out-loc security demanded that the officer should not be already well known through detective work, and this probably meant he or she would be young. The majority of young officers did tend to be hormonal and have sexual links. To exclude everyone married or shacked-up was impractical.

Naturally, the argument would apply even more to older detectives – that is, supposing one not familiar to the villain firms could be found. Although there might be some still single, or widowed or divorced, the bulk would be cohabiting and have children. Because of such liabilities, these officers were unlikely to volunteer for Out-loc, anyway, and only volunteers did undercover.

Esther tried to see from the corner of her eye how Mr Martlew took Channing's bleak evidence. She felt it would be an intrusion to turn and openly watch him, a kind of cruelty. He seemed to be still crouched forward in that settled position, still measuring every word. Although she'd managed to find in Dean someone with no partnership ties or responsibilities, it would be impossible to go further, of course – to look for a detective with no ties at all: no living parents who might be hurt by any disaster, no brothers or sisters. Perhaps her fussiness had been a token only, a slight and silly gesture to show she did genuinely worry about the risks to one of her people.

She'd read somewhere that panels selecting astronauts for space missions actually *favoured* candidates in established, steady relationships because this might indicate balanced, durable personalities. Well, Out-loc, too, needed balanced, durable men and women because their period under vast stress might be long, so Esther saw there could have been a case for actually *preferring* officers in long-term relationships. And although her own marriage would never be regarded as a thing of balance and steadiness, she'd admit some like that might exist. Just the same, she had decided that for the Cormax Turton Guild project, she wanted a total singleton. Dean Martlew had claimed to be that. They did additional research on him and this seemed to be true: no regular woman in the background.

It struck Esther later, including sometimes now, as she followed the trial off-and-on, that maybe she had let this celibacy requirement get too absolute, too inflexible. Might one of the other shortlisted people have done the Guild assignment better, despite a solid, ongoing relationship? Might he/she still be alive and undefaced? That's what 'better' meant to Esther now: unmurdered, unmutilated.

There'd been a woman detective constable, Amy Dill, on the list whom Esther had thought from her records the most promising, although due then to be married fairly soon. Channing considered her brilliant, also – in fact, made her his preferred candidate, with Martlew next, but not a real challenge. Esther had even driven over to the outlying nick at East Stead where Dill worked to take a look without her knowledge and without commitment. In fact, at the end of that trip there *had* been commitment – negative commitment. Dill was too lovely. If Out-located she'd be stalked by every straight, fit man in the Cormax Turton Guild. It would not be fair to her, not right by her, even if she volunteered.

'How eventually was the body of Dean Martlew definitively identified?' Longmuir asked.

'Bank cards in his jacket pocket, dental records, an appendectomy scar and finally, when most doubts had been removed, we informed the family. His father, Mr James Martlew, and another of his sons came to view the body and confirmed it was Dean Martlew.'

Esther thought she heard Mr Martlew mutter something, but something unintelligible, perhaps just Dean's name. He still made no movement in his seat. She wished she could go to him after the hearing today and say: 'Mr Martlew, I'm all the time conscious of your distress, of the family's distress, but will you believe Dean *wanted* to do it, virtually insisted? He hated the idea that we might settle on someone else. We couldn't. He was outstanding, far and away the most suitable.' That would have been defensive, though. Selfish? It might help console Esther, suggesting there'd been no option, but would it make things any easier to bear for Mr Martlew and the family? They might argue Dean was a youngster, a kid, and that Esther had let him follow the foolhardy impulses of a youngster, a kid, excited by the prospect of cloak and dagger work; had cashed in on them. Most probably no conversation would take place between her and Mr Martlew, anyway. That could only occur if he began it. She would not force herself on him. He and the family had built a wall.

And was it true Dean had been outstanding and far and away the most suitable volunteer? Did Esther's determination to get someone with no active love life distort her judgement? Did the information he provided in those four months through secret contacts with Channing add up to much? Might someone else have been more effective *and* still alive and unabused, with Cormax Turton destroyed by information he or she came up with?

But, as to Amy Dill, Esther had also worried about that possible trouble she'd heard of at Fieldfare – the Stockholm Syndrome. Suppose isolated, under stress, Out-located Amy Dill forgot her loyalties to the job and her fiancé, fell for one of the men chasing her and went over. Esther had realized she might be doing Dill an unpardonable injustice by thinking of her as potentially weak and a wanderer. But, in fact, Esther did pardon herself: the Stockholm Syndrome existed and was common enough to get itself a title and inspire serious learned studies. Finally, Esther took Amy Dill off the list. On the same day, she approved Dean Martlew and authorized his application for Out-loc training at Hilston Manor. Then, a fortnight ago Dill's scheduled marriage took place, and this did help comfort Esther: something good was saved from the mess-up. She knew her thinking to be stupid and evasive. She sent a wedding present bought with her own cash. In the job, Amy kept her own surname.

Of course, on top of all her other concerns, Esther had wondered about Channing's enthusiasm for Dill. Perhaps he fancied working with the gorgeous female DC in the kind of very close and confidential style bound to exist between an Out-loc and the senior officer managing her. There would be many secret, interdependent get-togethers. Though Esther had plenty of faith in Channing, and some in marriage and engagements, there could be limits. She'd wanted to keep the Guild project uncomplicated and clear of possible emotional pressures. And, yes, in the long run she'd got that, hadn't she: death *was* uncomplicated, just someone in a mimic suit washed up on the beach?

Chapter Seven

Channing's evidence-in-chief finished. Not bad, Esther thought. It came as answers to the helpful, chummy, complicit questions of Longmuir QC for the Prosecution, and did bring her bits of comfort. Yes, bits. Now, though, she knew she should attend at least some of the cross-examination sessions when the other side's QC would get to uninhibited crash-ball work on Channing. She had to show him, and show the jury and the court in general, didn't she, that he had total, continuing, official support? That's what she was, wasn't she, seated with the rest of the spectators – total, continuing, official support?

Of course, such total, continuing, official support meant not much here. Less. She couldn't say anything, do anything except listen and wish Channing didn't sound so fucking feeble. He stood in the witness box solo and had to deal solo with everything flung at him. Esther offered a presence, but a presence no more significant than Mr Martlew's or anyone else's in the visitors' corral. Occasionally, Channing glanced her way. She couldn't read his eyes. Did they say, 'Thanks so much for turning up to offer total, continuing, official support, ma'am?' Or, 'Thanks for landing me in this shit pit, Davidson': after all, (a) he'd opposed Out-loc; and (b), if they did do it, he'd wanted someone else, Amy Dill, for whatever reason: maybe she'd have coped better, survived inside the Guild, or at least been quick enough to read the warning signs, use the exit drill and get out in time.

And did Channing read *Esther's* eyes? Although she tried to make them signal, 'You're brilliant, indomitable and right, Richard,' perhaps they told him, 'Rather you than I, dear Richard.'

Parkhouse QC said: 'Superintendent, you mentioned in your evidence-in-chief that Detective Sergeant Dean Martlew was conducting inquiries, undercover, from inside a group of companies.'

'Yes.'

'This would be the Cormax Turton business complex, would it not?'

'Yes.'

'You said that undercover work could be very dangerous?'

'Yes.'

'Does this mean that it would be tried only when other kinds of inquiry were reckoned to have failed?'

'Not necessarily failed.'

'Which word would you use, then?'

'Perhaps the inquiries did not move quickly enough.'

'Very well.'

'Out-location can, in fact, operate alongside other kinds of investigation. They would complement each other.'

'Have such other kinds of investigation been carried out on Cormax Turton?'

'Yes. Exploratory inquiries without prejudice.'

'Over what period?'

'Some months.'

'How many?'

'About eight.'

'An eight-month "exploratory" inquiry without prejudice into Cormax Turton before resorting to Out-location?'

'Yes, and then in tandem, ongoing. A routine assessment of a business. Many are done.'

'Can you tell us how many officers took part in this "routine assessment" spread over eight months, and before Out-locating Detective Sergeant Martlew inside Cormax Turton, then ongoing?'

'That illustrates the strangeness of the term "Out-location", I think,' the judge said. 'You speak, Mr Parkhouse, of *Out*-locating the detective *in*side Cormax Turton.'

'This would be a matter of standpoint, Your Honour.'

'And a significant matter. I think of Harold Ross, first great editor of *The New Yorker* magazine, who used to look at cartoons offered for publication and ask, "Where am I supposed to be?"'

'Certainly an important question.'

"But perhaps this is a diversion,' the judge replied.

'Yet very worthwhile, if I may say,' Parkhouse replied. 'Superintendent, can you, then, tell us how many officers took part in this investigation spread over eight months, and before Out-locating Detective Sergeant Martlew inside Cormax Turton?'

'It would be a changing number.'

'"A changing number". What would cause such changes?'

'Some parts of the inquiry might require specialist officers who would be co-opted temporarily.'

'You mean officers with special investigative skills in some particular area, do you?'

'Yes.'

'What type of specialist skills?'

'For example, in commercial and business matters. Also dockside practices.'

'These specialists would augment and assist the officers already conducting the inquiries, would they?'

'On a temporary basis.'

'The specialists would come in for a limited period and deal with a particular aspect of the investigation?'

'Yes.'

'How many officers would comprise the central core – that is the ones permanently on the inquiries?'

'About ten.'

'About ten officers permanently on the inquiries into the Cormax Turton companies over an eight-month period?'

'Yes.'

'And then this number would be increased by the specialist officers, is that right?'

'On a temporary basis.'

'How many of these specialist officers might join the basic team at any one time?'

'This would vary.'

'What would be the lowest number?'

'Possibly only one.'

'And the highest?'

'Perhaps five.'

'This means, does it not, that over a long spell of eight months ten officers at a minimum and fifteen maximum were at work on an investigation of the Cormax Turton business concerns?'

'Yes.'

'Would you, then, regard this eight-month inquiry by what we might call conventional detection methods as a major investigation?'

'Yes, of its kind.'

'"Of its kind". How would you describe its kind?'

'Exploratory. Routine. Without prejudice, as I've said.'

'What does "without prejudice" mean?'

'That no adverse reflection on the company is necessarily involved.'

'An eight-month investigation and then an undercover penetration, but no adverse reflection is necessarily involved. Is that what you're saying?'

'Yes.'

Of course, Esther had already known in outline how Channing would deal with cross-examination, and thought that perhaps it would work. Now, though, she felt only the absurdity of his words.

Parkhouse said: 'Very well, Superintendent. You would agree, I take it, that as well as being a major investigation this was an extremely *thorough* investigation – about ten officers permanently concerned, plus specialists drafted in when required.'

'Yes.'

'Who was in charge of these ten-to-fifteen officers?'

'Detective Chief Superintendent Simon Tesler, head of CID.'

'This, again, confirms what you have told us, doesn't it, that the inquiries were major and thorough, requiring management by the most senior detective?'

'Yes.'

'Whom would Mr Tesler report to?'

'To Assistant Chief Constable Davidson, Operations.'

'And since these inquiries were "major" Assistant Chief Constable Davidson, Operations, would wish to know of them in day-to-day detail?'

'She would know of them.'

Yes, she would know of them, all right. Esther saw the tactics of this cross-examination and loathed them, and loathed Parkhouse QC. Feared them? Feared Parkhouse QC? The investigation into Cormax Turton would get apparent praise from him for its rigour and scale and energy. But this was so he could subsequently show it as null – a sheer, laborious, large-scale, dick-headed and perhaps malicious farce. And not so much subsequently. *Now,* for God's sake.

'Thank you,' Parkhouse said. 'Superintendent, could you tell us, please, what did this major and thorough eight-month inquiry produce?'

'Produce?'

Esther wanted to groan at the stupid stalling but kept it under.

Parkhouse said: 'The result, results, of this major and thorough inquiry. Such an inquiry would be aimed at reaching some result, some outcome, would it not?'

'In what sense?'

For fuck's sake, Channing!

'In the sense of discovering whatever it was you hoped to discover,' Parkhouse said.

'Much of the information is still being processed.'

'I'll speak plainly now. Have there been any charges arising from this eight-month investigation?'

'This was a routine assessment. Charges were not necessarily the objective. In any case, some information is still being processed. This is ongoing.'

Did the jargon make him feel safe – 'processed', 'ongoing'? These were his life-rafts?

'Police would conduct an eight-month inquiry, supported by undercover penetration, and not hope to make charges?'

'Not necessarily.'

'Have there been any charges arising from this investigation?' Parkhouse asked again.

'The investigation is not yet complete.'

'Have there been any charges arising from this investigation?'

'No.'

'Thank you.'

Esther thought: the answer gets agonizingly squeezed out of him and so becomes three times as notable, three times as disastrous.

Parkhouse said: 'It's true, isn't it, that we have a team of never less than ten, and sometimes as many as fifteen, working for eight months on one dedicated inquiry, led by the Force's senior detective, responsible to and guided by the Assistant Chief Constable in charge of Operations, and nothing incriminating has been found?'

'Rapid results are not usual from this type of major assessment.'

'Would you say that a result after eight months of intensive work by up to fifteen officers would be "rapid"?'

'Some business assessment operations are immensely complex.'

'If you please. Now, Superintendent, in one of your answers to my learned friend you said that an undercover, or Out-located, officer might be used with the aim of collecting information that would otherwise be unobtainable. I have a note and think that's right: "not otherwise obtainable".'

'Yes. In some cases.'

76

'"In some cases" certain information would be "unobtainable" except by undercover work? Is that your view and the view of police generally?'

'Yes, it's my view.'

'In *this* case?'

'I mentioned that Out-location of an officer will often supplement other, parallel forms of inquiry.'

'Or *replace* other forms of inquiry, because the other forms of inquiry have failed?'

'Usually *supplement* other forms of inquiry.'

'You told my learned friend that an Out-located officer would be in great, continuous danger – in danger of death and torture – didn't you, Superintendent?'

'Yes.'

'Even on what you described as a routine exploratory business inquiry?'

'I was asked a general question about the dangers of Out-location. I was answering in general terms. There are certainly instances where an undercover officer would be in danger.'

Oh, God, the wriggling.

'If you please. Now, one of the main requirements for a senior officer like yourself, or like the head of CID, or the Assistant Chief Constable, Operations, is to do all possible to ensure the safety and welfare of your subordinates, is it not?'

'Yes, naturally.'

'"Naturally." Does it follow from this that you and your superiors would not wish to expose an officer to the risks of Out-location unless all other means of acquiring the kind of information you and they were determined to find had proved unsuccessful?'

And Esther would admit that, yes, it did probably follow. Of course it followed. Esther wouldn't *have* to admit it, not to the court, because at her rank she was not likely to be called. But to herself she'd admit it. After all, this explained why she reluctantly went to Fieldfare. Esther had longed to be assured there that, given the right preparation and precautions, Out-location could work, and work within the limits of acceptable risk. And she *had* been assured of this, and gradually let herself come to believe it.

At Fieldfare the speakers – A, B and others – had not hidden or even downplayed the hazards, but their overall tone was positive. *Do it!* Again, of course. Of course, of course, of course. That's why this Fieldfare programme existed: it had been created to teach management techniques for undercover. Naturally, no outright and absolute condemnation of Out-location had been – *could* have been – voiced by platform personnel at Fieldfare: it would scupper the whole Fieldfare purpose. The fact that there *were* platform personnel at Fieldfare, who had done undercover and then turned up and talked about it, showed the work could be handled, and that those doing it could survive. Esther herself proved this, but she'd needed extra evidence and had got it.

If Iles had come he might have hissed influential dissent from the floor. However, unlike A and B and the others, Iles did not show. He considered his flagrant, picturesque, non-attendance should be sufficiently meaningful. Mountainously, imperviously, vain, he would naturally think this. Iles expected the stark gap created by his absence to turn out far more significant and vivid than the actual presence of anyone else. He was the dog that didn't bark in the Sherlock Holmes story, and this non-bark said a bucketful. As a minus quantity at Fieldfare, Iles added up to more than all the rest together as pluses – this would be his thinking.

And he had it cataclysmically wrong. She left there converted; not as spectacularly or completely as Saul on the road to Damascus, but enough: enough to get Dean Martlew into a spot where he could be carved and slaughtered. The only sustained bit of scepticism about undercover had come from Inigo Ivan Mullins, and she realized at the time that he was like her – secretly keen to be convinced in favour, though, apparently, with big doubts: he'd expressed his, she hadn't, but Esther felt his attack to be an exercise only, a token. Fieldfare persuaded him into approval of Out-loc, as it persuaded Esther. Fieldfare knew its business. Fieldfare recognized, treated and cured intelligent and very intelligent doubt.

Now, in this cross-examination, Parkhouse QC wanted to demonstrate that the police – she, Esther, Operations honcho – would do more or less anything, including risk a minion undercover, to manufacture usable material against the Guild because they – she – had pre-decided the Guild was crooked, pre-decided without any valid evidence. Parkhouse would probably go beyond that and say without *any* evidence. Routine, unprejudicial exploratory inquiries? Bollocks.

Parkhouse QC's chambers were in London. He hadn't lived in this city and watched the dark, expanding Cormax Turton operation on the streets, in the clubs and rave sites, at the docks; and, even if he had lived here and seen it all, he'd been hired at QC rates to argue that, because there'd been no charges, there'd been no villainy. He wouldn't know about the witness intimidation, protection contributions and the skilled and ample bribery. And, even if he did know . . . yes, even if he did know or could guess, he'd been hired to argue that, because there'd been no charges, there'd been no villainy. He'd suggest the argument was so simple as hardly to need an argument at all; QED, as they briskly and smugly said in mathematics when a problem had been dealt with: Latin for 'which was to be proved (and has been, thank you very much)'.

Having failed in a major and devotedly thorough, long-haul way to nail the Cormax Turton Guild, police eventually chose Out-location – this was his point. And he'd allege that, when the Out-loc officer turned up hacked and dead on a beach, Channing and the police generally would instinctively and instantly assume he'd been savaged and killed because people in the Guild discovered his identity and silenced and disposed of him, after the routine gangster mode of these things. Esther, battered by the lawyer's theme, dismayed by the neat way its sections interlocked, wondered, Oh, hell, did Parkhouse QC portray the situation right? Had her resolve to hit the Guild become an obsession, and drowned her judgement?

Parkhouse said: 'Superintendent, I suggest you were part of an unflagging campaign to prove what the police had decided must be proved despite a complete lack of evidence.'

'Our purpose was to gather such evidence by proper means, as in all such investigations.'

Robot-speak. But what else could he have spoken?

Parkhouse said: 'I suggest that when your undercover, Out-located, officer was found on the beach near Pastel Head you immediately concluded for no valid reason that he had been killed because he'd discovered something the inquiries over many months by up to fifteen officers failed to find.'

'No.'

'I suggest you at once decided he was eliminated to ensure he could not pass on this information.'

'That is not true.'

'I suggest it was on account of this totally unjustified rush to judgement that you and those above you in the police hierarchy sought to concoct a case against my client, Ambrose Tutte Turton, who appears here charged with the murder of Detective Sergeant Dean Martlew.'

'That is false.'

'I suggest you saw this death as tragic, but also as a splendid opportunity to do what you and your colleagues had failed to do previously – bring charges against Ambrose Tutte Turton.'

'Tragic only.'

'You told my learned friend during your evidence-in-chief that the reason an undercover officer might be murdered was to make sure he could not pass on information he had secretly gathered, did you not?'

'Yes.'

'Did you automatically think this was the motive for

Detective Sergeant Dean Martlew's death when you saw his body on the shore?'

The judge said: 'In his evidence-in-chief the witness told us there were *two* reasons an undercover, Out-loc officer might be killed, Mr Parkhouse. One was practical – to render him silent; the other philosophical, meaning there is an in-built, traditional hatred of police spies – or what, as I pointed out earlier, the Americans call "finks" – the same word they use as for informants. "Rats" is another term.'

'I'm very much obliged, Your Honour,' Parkhouse said. 'I believe the witness also mentioned that the two – the practical and the philosophical – could sometimes coalesce and act in unison.'

'You wish to argue, Mr Parkhouse, do you, that the Superintendent, and later his superiors, might have decided these two, linked factors explained the death of Detective Sergeant Dean Martlew? Very well, you should put that to the witness.'

'Thank you, Your Honour. I am very grateful for your help in general, and especially the advice on United States low-speak. Superintendent, I have to suggest to you that, when you saw Dean Martlew's body on the beach, you decided at once, instinctively, that he must have been exposed as a police officer, and then killed to silence him; but also because Out-located detectives have always been regarded by criminals as contemptible traitors by criminals – in the words kindly supplied by Her Honour, "finks" or "rats".'

'I had no instinctive response other than accepting it as my duty as a police officer to discover how the body in that state came to have been washed up at Pastel Head.'

The judge said: 'On the matter of American slang, it's perhaps worth noting, though as very much an aside, I admit, that the US term for an unmarked police car happens to be a "pastel".'

'Thank you, Your Honour,' Parkhouse said. 'Yes, fascinating, indeed.'

'I feel one should keep up to speed on these things,' the judge said, 'if only to correct the impression that the judiciary are out of touch with the basics of life, either here or across the pond.'

'A worthwhile aim, if I may say,' Parkhouse replied. 'Superintendent, I suggest you and your colleagues at once saw – imagined – a link between the discovery of this body at the interestingly named Pastel Head, and the abortive inquiries that had taken place over many months.'

'No.'

Yes.

'And I suggest this link, utterly unbacked by credible evidence, consisted of, first, the wrongful long-term assumption that the Cormax Turton business network was criminal in some of its activities,' Parkhouse said, 'and, second, the conclusion that the Out-located officer had information to prove this assumption, but had been revealed as a police officer and executed to keep him quiet, and to punish him for the deception he'd maintained for four months.'

'No.'

'I suggest you decided at once to try to construct a case against my client because of this instant, pre-determined, mistaken interpretation of the death.'

'No.'

'I suggest your case against my client is of the same, stubborn, unwarranted nature as the inquiries into the Cormax Turton legal business interests which preceded it – that is, presume guilt first, then attempt to amass facts to prove this, rather than the proper route: to arrive at an accusation of guilt because evidence, fairly and thoroughly examined, leads to that conclusion.'

Chapter Eight

So how did they get to this? Often she would think back:

Out-location of DS Dean Martlew: Esther's narrative

1. Preparation

In her view, this had broken into five stages, five choices. She started with the most basic: (a) should she go for Out-loc or not? Well, Fieldfare and frustration had settled that for her, hadn't they, though Fieldfare short of the agonized voice of Desmond Iles? She'd do it.

Next question: (b) who would day-to-day, night-to-night, take charge of things and be the Out-loc officer's controller and contact? Not herself. As Assistant Chief, Ops, she supervised all important projects, but at policy level. Fieldfare, and what happened to her thinking there, was absolute policy, and she brought a consignment of this back with her, like IKEA assemble-yourself furniture. Now, here, she had to pick someone to put it, get it, together. Assistant Chiefs, Ops, delegated the Ops, like most modern leaders of men and women. Adolf didn't spend much time at the siege of Stalingrad.

Of course, she had talked privately to Detective Chief Superintendent Simon Tesler, head of CID, about the job. At first, she'd more or less automatically thought him the likeliest. He would certainly want it. He exuded experience and drive. He had looks, good hair and teeth, some charm, some wit, and probably expected these to work on Esther when it came to big choices, and this was a big choice. She realized people thought her a bit susceptible to any man more up to snuff these days than her husband, Gerald, which meant virtually any man outside a Rest Home. And, yes, she'd agree, she could be susceptible, though not, as yet, slaggish, or even close.

On top of that, nobody knew better than Simon the Cormax Turton structure, financing, family links, internal politics and work patterns. Yes, most probably, he'd assume the role must come to him, and she didn't want to turn Simon snotty and resentful. For months, he and his investigative group had been struggling to get something usable in a court on Cormax Turton, and he'd reasonably feel slighted as a failure if Esther decided she'd now try a different kind of attack, and drop him. Simon had come up the accelerated promotion way and this brought extra width and hearty fizz to his ego. He could be touchy. Well, he might be entitled to some of that.

Esther had learned from many staff rank leadership courses that you should never humiliate your senior people, unless it became necessary. As it had been put at one tutorial a few years ago, 'Do not fuck up top lieutenants, nor fuck them.' Easy to say, she'd thought. On the whole, she liked the way the verb to fuck had become de-gendered, bi-gendered, so women could now say they fucked men, as well as getting fucked by men, as per the old usage. But she saw this might also be not much more than illusory, feminist word-play. Basically, it remained the zoological case that men fucked women. Cows didn't fuck bulls, hens didn't fuck cocks. Cocks fucked. Men provided most of the necessary violence. Yes, extremely necessary. One of those largish US women writers on the metaphysics of shagging had declared, as if it were a revelation – and a terrible one – that the sex act inevitably entailed violence on the female. Well, of course it did, you well-meaning, trite, benighted duck.

'Out-location?' Simon Tesler replied with really positive positiveness when she spoke to him about it. People who came up on the accelerated promotion route did tend to be very positively positive. Esther had been chosen for that career boost herself but it would have involved a course away from home at Bramshill, Hampshire, and Gerald had objected. At the time, Esther herself hadn't wanted that kind of separation, so she'd turned the offer down. It hadn't mattered much: she climbed fast through the ranks. 'Out-location is clearly an option, ma'am,' Tesler said.

Oh, thanks, Chief Superintendent. But she actually said: 'I've had some advice, Simon.'

'Wise – I mean for a new kind of work.'

'It's not entirely new to me. I did some undercover myself way back.'

'Yes, of course. But new as organizer, rather than operative.'

'Luckily there's good, balanced, up-to-date guidance around.'

'Would this be at Fieldfare?'

'It's from experienced people,' she replied.

'Yes, I've heard they do intensive Out-loc sessions for staff rank officers at Fieldfare.'

'All-round treatment of the topic.'

'Of course, I'd noted you were away a while lately.'

'Undercover's become a kind of science.' She resented his guesswork, especially as it was so sodding correct, the smooth, speculative git. If she went on a secret scheme, she wanted it secret, not wondered about intelligently by some very intelligent inferior. 'Yes, a kind of science but it's still going to be difficult to place someone in Cormax Turton. Gangs have their own science.'

'It's always difficult, wherever, isn't it, Chief, but I do think we can bring it off here.'

'Family firms are the trickiest.'

'Yes, they can be tricky.'

'All right, most firms *are* family at the top, but clan connections in the Guild are exceptionally strong and established, as you know, Simon. Blood lines in all directions, like the Royals. We're fighting genealogy charts.'

'So, we don't try to get in that way, do we, Chief? We accept there are areas of the firm beyond us, at least immediately. The good thing about family outfits is that all the members – father, sons, sons-in-law, cousins, cousins-in-law, godsons – they all think they're lined up for a major job, and won't take anything less. And that's without even mentioning the women. Rivalries burn, the way film stars scrap for top credit. Family gangsters watch one another. The hates are real, unwholesome and imaginative, as in any family. People with even the faintest claims to lineage refuse to take a down-grade post because it would disrespect them, dis them – make them marginally less than some despised son-in-law or second cousin. This means there are openings. We get our man or woman in at that sort of level – courier/messenger, shop-doorway pusher, jetty lookout, protection collector, ship-to-shore loot truck driver. We recognize the family aspect – and we turn it to our favour.'

So, yes, it had been drilled into him to go for the positive – to locate someone's strength and brilliantly adjust this into a weakness, or adjust how it *appeared* into a weakness. Think Ho Chi Minh. Ho knew the US and South Vietnam together could blow any enemy off the battlefield. So, don't gift them battlefields. Do your Charlie hits from the jungle, then disappear. Esther had some of this buck-the-odds thinking herself. Almost everyone who got on in the police – or in any organization worth much – had a slice of it. You must believe an opponent's main assets could be upended, and you must make it obvious you believed it, or what use soccer managers and cheerleaders? The world might be a shit heap but it had to be climbed.

Just the same, it troubled her now to hear Tesler reduce the perils of this proposed Out-location to a rosy 'think win' formula, even if, by deciding to go for the Out-location solution, she showed she, Esther herself, believed it could work. After all, she wouldn't send someone into

Cormax Turton expecting him/her to get exposed and annihilated, would she? But it was hearing Simon Tesler trot out his analysis with such confidence and energy that unsettled Esther – the sheer words, the style, the plonking fluency. He had made everything sound entirely simple and cut-and-dried. *So we don't try to get in that way, do we, Chief?* Kindly, gentle, step-by-step reasoning. Teacher to pupil. Old hand to novice. Naturally, she felt not just ratty but perverse.

When she and others had interviewed Tesler for the top CID job, confidence and energy, and even style and fluency, would have been qualities she looked for. Now, they came back to piss her off big. Spiel king. Lists – he loved lists, to back up his logic and batter a listener into acceptance. *We get our man or woman in at that sort of level – courier/ messenger, shop-doorway pusher, jetty lookout, protection collector, ship-to-shore loot truck driver.* Admittedly, Esther liked to tabulate when assessing a situation, but Tesler talked like some page from a tactics manual. In Esther's view, confidence, energy, style and fluency were certainly OK when they were OK – that is, when directed right: say at a selection panel or a trial jury. But she had enough of general, all-round confidence, energy, style and fluency at home from her bow-tied, prat bassoonist, Gerald. And these days he seemed to be at home a lot, so she got a lot. He would theorize and incant and come to very downright conclusions, on a par for unshakeable tone with Tesler's, *We recognize the family aspect – and we turn it to our favour.* No problem. No?

To stick with Gerald a minute, he used to tour with orchestras, which brought some domestic peace. She thought his bassooning must have begun to go clumsy with age, though she couldn't ask him about this sympathetically or he might get nervy and perform even worse, attract less work, and be at home more still: he loved sympathy but would melt into paralytic self-pity when it came. Concert engagements had grown scarce. Impossible to write to orchestra chiefs, either, saying, 'For fuck's sake and mine give my hubby a job,' though she'd considered it. How exactly might bassoonery become clumsy through age? A matter of lung strength and wind power? Lip tension? The spit element? – too much, too little? She would be very willing to pay a gym subscription for him if it upped his puff. And some cosmetic surgeons specialized in lips – plumping them for a more sexy pout, and that sort of thing. No treatment – lips or elsewhere – could do anything for Gerald's sexiness, but he might be helped get a better mouthpiece grip; also benefit one way or the other from saliva control. But perhaps it was just that his fingers had grown too shaky to open the instrument case. Could he carry the bassoon in a carrier bag to concerts – one with a good name on it, like Waitrose?

'Of course, there is a very legitimate question to be asked about my commentary on possible Out-location in the Cormax Turton Guild,' Tesler said.

Well, let me ask it, you gabby bastard. Don't try to kill objections by pre-empting them. Esther did not say this either. 'There is?' she replied, as if startled that anyone might challenge a mind like his.

'Undoubtedly. Vain to deny it. Obviously, the question is: if our undercover officer is in such a lowly position and so far from the sources of family power – the main or, as it were, *mains!* power – how is he/she going to discover much of use to us? Information about the Guild's major activities will not seep down to our officer, driving a lorry-load of nicked cargo, or pushing packets in a shop doorway. This is a firm that's been in operation since 1986. Since 1986! Survival-wise, it's getting close to the Church of England, Murdoch media and the Great Wall of China. Cormax Turton didn't get to where it is today by careless-ness on security. The Out-loc officer's range will be small, and he/she would be unable to give us even these chicken-feed tip-offs, because if some of their minor projects get jumped on by police the Guild will know it's got a spy guest, and will set out to find him/her and silence him/her before he/she can get on to the bigger topics.'

'Why it's crucial to select as our undercover lad or lass someone who understands how a firm like Cormax Turton works, and so might be able gradually to move him/herself up the hierarchy.'

'Right.'

Again she thought the response too quick, the agreement too easy. No matter how talented the undercover detective, it would be appallingly difficult to move him/herself up the hierarchy. And exactly which talents would help with that? Bravery? Yes. Plausibility? Yes. Determination? Yes. Business skills? Yes ... and about fifty other qualities. Tricky to find them all in one detective? Probably. Very probably. 'Selection is the key,' Esther said.

'Cormax Turton has solidity, no question. It also has splits, famous splits, splits that might widen. Surely, these can be exploited by us as an aid to placing our Out-loc man/woman, and possibly getting him/her advanced. The Turton–Crabtree alliance *looks* stable, in some respects possibly *is* stable, but behind it always is that 17 November 2004 episode and the repercussions for Palliative Crabtree and Ambrose Turton. These are rivals for the eventual leadership. Yes, yes, I know they combined together well enough after that Preston Park incident to do Seraph Bayfield, but things between the two are still fundamentally troubled. It can be argued that the new shape and purpose of the Guild dates from the November 2004 business, so it's inherently, fundamentally shaky. Also, there's Cornelius's deep-grain envy of Palliative's dead dad, Brent Holywell Crabtree. That fine, touching tale about the *Times* obituary! Turton, Crabtree. This link is only through marriage, not blood, and perhaps flawed.'

'You mean we and our Out-loc girl/guy should side with one of the families against the other – the Turtons or the Crabtrees?'

'We have to feel our way. In one scenario – admittedly the most ambitious – Ambrose or Palliative might even get to rumble our girl/guy but agree to say/do nothing about it as long as there's an understanding that any prosecution based on the Out-loc evidence is directed only against the rival – that is, against Palliative if it's Ambrose cooperating with our officer, Ambrose if it's Palliative. Immaterial to us which. We could help one or other of them towards the succession, by getting rid of an obstruction – Ambrose or Palliative. My enemy's enemy is my friend.

'Agreed this is not the most ethical bargain I've ever heard of, but it might be a goer. And it wouldn't preclude us from later – not very much later – doing the job on whichever of them survives our first prosecution, Ambrose or Palliative, and is by then probably head of Turton–Crabtree. We'd pick them off in stages, as it suited. Ultimately, we set up the new leader, then nick him – decapitate the firm. Dealing with an internally troubled Guild, we have a thousand opportunities, a thousand! They've always been there, but it's you who intuited this and brought them into the reckoning.' He turned full on to Esther and gave her a disciplined but very appreciative smile. 'If I may, ma'am, I'd like to congratulate you on going for Out-loc, even though I know it is, or very much *was*, against some of your instincts. You have done what should always be a feature of leadership – developed your views in accordance with the developing scale of the problem. Yes, I know you've had guidance at Fieldfare, but the culminating decision is yours, utterly yours. This is the ability to act on an overview, so vital and good in a staff rank officer.'

The interview with Tesler drifted to an end soon after, and Esther chucked any consideration of him as manager of the undercover project. He could keep the windbag optimism and high-flyer buoyancy for his usual, standard role as head of CID. They'd be useful there. It was why she'd agreed with his appointment. He *knew*, did he, that she'd been at Fieldfare for guidance? He had it right, of course, and this enraged her. How could he *know*, the know-all bastard? And did he *know* that the 'guidance' had been crucially incomplete because Iles opted for absence? Esther read poetry now and then and had come across something by a Welsh clergyman called R. S. Thomas that seemed to fit Iles's thinking about Fieldfare: 'It is this great absence/that is like a presence.' Iles might have imagined his cruel truancy would speak like a presence, but she could tell him not a fucking bit of it. Did Tesler *know* how this unforgivable failure by Iles still troubled her, still put a shadow and a shudder on her Out-loc decision? She consoled herself with the argument that, if Iles's judgement was bad enough to get wrong the impact of his non-appearance at Fieldfare, perhaps it was also bad, misdirected, in campaigning against Out-loc. In other words, Out-loc might be fine, despite Iles.

When later on she spoke to Richard Channing about the possibility of undercover, he, of course, came up with one of those production-line objections to helping turn a colleague into a 'rat'. And – also of course – he mentioned the refusal of people like Iles to risk an officer in such operations. She dealt with all that, and then with his fears over trying to get someone into such a tight, family-based firm as Cormax Turton. 'The strong family element can actually be its chief weakness,' she said.

'Don't get that, ma'am.'

'They all compete with one another – are on eternal, bitter watch for disrespecting – so won't take the floor level jobs. Families are like that. This is the opening for our man, or woman.'

'Is it? Something menial? But how does someone so low in the firm get to see anything worth telling us about? We have to hit the main people, not nobodies.'

True, damn true. 'First and vital stage – implant the officer. Then, movement up the structure might be possible. Differences between major members can be exploited.'

'Oh, you mean Palliative and Ambrose?'

'The Guild is ridden with rivalries, envies. There's bound to be a Turton–Crabtree divide. Do you recall that mad business over the *Times* obituary for Brent Holywell Crabtree?'

'Buying up the papers. Yes. Maybe some grudges do exist, but I don't see how they help us.'

No. Esther didn't either. She tried to remember Tesler's mad, assured scenario. 'It's possible one of them – Palliative or Ambrose – might rumble our officer but would blind-eye her/him if we guaranteed to prosecute only the other. This would clear the way to the Guild leadership for a contender. For either contender. We don't care. My enemy's enemy is my friend.'

Channing thought about that. The idea had obviously never occurred to him, and *would* never have occurred to him, nor to anyone else but Tesler, if she hadn't mentioned it. 'Excuse me, ma'am, but you really believe that could happen?'

No. It was bloody ludicrous. The one factor that could unite any gang, firm, guild, was hatred of an Out-loc detective. 'These are people who'll do anything to improve their position in the Guild, Richard,' she replied.

'Excuse me, ma'am – *anything*? Even betrayal of a relative to the police?'

No. Never that, though they might fight each other. 'A relative who's in the way, and who isn't blood,' she replied. 'By marriage, only. We have to try to think as these people think.'

'Well, I do,' Channing said. 'I understood loyalty to the firm came top of everything – more important than anyone's personal ambitions.'

'Yes. But we have to ask, don't we, what does loyalty to the firm *mean*?'

'Well . . . that. The firm's interests are supreme.'

'There's short-term loyalty and long-term.'

'I don't get the difference.'

'Look, Richard, long-term loyalty could mean providing the firm with the chief most likely to make it go on working well, and improving. Palliative might think he's that man. And Ambrose might think *he* is. This is the point where personal ambition and the future health of the firm overlap – in the eyes of the people concerned. Each thinks he's God's gift to the firm. It's just normal top-man arrogance and sense of misssion.'

'Excuse me, ma'am, but are you saying they'd regard selling somebody down the river as good for the Guild?'

'One of them might. A twisted view, agreed. But not impossible.' No? It made her half sick to know she was using Tesler's arguments against Richard Channing when she had rejected Tesler for spouting these arguments to her. Perverse again? Yes, damn perverse. But it was the *way* Tesler had spouted them, wasn't it, wasn't it – so bland and dogmatic? Now, the entire conversation with Channing brought difficulties, and promised more. Simon Tesler would almost certainly hear about this interview, and realize she must be thinking of Channing, not himself, as manager for the Out-loc scheme. Dodgy. She'd considered asking Richard to come to her house for the meeting, to get away from headquarters gossip. But Gerald might be around at home, nosy, tearful, loud, opinionated, wearing one of his fucking horrible bow-ties so he'd look more pitiable. Instead, she saw Channing in her suite. Tesler would have to be told, anyway, once Esther decided Richard should do it. Occasional moments of brutality came with her rank. 'I want you to run this for me,' she said.

'You're sure?' Channing said.

'Absolutely.' Well, more or less.

Channing paused again. He had to consider the politics. 'What will be the relationship between this operation and the long-time investigation into Cormax Turton under DCS Tesler?'

'They are interdependent. Simon will understand that. He is obviously preoccupied with his exceptionally useful work there. He couldn't take on this as well.'

'One rumour said the investigation – I mean the established investigation – would be shut down, because it can't get past the silence brick wall, and that undercover will replace it.'

'Our established, ongoing investigation and this new Out-loc project should complement each other really well, I feel, don't you?' Esther replied.

Chapter Nine

'Ladies and gentlemen of the jury, you have heard from witnesses how, under an assumed name, and with his police identity concealed, Detective Sergeant Dean Martlew was placed in the Cormax Turton organization, performing a variety of duties, as if an ordinary working member of the company, but in touch secretly through telephone calls and meetings with a superior officer.'

Esther attended court for slices of the judge's summing-up in the trial's last days, and saw Iles had also come. Wearing a grey, single-breasted suit, he sat again in the public gallery, not far from Mr Martlew, to the left of Esther and one row ahead of her, so that off and on she could watch Iles in full or part profile. Most of the time, he stared at the judge, his head still, a gundog pointing prey. Occasionally, he switched this gaze to Ambrose Tutte Turton in the dock, gave him the same sort of hard attention, before switching back to the judge. Iles's tie seemed to have strong silver and red stripes on a dark blue background, perhaps the colours of some rugby club he played for when young.

Esther tried to read what she could intermittently see of his face. Of course, she wondered if he'd decided this prosecution was halfway down the tubes; just as that earlier one went down the tubes on his domain after an under-cover man's murder. But she could not make out a lot from his appearance. His lips looked magnificently dry, although she understood he sometimes frothed if put to exceptional stress. This could happen, she'd been told,

when quite frequently he berated two of his senior detectives in public, and presumably in private, about adulterous
affairs conducted with Iles's wife – at different times, as
Esther heard it. Also, it would sometimes occur during
funerals if, by invitation or not, and usually not, Iles got
temporary control of the pulpit at a service for someone
wiped out on his ground in a particularly unnecessary and
possibly monstrous way. He'd use the chance to rage and
foam against named criminals, and/or God, and/or the
judiciary, and/or Fate, and/or the Home Secretary and
Inspectorate of Constabulary, and/or medics. Esther felt
almost certain, though, that Iles would never make such an
open, fierce display in a fully fledged court of law like this,
nor forcibly attempt to take over from the judge, whether
male or female. His training surely made that impossible.
Churches and chapels he'd have a different attitude to. He
could be more brutal and competitive there. The rugby side
of him might come out then. Pulpits he seemed to regard
as up for grabs, like a ball fought over by players.

The judge said: 'A police witness has explained why it
was thought necessary to infiltrate – to Out-locate, in police
terminology – the detective sergeant into the Cormax
Turton organization. You would, no doubt, have made
your own deductions about this, even without the reasons
given by Superintendent Channing. Put briefly, the police
wished to know more about the workings of the Cormax
Turton group and had determined to seek evidence by
Out-location, as well as by other methods of investigation
already under way. Police witnesses have been guarded
about saying why these inquiries were considered necessary, but it is plain that the Cormax Turton group was suspected of some kind, or kinds, of lawbreaking. This is an
important factor in the case, members of the jury, because,
according to the Prosecution, it provides the background
and, indeed, the reason for the death of Detective Sergeant
Martlew. I shall speak more about this later.

'I must emphasize to you now, though, that no evidence
– I repeat, no evidence – has been put before you during

95

the trial of criminal activity by the Cormax Turton organization. In fact, it could even be said that you have heard
evidence to suggest the reverse. The Out-location project
became necessary, according to the police, because a
lengthy investigation by a team of officers, under the head
of the Criminal Investigation Department himself, produced nothing to justify charges against anyone in Cormax
Turton. We have been told that this investigation was still
"ongoing". Nevertheless, you might feel that the failure
to find anything to warrant charges after eight months is
significant.

'Further, Detective Sergeant Martlew had been installed
at Cormax Turton for four months at the time of his death.
Detective Sergeant Martlew and Superintendent Channing,
who had charge of the Out-location project, maintained
covert contact – or contact they hoped was covert – and
several meetings took place, as well as telephone calls. We
have heard no evidence – I repeat, no evidence – from these
debriefings that anything criminal had been discovered
by the detective sergeant. Superintendent Channing has
said that it could take some time before such a flow of information might be expected from an Out-located officer.
This is understandable, but does not change the fact that
from neither of the types of inquiry run by the police – the
team investigation and Out-location – had any evidence
been gathered at that stage – I mean before the death of
Detective Sergeant Martlew – to justify a prosecution of a
member or members of the Cormax Turton Guild. This you
must keep in mind when considering matters of motive in
the case before the court now. You should not regard suspicion as fact.'

The judge adjourned her summing-up soon after this. In
the evening, Esther went to a retirement party for Bernard
Stonevale, one of the eight-month investigation team into
Cormax Turton. Bernie had done his thirty years and, obviously, the eight months made only a tail-end fragment to his
career. Just the same, she felt a kind of grim symbolism in
these proceedings. Generally, Esther didn't go much for

symbolism and its realms of wool. But tonight, during the presentation and speeches, Esther heard something beyond the usual fond, formal leave-taking. Cormax Turton lived and prospered, whereas Detective Inspector Bernie Stonevale, who'd sweated and intrigued to wipe out the firm, now withdrew, passed on. And if the judge's summing-up resumed tomorrow with the same slant as today's, Cormax Turton might continue to live and prosper, with Ambrose Tutte Turton back near the top of the Guild and pretty well fireproof. Of course, it was a fluke that Bernie should be going out of the job now, but Esther found herself for more than a moment or two conscious of a signal in his departure: a white flag signal, a retreat, a capitulation. God, so damn unjust to Bernie – yet the idea clung and seemed particularly strong and troublesome, because a few years ago hadn't Bernie helped tutor a lad new to plain-clothes duty in the mysteries of detective work: Dean Martlew?

Iles had disappeared very quickly this afternoon when the judge ended proceedings for the day. He plainly did not want to talk, most likely because any talk between Esther and him after the judge's words could be only miserable. Mr Martlew had also left quickly, but then he always did, as if preoccupied by his own private sadness and despair, and uninterested in the reasoning and explanations of the brass who caused them. She could sympathize with him. Sometimes brass had to take a hammering.

Now, at the evening do, Simon Tesler handed over three farewell gifts and Bernie spoke his thanks and ran through some formula farewells. Soon, the main drinking would start. Esther did not intend staying. She might inhibit things. Brass. Gerald sometimes came to this kind of function with her and had wanted to tonight. Esther put him off, though. There would be tensions here: the failure of the investigation; the possible failure of the court case; the hints of resentment from Tesler over the Out-loc management, despite its bad end. Gerald couldn't always cope with social tension. Actually, Gerald couldn't *ever* cope with social tension, and it always seemed wrong to

Esther for someone to look so deranged or crushed in company while wearing one of his foully bright bow-ties. To dissuade Gerald from coming to the Stonevale party was not easy. Months ago, Esther had given up suggesting to him on occasions when she wanted to leave him at home that he should settle with a six-pack and listen to some radio music. He had come to hate any performance he wasn't in, which these days meant all performances.

Eventually, tonight, he said he'd go to his club, a dismal little place near the city centre with some similarly arty members in various routine difficulties about getting or selling work. They consoled or incensed one another, and he'd often spend a few uncheerful hours there. Money could be a tricky topic. Obviously, as an authentic bassoon player, he would have been insulted if Esther offered him a twenty for these evenings. Luckily, though, the owner of the club had been an army officer and to some members, including Gerald, he allowed the same kind of civilized arrangements he'd enjoyed in the mess: not cash over the bar but a monthly bill, in Gerald's case always paid by cheque very much on the nail – from the joint Esther-Gerald account.

At the leaving party, after Stonevale's speech and some hand-shaking he crossed the room to Esther. 'Well, as Simon Tesler said, we'll miss you, Bernie,' she told him. Stonevale was squat, strong-looking, boyishly open-faced although into his fifties. He had a job lined up with the Health and Safety people.

'It's all going to collapse, isn't it, Chief?'

'What is?'

'We'll never get Cormax Turton. But maybe I shouldn't say "we" any longer. I'm gone.'

'Someone will take over your work, don't worry.'

'I know I'm not irreplaceable. That's not what I meant.'

'We stick at it.'

'But you'll never get Cormax Turton, will you?'

'It's uncertain at present. Yes, it's uncertain.'

'We heard about the summing-up today.'

'Not over yet, Bernie.'

'But, so far, bad?'

'The judge had to say what she did. It was fair.'

'"No evidence against Cormax Turton,"' Stonevale replied.

'It's true, but marginal. Ambrose Tutte Turton is on trial, not the Guild.'

'I feel like I'm going out a failure. I've done a lifetime, but it's all made nothing by Cormax Turton.'

'Not at all, Bernie. You –'

'As if I'm deserting.'

Yes, it had been her thought, too, hadn't it, cruel and absurd? 'Nothing's finished yet.'

'If he gets off it's finished, though, isn't it?'

'Inquiries were, are and will be ongoing.'

'You can't do undercover again.'

'No, not undercover.'

'So you're back to what – back to the kind of stuff we've already tried and tried, and it's hopeless, isn't it?'

Yes, fairly hopeless. But Esther said: 'You know how it is with this kind of investigation, Bernie – suddenly we get one piece of evidence that makes everything else add up right.'

'If he's acquitted, any other move against Cormax Turton will look like grudge tactics – malicious prosecution. And they can afford top briefs to say so. My view? We should have been a lot *more* fucking malicious way back.' He frowned: 'Oh, sorry, but I can fuck and blind in your presence now I'm nearly through the exit door.'

'We've done it absolutely straight.'

'Which has got us where, Chief? This judge wants evidence. Fair enough. They all do. That's the kind of minds they have. All right, we should have supplied it.'

'We've tried to. You as much as anyone know that, Bernie.'

'We should have tried harder,' he said.

'I don't think we could have.'

'Tried harder and been cleverer.'

'Cleverer?'

'*Really* cleverer.'

'"Cleverer" meaning . . .?'

'*Really* cleverer.'

'You mean try to fit people up – Cornelius himself? Ambrose? Palliative?'

'I think you did right to go Out-loc, despite the disaster,' he replied. 'Yes, you had to risk it. Not everyone around here thought so, but me, I was in favour. You chose well. Dean had talent. He might have brought out seeming little items, inklings – items that could be fashioned up into something that would impress a jury, even impress a judge. Dean would have been good on inklings. He'd see the potentials.'

'Fashioned up?'

'And these would also have helped us plump out some of the material we'd been working on in the investigation.'

'Plump out?'

'All right, they have top lawyers, smart at knocking our case, smart at looking for flaws and so-called make-believes and contradictions in our stuff, but we still might have been able to get enough past them and convince the jury. After all, evidence is not something pure and absolute, is it, Chief? One scientist looks down the microscope and sees Life's First Cause. Another scientist looks at the same slide and sees not much at all. Evidence is what you make of it. Often it needs some . . . some shaping, some helping hand. Think of Tony Blair and the weapons of mass destruction.'

'I do.'

'We need to win, Chief. *You* need to win. We – you – know what Cormax Turton really is.'

'Of course we do. That's not enough, though, is it?'

'We – you – should make it enough, somehow.'

Well, yes. That's what it had all been about. It was why she chose Dean, or made Channing choose him. Dean had talent. *Enough* talent? It hadn't been enough to keep him alive. 'Enjoy Health and Safety, Bernard,' she replied.

Chapter Ten

Out-location of DS Dean Martlew: Esther's narrative

1. Preparation (continued)

To date:
    (a)   Out-location project approved.
    (b)   Manager approved – Superintendent Richard
Channing.

Pending:
    (c)   Who? Selection of suitable officer to Out-locate.

Yes, who? Esther had felt herself getting too involved in
the choice, and yet couldn't back off. She knew that picking the officer actually to go undercover should be left
almost entirely to Richard Channing. No, not *almost*
entirely, damn it, damn it, damn it, Esther. Absolutely
entirely, Esther, damn it. If you appointed a manager you
let him manage, and particularly on a job like this one.
After all, it was he who must work with the selected
detective in the kind of exceptional, tense, indispensable
closeness natural to undercover. He would search for
someone whose general temperament might suit his own.
Naturally, he'd also be looking for the full bag of basics –
of essentials – for a spy: plausibility, observation skills,
courage and more courage, coolness, memory, an unspec-
tacular career past, confidence, and still more courage. But
the need to find an officer whose nature might harmonize

with his own probably rated higher than any of these more obvious wants.

Only Channing could sense – guess? – who might fit. It would be an instinct, though an educated, trained instinct about people. Nobody should try to advise him on that mysterious bonding aspect of selection. Nobody. Esther knew this included her, and her above all. But . . . But she had instincts of her own, educated, trained instincts about people, and about bonding, mysterious or not. Although she'd attended God knew how many leadership courses that stressed the crucial role of wise delegation in police work, she'd always been poor at this, and knew it. Having appointed Channing, she should give him autonomy. She knew this, too, but couldn't deliver.

From the start of the selection process there were difficulties. Channing could not at first reveal to people the purpose of his trawl. He, and Esther, had to avoid gossip. Although it would start as restricted police gossip, it might spread. And Cormax Turton were gifted, wise listeners. They heard a lot. Firms didn't last two full decades without ears and a flair for information. If a tale went around that Superintendent Channing wanted somebody for Outlocation, Cormax Turton would grow interested and expect to be one of the intended targets; would expect to be top of the intended targets. Or the only. They prized, and, naturally, denied officially, their crooked status. They'd get super-alert and prepare a reception.

Cormax Turton, of course, knew about the eight-month, brickwalled, blank inquiry into the Guild. Although they might also know about Esther's long, dogged resistance to undercover, perhaps if they heard whispers of Channing's search, they'd quickly deduce that eight months of failure could bring a mental turn-around in his boss. This was another thing about firms that lasted two full decades: they tried to understand the opposition, and did a bit of psychologizing.

So, Channing went very delicately. He did all his early research by computer-sift, working through the personnel dossiers of detectives who met the first, utterly elementary requirements: no prominence in previous cases; not too old; not too loaded with dependants. For undercover, these could be only very crude selection criteria. Dossiers might say who'd had business training and would be useful on fraud inquiries; or who spoke fluent Polish or Mandarin or Albanian, a nice plus in some situations. But undercover abilities? There was no way of assessing these from stored profiles, unless an officer had actually done that kind of work and made a go of it. Until now, though, Esther had forbidden undercover so nobody with experience lived on her ground, except for Esther personally. Age and rank would disqualify her. And, these days, because of civic functions, and media interviews on police themes, she badly lacked anonymity.

No, Esther would not be sidling herself into Cormax Turton. Besides, she had a chronically dependent dependant – Gerald, the job-seeking bassoonist, those talented, subsidized lips yearning for a double reed reblow at Mozart. Esther knew not much about music, but years ago she heard Gerald play the Bassoon Concerto and thought it one of the loveliest and wittiest performances ever. Could he get back to that? He'd been in a tuxedo for this show and the fine white shirt and black bow-tie conferred something close to dignity. It was only lately that he'd taken to the appalling coloured and dotted dicky-bows he wore these days. What did they signify, for God's sake – someone trying to appear jaunty and undesperate? They looked desperate.

'I note bravery commendations,' Channing told Esther when they discussed the first-stage sieve, 'but sensible, calculated bravery, no derring-do.'

'Everything about undercover working has to be calculated.'

'On the negative side, I tend to discount anyone who has actually asked to work in Traffic or Licensing.'

'Yes, probably not the right sort of ambitions. How about visuals?'

'Pictures?'

'Are you affected by appearance?'

'By mug-shots on the screen?'

'Do you read anything from their faces?' Esther said.

'Maybe some of them do look cop and will always look cop. No good at all for Out-loc.'

'They might look cop because you *know* they're cop.'

'It's possible. But many *don't* look cop, Chief, although I know they are.'

'How does somebody who looks cop look? Do I look cop? Do you?'

'It's not a question of their looking cop to me, is it, ma'am?' Channing replied. 'I have to consider whether this cop would look cop to people in Cormax Turton.'

'Sure. But how do you judge whether this or that one might look cop to Cormax Turton? How do you get to see things the way Cormax Turton sees them?'

'*Might* see them. It's speculative. Obviously, I have to make a leap. A guided leap, but a leap.'

'Guided by what?'

'Call it intuition?'

'Right. But when you make the intuitive leap, what is it in a face that says to you – you acting as Cormax Turton, after your intuitive leap – yes, what says to you, supposedly looking at this prospective recruit to Cormax Turton, what says to you that this is no thoroughbred, wholesome, trustworthy novice villain, but a dirty undercover pig masquerading as a thoroughbred, wholesome, trustworthy novice villain? Eyes? Chin? Smile? Lack of smile? Composure? Lack of composure? Incipient or actual moustache?'

'Many factors.'

'Many? Well, we should do something about that, shouldn't we, Richard? They might jeopardize an Out-loc project.'

'No, they couldn't, you see, ma'am, because if I'm aware of any degree of copness I reject them.'

'But you can't be exact about why?'

'Combined factors.'

'Which?'

'The overall count,' Channing said.

'Does this go for men *and* women?'

'Certainly. I must believe in my response. For now, it's all I have.'

Yes, she'd agree. If she put him in the job, she also must believe in his response, mustn't she? That's certainly what delegating meant, and, yes, delegating *was* important. She might have responses of her own, though, and in any dispute, she thought she'd prefer these. Knew she'd prefer them.

'The more or less instant and complete belief in each other – that's the kind of relationship I'm looking for between the Out-loc officer and myself,' he said.

'I don't know whether I *ever* achieved that with the guy running me when I went undercover, on a different patch,' Esther said. 'He had big rank, or big to me at the time . . . but as to his judgement . . . I couldn't rely on it. And then sexual complications. He thought he had an entitlement. All those furtive meetings – dark corners, dark cars. He regarded Out-location as an In-location chance, for his person, as we'll call it. I was young and, I suppose, reasonably all right to look at, so such things came into serious play.'

'Oh, that must have been a nuisance.'

'Yes, a nuisance. It shoved the whole operation off balance. Exceptionally dangerous.'

'I can see that. "Nuisance" – a feeble definition. Sorry, ma'am. Yes, dangerous.'

'Dangerous in the sense that he wanted to keep the undercover going even though I'd started to see bad signs in the firm where I'd been placed. I mean, signs people there thought I might not be what I was supposed to be – the thoroughbred, wholesome, trustworthy, novice villain. He liked the situation, didn't he – me on a string to him because of the job? He needed more time to get where he hoped to get. He wasn't going to, but wouldn't give up. So, he thought I only imagined the peril signs, because he wanted to think it. It's true that the continuous stress can sometimes make undercover officers imagine they're about to be exposed. I knew that, and naturally wondered whether my manager – so much more experienced than myself – had it right. Was I panicking? Eventually, though, I had to ignore him and come out, anyway. I don't say he knowingly kept me under big risk, only that he'd let his mind get clouded.'

Channing said: 'Rotten for you.'

'There was an inquiry, and it didn't endorse him one hundred per cent – unusual when he, manager of the show, had been defied by a nobody like myself. He took early retirement and ran a stall in the Town Market. I bought chestnuts from him one Christmas. He'd forgotten me, or pretended he had. I hoped he really had. Undercover people should try to be forgettable. It's a flair.'

'I'm looking to set up a link with my chosen officer where she – I'll say she, because I'm thinking of the experience you've just described, ma'am – where she knows I'll accept without question her estimate of how she's regarded inside the firm at any time, and not act too late in ordering her out,' Channing replied. 'And where *I* will know that she is telling me the whole tale of what she has seen, heard, with nothing left out or exaggerated, so I can make my recommendations on the basis of totally accurate briefings. Things could still go wrong, I realize that. It's why I've always shared your worries about undercover, Chief. But, if it's got to be done, I'll want it done to foolproof standard, or better. More than an alliance or a mere working arrangement between her and me. Let's call it a fusion.'

She did not much like this word, any more than she had liked 'nuisance', but undercover work would often involve strain on vocabulary. For instance, 'Out-location', itself, an ugly title meant to hide more than it told, if it told anything. After all, the homeless sleeping in London shop doorways could be called Out-located; and an Old Testament leper sent into the wilderness. Undercover reversed and even trampled on so many principles of policing, yet somehow had to be acceptably described, because undercover was also a valid and often invaluable type of detection. As Officer A had told them at Fieldfare, for the sake of disguise and ultimate success, Out-location might – probably would – require a detective to blind-eye or even take part in exactly the kind of criminality that police forces were set up to stop. Jargon phrases had been concocted to explain away this kind of deep contradiction, but they always sounded hazy, far-fetched and two-timing: 'conditional permitted complicity'; 'necessary temporary suspension of law-keeping'; and then the one mentioned by Officer A, and given the weird Oscar Wilde reference by him, PPA – 'Posed Participation as Accessory'. Oh, God.

Undercover also ran against one of the fundamentals of police training – corporate responsibility. Normally, you acted 'as one', showed absolute loyalty to the team and knew the team would show absolute loyalty to you: 'canteen culture' as critics curtly dubbed it. But an undercover officer worked solo. Goodbye, team and team talk. True, there was a rescue party if things went very bad, but routinely the Out-located detective operated alone, or alone except for the senior officer managing her/him. Perhaps the description by Channing of this powerful, one-to-one intimacy as a 'fusion' did have some truth, although the idea made Esther uneasy. But, then, so did her own name for it – intimacy. She recalled that old joke about the prostitute talking to her lawyer in a rape case: 'So this fucking tom turns out to have no money, so I say "No fucking way, mate," but he pushes me into the fucking bushes, tears my fucking clothes off, and it was there that intimacy took place.'

'Are you near a shortlist yet, Richard?' Esther said.

'Down to three or four.'

'So, you'll have to start talking to them soon.'

'Very roundabout, at first. They don't know what the job is. I'll mention some general, prestige role we want to fill and make up my mind as we go along.'

'Make up your mind how, if the actual prestige role hasn't been specified?'

'Intuition. What else is there, ma'am?'

'Intuition again?'

'What else is there, ma'am?'

'Not much.'

Chapter Eleven

'Ladies and gentlemen of the jury, it is not in dispute that Detective Sergeant Dean Martlew worked for the Cormax Turton companies, or Guild as it was – and is – familiarly called by the police and media. What *is* in dispute is whether members of Cormax Turton knew – came to know – that Dean Martlew was not an ordinary employee but an undercover police officer. Also in dispute and important is the period or periods of time that Martlew remained with Cormax Turton. I will consider first, then, the view, the appraisal, of Martlew while he was with the group, taken by the main figures of Cormax Turton, his ostensible employers.

'You have heard from the witness, Mr Nathan Garnet Ivan Crabtree, a director of Cormax Turton, and a grandson of the chairman, Mr Cornelius Max Turton, that the companies routinely recruited what he called "freelance labour" as and when necessary. That is, such engagements were for specific tasks and of limited duration. They were not what might be denominated "staff appointments", which carried a longer-term, more established, status within Cormax Turton. A "freelancer" might be hired, for instance, during exceptionally busy spells to help with, say, delivery matters arising from the courier business or the dockside interests of Cormax Turton. Mr Crabtree said it was for these kinds of duties that Dean Martlew had been taken on in a casual appointment. One thinks of strawberry pickers, hired for that short spell when the fruit is ready for harvesting; and of students helping gather grapes in the limited period of the French *vendange*.

'Mr Crabtree told the court that at no time did he, or, to his knowledge, anyone else in Cormax Turton, suspect Dean Martlew might be a police detective. They, of course, knew Martlew as Terence Marshall-Perkins, his assumed name for these duties. I'll read Mr Crabtree's words: "We would regard any locally recruited temporary employees as simply that. We do not need an elaborate checking procedure for such labour, though there has lately been more emphasis on security at the docks, because of possible use by terrorists. That apart, we would have no reason to suspect the companies had been targeted by the police and infiltrated, since Cormax Turton always acted legally and should not have been of concern to the police." Mr Crabtree said that even if he and colleagues *had* thought Terence Marshall-Perkins to be other than an ordinary casual employee, it would not have affected their attitude to him, as the Cormax Turton companies had nothing to hide. Had they discovered he was a police officer, he said, they might have thought he entered the firm concealed to make sure its anti-terrorist precautions had been brought up to date.

'This was contradicted by police witnesses. They said that Dean Martlew *posed* as someone available for freelance work so he could penetrate the companies and collect confidential information on the finances, structure and trading of Cormax Turton. It's clear that the police believed the companies to operate outside the law in at least some of their activities. As I have said, no evidence has been adduced as to the nature of any criminal behaviour, but you may think, based on media reports of possibly similar cases, that police suspected the courier business to be what is known as "a front" for dealing in illegal drugs; and believed the dockside interests centred on organized theft of cargo. As police witnesses have told the court, this explains the role of Dean Martlew: clearly he was *not* simply someone from a pool of day-by-day labour, temporarily useful to Cormax Turton, but an undercover officer charged with the secret collection of evidence possibly to be used *against* Cormax Turton. According to Mr Crabtree's evidence, he and others in the group entirely mistook Martlew's (Marshall-Perkins') real identity and were deceived by him.

'What we do not know, and what must be a matter for your judgement, is whether the reason for assigning such work as a spy to Dean Martlew by the police had any basis in fact. Mr Crabtree has said it did not, and that he and Cormax Turton had no cause to expect infiltration. Superintendent Channing and other police witnesses have represented such infiltration as not only justified but inevitable. In so far as this difference is relevant to the charges against the accused, you must decide whom you believe.'

In her office, Esther read the transcript of this later slice of the judge's summing-up a long time after its actual delivery in court. By now, the transcript amounted to ... amounted to a transcript ... to not much more than an historical document. It had its controversial sections, but nothing of any present importance; nothing that would warrant an appeal for misdirection. True, after the trial, queries had been raised in the Press about the judge's invitation to the jury to speculate on the cause of police suspicions before placing Dean Martlew in Cormax Turton: the courier business as a 'front' for drugs dealing; and a waterfront theft industry. Law experts quoted in these articles asked whether a judge should put unsubstantiated notions into jury members' heads like that, or suggest they might assume something because of apparently similar previous cases. But Esther didn't think a protest worthwhile, and not in police interest. For God's sake, didn't the judge have it spot on? Those *were* the precise suspicions about Cormax Turton that led Esther to decide on undercover intervention.

Whether the judge should have spoken them, rather than just silently chewing them over in her forensic brain, was a technical, legalistic point only, and, in Esther's view, best ignored. She thought that, if she *had* been present on the day for this portion of the summing-up, she might not even have noticed the blunder by the judge, suppose it *was* a blunder. Esther had certainly planned to attend all the closing sessions of the trial. But then, suddenly, and utterly unpredictably, came that terrible business at East Stead, near the boundary line of their patch, and she'd felt compelled to get over there immediately. To have idled again on the court's public seats in the Ambrose Tutte Turton trial became impossible. It would have seemed like a lapse of duty: or, at least, it would have seemed like that to her, personally. Some might argue she needn't have become so directly involved at East Stead. After all, she did not really know the girl destroyed in this tragedy, and in fact had deliberately opted a while ago *not* to know her: had very carefully and categorically excluded her. Yet Esther realized that this negative link exercised its own strange, irresistible power, and had somehow tugged her away from one of the concluding sessions of the Ambrose Tutte Turton trial, and perhaps one of the most significant.

'Negative link.' 'Strange irresistible power.' 'Somehow tugged her away.' Jesus, she thought, what fucking, slap-happy verbiage – am I ready for a Rest Home, or even a seat in Parliament? She hadn't been tugged '*some*how'. She knew exactly how. The power was not 'strange', though possibly, yes, negative, and definitely irresistible. Look at it like this, Esther, dear, you barmy prat, she'd told herself: she, or she and Channing, had finally settled for a shortlist of two officers from which to choose their undercover man/woman. And now, of these two, two were dead: Martlew while Out-located; Amy Patterson, neé Dill, while *not* Out-located, because ultimately refused Out-location by Esther overruling Richard Channing. So, one hundred per cent wipe-out. The conjunction of deaths did undeniably and entirely *un*strangely create a powerful link, and, OK, maybe it *was* hard to see such destruction as other than negative. Yet did it also have a positive bit: didn't it make Esther get to East Stead regardless, and hang around East Stead regardless, where Amy Patterson, neé Dill, was killed?

'Now, members of the jury, I will turn to the matter of the spell, or spells, of time that Sergeant Dean Martlew worked as an apparent casual employee of Cormax Turton.' Esther read on in the transcript. 'You have heard deeply conflicting statements. The differences can be simply put. The Prosecution maintain that Martlew remained in the Cormax Turton group until two days before his body was washed ashore on the beach below Pastel Head on 10 June. It is the police case that his real identity had been discovered, following which he was murdered on 8 June by the accused somewhere on Cormax Turton property, and his body dumped in the sea, probably from a docks jetty. This is denied by the accused and by Mr Crabtree, whose responsibilities as a director included Personnel. They say Dean Martlew left the group after two months' work on 27 May and that his whereabouts from then on were unknown to Cormax Turton, and of no concern to Cormax Turton. This would be a standard situation: witnesses for the firm described two months as a typical stint for a casual worker. Mr Crabtree produced employment records apparently showing that Martlew was paid off and left on 27 May. You saw these as exhibits. Medical evidence puts the death of Dean Martlew at around 8 June. This means that establishing the latest date of his employment at Cormax Turton becomes highly relevant.

'According to Superintendent Channing, Dean Martlew's manager and liaison officer during the undercover operation, a secret meeting took place between the two on 4 June. And the Superintendent said he received a brief call from Dean Martlew on his mobile telephone in the evening of 6 June, Martlew using a public pay line. The Superintendent told the court that in both of these exchanges, Dean Martlew spoke as if he were still in place as a bogus, freelance member of the Cormax Turton work force. He said the unscheduled 6 June telephone call was to report

113

that the chairman of the group, Cornelius Max Turton, intended entering hospital soon for a knee operation, and that the accused, Ambrose Tutte Turton, and Nathan Garnet Ivan Crabtree would both take on increased responsibilities in the companies.

'Superintendent Channing also told the court he thought Martlew had sounded especially uneasy during this telephone call, as if afraid some members of Cormax Turton doubted his cover. Martlew did not say this explicitly, nor mention any new warning signs. It was the Superintendent's impression – the impression of an experienced senior police officer, though not specifically experienced in managing an undercover operative. Channing felt so troubled that he asked the twenty-four-hour rescue party to be on special alert.

'Now, it's clear that meetings and telephone conversations between the two men would always be tense, because they might be seen or overheard. But, according to the Superintendent, voice stress during the 6 June telephone call became exceptional. The cell phone conversation between Dean Martlew and Superintendent Channing was not recorded. We heard this is normal in undercover work, even for landline calls, because preservation of recordings might endanger security. The Superintendent said he did, however, keep a coded log of all meetings and telephone calls. Each log entry is timed and dated and comprises a summary of what the witness tells us was said by both parties.

'Members of the jury, you also saw extracts from the log as exhibits, with Dean Martlew referred to under the code name Wally. I should say, names are bound to take on some complexity in undercover operations. There will be the real name of the officer, in his case Dean Martlew. Then there will be the assumed name used in the target firm – Terence Marshall-Perkins. And, because the real identity of the detective has to be kept secret even from most other police officers for fear of leaks, there will often be what is termed a "working" name – this being the name by which the

Out-located man or woman is known, say, to those who might have to conduct a rescue. Dean Martlew's "working" name was Wally. We heard in an amusing aside from Superintendent Channing why this had been chosen and its origin in the name of the poet Walter de la Mare, author of "The Listeners".'

Esther recalled Officer B on monikers and her anxieties when people in a penetrated firm repeatedly used her assumed name in conversation – Dawn, Dawn, Dawn, as if to prove they believed absolutely in it; which meant they didn't. Did Cormax Turton people start calling Martlew Terry, Terry, Terry? Had that been one of the factors troubling him?

The transcript said: 'Relevant times and dates in the log are 1845, 4 June for the latest meeting; and 2015 on 6 June for the phone call. The summaries are written as if Dean Martlew (Wally/Marshall-Perkins) was still Out-located and functioning in Cormax Turton. The 6 June summary contains a reference to the possibly impending knee operation for Mr Cornelius Max Turton.'

Esther thought that if she'd been in court to hear this she might have felt cheered for a while by the judge's reminder to the jury of Channing's impeccable, methodical note-making, carefully dated and timed. But Esther was over at East Stead then, observing – some would say interfering – and mourning. She had spent several hours there, drawn by that compulsive, haywire, farcically illogical, sense of connection with DC Amy Patterson, neé Dill.

Esther came to one of the chief passages in the transcript. 'Members of the jury, the disagreements about time are obviously very profound and are one of the main issues in this case. The Prosecution says Dean Martlew remained in place with Cormax Turton until 8 June, when he was murdered by the accused, acting out of hatred for a spying intruder, and in order to silence him. The Defence says nobody at Cormax Turton had any reason to hate an undercover officer, and that Dean Martlew left the group on 27 May but, apparently for private reasons, did not

115

inform his police superiors. If the Defence argument is correct, there are considerable gaps in what we know of Dean Martlew's activities and whereabouts from 27 May, until he was killed by a person or persons unknown and his body found on Pastel Head beach. The only information we have about Martlew during these ten or so days is Superintendent Channing's report of the meeting on 4 June and the telephone call on 6 June. The Superintendent says he believed Dean Martlew to be still installed at Cormax Turton on these dates.

'The Defence argument which aims to refute this produces two possible implications. First, the Defence suggestion could mean the liaison officer, Superintendent Channing, was deceived into thinking that at the time of the 4 June meeting and 6 June telephone call Dean Martlew continued as an Out-located officer in Cormax Turton, and therefore the Superintendent's notes on this meeting and telephone call are entirely unreliable. The Defence cannot say where Dean Martlew was or with whom, only that he was not in Cormax Turton with former work colleagues. The Defence is, of course, under no obligation to provide evidence of where Martlew spent those intervening days. It is not the duty of a firm like Cormax Turton to remain in touch with freelance labour that has been paid off.

'The second implication of the Defence's argument is considerably more serious. Does it suggest that the meeting and telephone call might not have taken place but were invented as part of a strategy by the police to make conviction of the accused more likely? The Superintendent's account of special stress in Dean Martlew's voice on the telephone could be seen as contributing to this aim, and his warning to the rescue group. In other words, the allegation would be of perjury, a very grave crime, and especially when committed by a police witness. This will be a key matter for your deliberation and judgement, members of the jury.

'I come now to the matter of Mr Cornelius Max Turton's knees, age and general state of health. These may sound

116

marginal and even a little humorous, but are nonetheless important. Superintendent Channing suggested that the telephone call of 6 June in which he said Mr Turton's knee trouble and possible hospitalization were reported proved Dean Martlew to be still embedded in the group and so able to pick up new, private information. But Mr Cornelius Max Turton said in evidence that there had been talk about his knee trouble and possible surgery for many months, if not years. No hospital appointment has, in fact, ever been made. He said it would be quite possible for Dean Martlew to have heard talk about these matters much earlier than June. In fact, MrTurton's knee trouble and other complaints were widely known about outside Cormax Turton.

'Mr Turton said Dean Martlew might also have heard earlier than June discussion of how the companies would be run if Mr Turton did, one day, decide to go into hospital and subsequently cut down on his work within the group, possibly handing over further shared responsibilities for leadership to the accused and Mr Nathan Garnet Ivan Crabtree. We heard they had already taken on some aspects of leadership because of Mr Cornelius Turton's age. The Defence argued that long-term, contingency planning of this kind was natural for any mature company, and would have been in the minds and discussions of directors as soon as Mr Turton's knee problems began to look chronic. In other words, ladies and gentlemen, a mention of Mr Cornelius Max Turton's knees in the telephone call referred to by Superintendent Channing would not necessarily have the significance suggested by him.'

According to the transcript, the judge didn't add 'supposing, that is, the 6 June telephone call ever took place,' but Esther thought she could almost hear the words. And the jury might have thought they could, too.

Chapter Twelve

Out-location of DS Dean Martlew: Esther's narrative

1. Preparation (continued)

To date:
- (a) Project approved.
- (b) Manager approved – Superintendent Richard Channing.
- (c) Final shortlist (alphabetically): (i) DC Amy Dill, (ii) DS Dean Martlew.

(i) Amy Dill
From the days of the first, wide-focus computer searches for someone to do undercover, Esther agreed with Channing that this girl looked extremely likely. No question, she'd be there among the last few or pair at the final choice. Of course, Esther realized that what she saw and assumed in Amy Dill might not tally altogether with what Channing saw and assumed. For a while, Esther had thought this didn't matter too much, though. They both liked what they read of Dill on file, including no dependants, and all the requirements for a reasonable shot at anonymity undercover: she was young, hadn't figured in any cases covered big by the media, and she worked in a fairly remote part of the domain over at East Stead. Her dossier contained praise from two chief inspectors for her calm and resourcefulness in bad situations. Naturally,

though, these situations didn't much match the kind of situations she might meet when Out-located. What did?

Dill had helped disarm and arrest a man who'd gone wild with a shotgun; and, solo, she'd chased and caught a thief on a warehouse roof. Great ... brave ... nimble, but ... But (a) could she convincingly act villain in a villain scene over weeks and maybe months? and (b) come up with information/insights obtainable in no other way, and likely to at least maim and possibly dismember Cormax Turton?

In fact, it was trickier than that because the villains in the Cormax Turton villain scene pretended not to be villains at all. They would like to be regarded as a legitimate, successful business outfit; and, above all, they would like to be regarded as a legitimate, successful business outfit by the police and the Crown Prosecution Service. CT really worked at this. Many firms did. Some meant to move gradually away from all crookedness and become genuinely law-abiding and auditable, though still in profit. Or they half meant to, or hoped to. Robert Maxwell, newspaper owner and notable swindler, might have hoped along those lines, though he made the mistake of getting found drowned from his yacht before he could manage it. But Cormax Turton *had* more or less managed to keep up the pretence they were pure. That is, they continued to perform as if a legitimate, successful business outfit because the police – meaning, as she saw it, Esther, in particular, poor, poor cow – yes, because Assistant Chief Davidson – that is, Assistant Chief Davidson (*Operations*) – had, in fact, failed to lead an operation that produced enough black evidence on CT's operations to persuade the Crown Prosecution Service to get operational and bring a case.

It followed from this that an officer Out-located to Cormax Turton would have to act villain, but villain acting lawful. There would always be an element of this in undercover work, naturally, because few villains went about proclaiming themselves villain. They tried for a respectable front. With Cormax Turton that front was brilliantly, superbly, presented and guarded by the combined families, and any credible undercover officer would have to help maintain this grand façade, while getting deep into the day-by-day villainy that made the grand façade so necessary. Maybe potential Out-loc detectives should be sent to the Royal Academy of Dramatic Art for a stint. At Fieldfare hadn't Officer A struck her as someone theatre-trained?

Esther saw again that it must be an eternal, eternally cruel, problem when selecting for undercover: you wanted someone with reassuring experience as an effective multi-face spy in the past; but not someone who'd been *so* emphatically effective that his/her fame and description spread among bent firms, making any future Out-loc a total and potentially suicidal no-no. Regardless of the hints in Officer A's talk that he, personally, had taken on several undercover assignments, Esther found the two fundamentally dissimilar demands couldn't live together, and decided she'd probably have to settle for a detective wholly new to undercover.

That's how it had been for herself far back in Esther's career. *Davidson, we'd like you to get yourself into the Beeling crooked outfit as one of them and bring us back untold goodies. OK? You're new to that kind of work? Great! We'll get you some training, dear.* Esther considered she'd done the job then reasonably all right; all right enough for the word on her to get around the firms that some young female cop had sneaked into the Beeling outfit and, despite having to bale out early, sent half of it to jail and the rest to the Job Centre. She could never go Out-loc on that patch again. She, Esther Davidson, had exactly typified the selection dilemma. Occasionally she dreamed up recruitment ads for Out-loc: *Experience indispensable and will disqualify. Good, non-existent track record vital.*

Channing also could come up with a phrase or two. For instance, 'the *Dirty Dozen* factor'. By this he meant that perhaps they should note and enjoy some of the thumbs-*down* comments in the dossiers of Dill and others, as much as the praise. What might be bad qualities for general policing could have unique, plus qualities for Out-location. And so, Channing suggested, consider *The Dirty Dozen,* regularly rerun on the Movie Channel: Lee Marvin leads a gang of hardened ex-crooks on an important, perilous mission in Nazi-occupied France, their villain skills and savagery suddenly alchemized to the side of good. All right, all right, nothing in Dill's dossier – nor in any of the others – suggested lawlessness. But some of the character judgements there pointed to apparent defects which might, in fact, turn out brilliantly, unmatchably useful for undercover work.

Esther didn't altogether buy the *Dirty Dozen* comparison, though. Marvin's platoon naturally showed plenty of tough individuality and had terrific, manly, snarling contempt for normal army discipline and organization. OK, these might be sexy and box-office in a war drama, but the mixture wouldn't do for Out-loc. Individuality, yes, oh, yes, as tough as you like: an undercover operative must be able to exist alone, unsupported from the police side for long spells, unsuspected and, if possible, untainted by the outlaw side. But Fieldfare taught Esther that discipline and organization in a successful undercover project had to be faultless, or as close as could be; which, admittedly, might not always be *very* close. Although Esther did seek someone with stacks of individuality and self-reliance, this someone also had to recognize the dull necessity of planning, timetabling, coordination, communications rules, and overall senior rank control. She and Channing both enjoyed one apparently half-adverse comment on Amy Dill's dossier: 'She has a quick and astonishingly thorough appreciation of strategic purpose, but will sometimes improvise unpredictably, and therefore unfruitfully, on the detailed, tactical working out of such strategic purpose.'

Esther had a smirk at 'unfruitfully', a delicate, punch-pulling term. Most probably it soft-pedalled some wondrous, all-round, Dill-based fuck-ups: pity they weren't described in the dossier. Just the same, she and Channing read the full sentence to mean Dill had excellent abilities that needed only fine tuning. Channing might fancy giving her some of that. Yes. In any case, if they picked her, the training and psychology tests at Hilston Manor should define and sort out any lacks. Esther noticed the reference to improvisation. Plenty of this would be needed, predictable or not. The achievements of undercover didn't come by schedule. Esther also noticed the praise for Dill's ability to cotton on to the main thrust of an operation, the 'strategic purpose'. It should help keep her morale healthy when stuck in Cormax Turton for a stretch without real progress; possibly without any progress at all, and for a stretch that really stretched and stretched. Dill's dossier showed no husband or dependants, but that might not be the full picture. 'Unofficial' liaisons would not be recorded – a boyfriend, even a fiancé or live-in partner. And if she *were* into a lasting relationship, separation could become irksome. She might need to remind herself frequently then how much her work mattered, and how it cornerstoned a major, overall design.

'I've been to East Stead to talk to her,' Channing said.

'Well, yes, I expect so.'

'Just recce.'

'Right.'

'When I say "talk to her" I mean, obviously, in a wholly informal way, at this juncture.'

'Which way is that?'

'General.'

'In what sense?'

'Yes, reconnaissance only, for now,' he replied. 'Very much so. As you'd expect.'

'In what sense?'

'Within quite definite parameters.'

'Which?'

'No mention of the specific upcoming undercover task yet. General only.'

'How do you explain yourself, then?' she said.

'In what sense, ma'am?'

'Why you're talking to her. Why you've done the mileage to a bird-nesting division like East Stead.'

'I talked to several young detectives over there. It seemed wiser like that. As if a pattern of interviews, of equal rating.'

'Did someone at East Stead have to line up the meetings for you – these talks? You gave a list of people you wanted to see?'

'I said I'd be conducting routine informal "get-to-know" sessions, reciprocal "get-to-know" sessions.'

'But they're not routine, are they? You don't normally run them. People would wonder about the real reason. That's how leaks can start.'

'"Routine" in the sense of nothing special. Informal.'

'And when you spoke to the others, would it be along the same lines as for your meeting with Dill?'

'Informal, yes. General. It has to be at this stage.'

'Juncture. The others are a sort of smokescreen, are they? You're really only interested in Dill.'

'I tell them all, including Dill, that we like to keep in touch – face-to-face, not just personnel files at head-quarters,' he said. 'The human approach. Very much a part of modern police practice.'

'Who?'

'In what sense, ma'am?'

'You said "we like to keep in touch". Who likes to keep in touch?'

'The whole command structure.'

'Oh? Myself?'

'*Your*self, *my*self, the Chief Constable, Mr Tesler. Everyone concerned with leadership, surely. And a natural departmental interest – CID. I'm there at East Stead as CID Number Two, after all. Keep in touch with all levels. Oh, yes, very much a feature of modern police practice.'

'Do you think they wear it?'

'Who?'

'The people you talk to. The officer who provided the people for you to talk to in a routine fashion.'

'"Wear it" in what sense, ma'am?'

'Do you think they believe there's nothing exceptional in the visit, nothing secret – just some humanizing face-to-face, very much a feature of modern police practice?'

'I keep it all informal.'

'And general.'

'Yes, and general.'

'So, is it of any use to you?' Esther said.

'In what sense?'

'If it's all informal and general, what are you getting out of it? You're there to discover more about Dill – her suitability or not for Out-location. In depth. That's crucial. How do you do that if the talk is general? A tonne of chat with her and others and where does it take us?'

'It has to be oblique, yes, so far. Uncommitted. Secure, at this juncture. I'm not going to come out with, "Look, Amy, I'd like you to think about undercover." It would be premature.'

'General in what sense?' Esther replied.

'Oh, yes, I'll range across a number of seemingly random topics, always in a lightish tone, putting her and the others at ease.'

'This is a clever girl, isn't it?'

'Dill?'

'She's the reason you're over there.'

'I'd say she's clever, yes,' Channing said.

'We don't really want her for the Cormax Turton job if she's not, do we, Richard? She's got to be clever enough to come back alive eventually, with usable insights and her legs the same length.'

'It will be a big help if she's clever, yes.'

'That's what I mean when I ask did she wear it.'

'In what sense, ma'am?'

'Did she guess you were bullshitting her by talking general in a lightish tone? Did she realize that the other people you met were only masks? Will the word go around?'

They were in Channing's room at headquarters. He had a page of Dill's CV on the computer screen and now replaced it by a series of dossier photographs captioned with dates and locations and covering her career from uniformed basic training depot and early service to plain-clothes detective a few months ago.

'What kind of general topics?' Esther said.

'Although they might be general, I could get good insights into her. That's what I meant by oblique,' Channing replied. 'It's a listening skill. I'm very much a believer in listening skills. I'd start an idea and then wait to see what she'd make of it, where she'd take it. This is how the listening comes in. What she opts for. It can be character-revealing.'

'Do we know anything about her sex life?'

'Listeners might appear merely passive, but not a bit of it in my case – something is happening throughout, and very much so,' Channing replied. 'Oh, very much so.'

'There's a poem called "The Listeners".'

'No surprise,' he said.

'It *seems* to be about a traveller banging very insistently and forcefully on a door while his horse champs the grass in the moonlight, but really it's about those inside simply staying quiet and listening to him banging on the door.'

'That would catch what I'm after exactly,' Channing replied.

'You're not the one banging on her door?'

'No, a listener.'

'When you say "topics", were they police topics?'

'A range. I imposed no limits. It's more productive. That's why I call the chats informal.'

'Where *did* she take it?'

'What?'

'The idea. The one you started.'

'Yes, very various. A range.'

'But not to do with undercover?'

'Not at this juncture.'

'Do you think she guessed it *was* actually to do with undercover? Maybe there's a buzz about. People know we're stymied on Cormax Turton after using ordinary methods for months and months. Would she pick up your real purpose? We agree she's smart.'

'Politics, sport, cookery – a spectrum,' Channing replied.

'Well, take cookery. What could you learn about her from that as a topic – relevant to undercover? Does she favour a particular kind of cuisine – say Mex or Estonian? Can you deduce something about her from that?

'And then by a sort of lateral thinking on to some other subject. An amazingly smooth switch. Speedy.'

'Is lateral thinking good for undercover? Well, I can see it might be.'

'And all the time I'm observing her, without getting obtrusive, I hope, but really observing – her breathing, her eyes, speech patterns, hand movements. That kind of thing.'

'Well, yes.' Esther had seen the pictures of Dill before. They worried her then, and still did. Part of that worry she recognized as inane. It centred on the photographs of her in uniform. She looked so totally right as a police officer, although more beautiful than most. Strangers might queue to ask her street directions. Thieves might flee from her across warehouse roofs. Esther knew that almost anyone stuck into a police uniform would look like police, and it was absurd to think these photographs eliminated Dill from undercover because she seemed too obviously cop. Esther's worries lingered, though.

'Chief, when I say "lateral thinking" – that's just a phrase, perhaps a bit high-falutin – when I say "lateral thinking" I don't mean her mind skids about all over the place willy-nilly. She can bring it to bear, really bring it to bear. Your word – "clever". A true brain there. If, for instance, we got her into Cormax Turton as a pusher she could handle all the selling side, no bother. She wouldn't have trouble with price changes day by day on the street, or bulk discounts on stuff for, say, a wedding reception or Social Services conference in the Mutalle Centre. She'd be able to keep all that in her head and when she handed over takings to Palliative or Ambrose they'd be spot on, no cause for possibly awkward queries. This is important. We need to establish competence, reliability. We've got to lull. Someone who can give them an assured trading flair like that is sure to move up the system. And that's what we're after, isn't it? She must get to the leadership and get trusted by the leadership – where the real information is.'

'She's a looker, isn't she?' Esther replied.

'In what sense?'

'The usual sense. A man about somewhere?'

He took a good squint at the pictures. 'Yes, I suppose to a degree she could be called a looker.'

'Is she as good as this in the flesh?'

'In the flesh?'

'Face-to-face. While you were observing her breathing and so on, I expect you noticed whether the photographs had her right.'

'When I say "observing" I don't so much mean gazing at her face and body in the usual sense, but observing her various reactions to what was going on. This is coupled with the "listening" technique I mentioned previously. It's the sort of dual function of the interview, the two things complementary. I'm waiting for her to, as it were, emerge – letting her emerge.'

'From?'

'Yes, "emerge" is the word, I think. I want the complete Amy Dill.'

'Well, yes.'

'Time is necessary.'

'When you observed her breath alternately emerging and getting sucked in what struck you about it?' Esther replied.

'About her breathing?'

'This told you something?'

'Very much in line.'

'In line with what?'

'When combined with other evidence.'

'Her eyes, speech patterns, hand movements?'

'The totality. One's overall impression of her. The, as it were, Amy Dillness of her. Consistent.'

'Consistent breathing must be a real plus,' Esther said.

'This is a remarkable officer, in my view.'

'And did *she* do any listening?'

'In what sense?'

'You said you went in for a lot of listening, as in a quite passive state, but not really – *seemingly* passive, but in fact the opposite. All the time you were geared up. What about *her*, did she listen, or was she chewing the various topics non-stop? Did *you* do any of the talking, say about cookery or sport, while *she* listened? Reciprocal, as you mentioned. For instance, did you tell her about some hop-skip-and-jump at your school sports?'

'My main aim was –'

'It's obviously vital she *should* be a listener, isn't it? Undercover, she's got to be able to manage that appearance of passivity we've spoken of. She has to find and record what Ambrose or Palliative, or Cornelius himself, are thinking and bring it back to you. That's the acme of listening jobs. She needs to be present when such talk is taking place, but part of the background only, forgotten about, blending in. It's what Keats calls "negative capability". If you ask me, there'll be a lot of blokes in Cormax Turton banging away and longing to get her door open, like the horseman in the poem, but she has to ignore all that and stick with the listening.'

'I must have a look at this poem, and Keats.'

'"The Listeners" is by Walter de la Mare. Clearly, he knew undercover first hand. They should get him into the Out-loc manual.'

'Poise,' Channing replied.

'Yes?'

'Oh, yes.'

'She has poise, you think?'

He chuckled with bemused satisfaction: 'You know, ma'am, I've been trawling for the single word to describe her, and suddenly it was here, with me, and is so suitable

I can hardly believe it took that long to surface. It must have been all the while in my subconscious.'

'Break it down.'

'In what sense?'

'The subconscious idea of poise sneaked into your subconscious subconsciously because of her conversation and behaviour. But when you think back consciously instead of subconsciously you'll probably say to yourself, "Yes, this, or this, or this, showed something that can only be called poise." How exactly did it show itself?'

'Not ostentatious. Not arrogance or presumptuousness. Those could go against her in undercover,' Channing said. 'They'd push her into prominence. They'd be the reverse of that passivity we spoke of as necessary.'

'Poise is to be at the point of balance, as I understand it. Between what and what, though?'

'In her case, poise will certainly turn out a plus.'

'How do you see it functioning if she's Out-located? What kind of situations?'

'Yes, when she gets to Hilston Manor I'm certain the psychometrics will prove she's exceptionally high on poise,' he replied. 'It wouldn't surprise me to hear they've never recorded anything comparable in the poise category. The data reading will come up on her profile screen there and people will whistle and call others over to see.'

'What about you?' she said.

'What?'

'How do you respond to it?'

'What?'

'The poise.'

'In what sense?'

'The usual sense. Men could find it exciting in a woman, I imagine.'

'Selling at street corners, or clubs or raves – that sounds furtive, menial, but some poise is needed even there,' Channing said. 'Customers have to be made to feel all right – safe and secure. Poise in the dealer will settle them, and bring them back next time. The recommendation goes around. They don't use the word "poise" themselves – that's a special sort of term. But they say about a dealer, "He/she's all right," "She/he knows the scene, *really* knows the scene," "He/she's always where he/she says he/she'll be and at the time she/he says." But what they're really getting at is poise.'

'It's part of the charge if a dealer's caught, isn't it – trading in illegal substances while poised?'

Esther drove herself over to East Stead. She felt she owed that to Channing. Afterwards, she would tell him she'd been there. Definitely, she would. She wanted him to see she gave very serious attention to his approval of Amy Dill, before, of course, overruling him and turning her down. In fact, Esther had absolutely rejected Dill before leaving for East Stead and knew that nothing she saw there could affect her view. But so that Channing would not feel slighted or trampled, Esther meant to make a considerate show of open-mindedness. Channing obviously wanted Dill for the undercover duty. Her poise had won him and whatever poise meant for (a) the coming Cormax Turton infiltration; and also for (b) Channing personally.

Esther couldn't tell which was the more influential with him, (a) or (b), but thought (b), though with (a) not a total non-starter. After all, if Dill failed in the job he would have no chance of scoring with her, because she would most likely be dead. So he could not altogether forget about (a) – because (b) depended on it.

For a few seconds Esther felt ashamed. God, what a cynical bit of reasoning that was. Where did such viciousness come from? Jealousy? Well, yes, maybe a kind of jealousy. 'A kind of'? Which kind? Jealousy was jealousy, wasn't it, destructive and pathetic? Did it anger her that Channing so gibberingly and obviously and verbosely fancied Dill? Yes, a bit. So, how big a bit? Esther thought she could fairly honestly say Channing rang few sexual bells for her, although to a point she liked him. He was affable, sceptical and sensible in a style she admired, and bright enough to keep up with her waggish talk and to tease her in mild, playful fashion: for instance, the way he had picked up her question, 'In what sense?' and repeatedly returned it; and his manner of killing certain questions by answering different ones; another trick he might have lifted from Esther, or from lags under interrogation.

He was thirty-eight, slim-to-thin, small-featured, untattooed on his arms, mousy hair very fashionably cut and arranged, nimble, cleft-chinned, alert. She found it pleasant to look at him after Gerald as he had become lately, but this amounted to very faint faint praise. No, Channing didn't get to her hormones, at least so far, but, as to jealousy, she envied and nostalgized for Dill's youthfulness, beauty, poise, if that meant anything. These combined could reach out and plainly, devastatingly wow a middle-aged, married-with-children, generally wise senior policeman. The pretence that he hadn't noticed Dill's attractiveness until Esther referred to it tickled her. And riled her. Esther might not want him herself at this juncture but it infuriated her to see the pull someone like Amy Dill worked on him. So, OK, a kind of jealousy, but a kind that Esther could tell herself, and keep telling herself, was sane, businesslike, responsible and humane.

Her reasoning – sharply slanted, as she knew – went like this: Channing seemed enraptured by Dill and this must affect his verdict on her suitability or not for Out-location; perhaps dangerously affect: his judgement had gone blackberrying. If the choice were left to Channing it would probably be made mainly for the wrong reason: pussy. One of the questions he'd dodged had been about her sex life. Perhaps he'd discovered she had one, a serious one, but Channing didn't want to give it recognition, because he had plans. This could mean Dill suited Channing but not Out-loc. And that would increase the already plentiful hazards of undercover: she might be unfit for the job and very liable to fail. Therefore, Esther decided she had a duty to veto Channing and possibly save Dill, but to show him managerial consideration while doing it. She wanted him to see that she gave every respectful attention to his selection before booting it out. Esther would be able to concoct major, credible reasons to give Channing for the rejection: probable harassment in Cormax Turton because of her looks; and possible Stockholm Syndrome. And these did count for something in her mind. Yes, for something. Memories of those sexual complications during her own undercover stint counted, too.

The scrutiny of Dill at East Stead could be kept to a glimpse, and *should* be kept to a glimpse. Esther would not give it much time. Certainly there would be no meeting and no talk. These might have affected Esther's verdict. She wanted quick, formal confirmation that Dill emphatically ruled herself out of undercover by being too lovely. *'You're gorgeous, so no go, kid.' 'She's a doll, Channing, so hard luck.'* It pissed Esther off in retrospect that nobody had considered *her* too sexy to be Out-located.

She got Dill's shift pattern for the month on screen and then her private address. Today Dill should be working from 2 p.m. to 10 p.m. Esther went to East Stead in an unrecognizable car from the pool and waited around lunchtime near the flat. It was like secret surveillance. Secret it had to be: she knew that a call at East Stead nick by yet another big-timer from headquarters would up the suspicions there that something special must be under way. Police lived by suspicion, especially of one another.

Dill had a flat at the top of a stately, stone-built Edwardian house in a suburban road near a big park. At just after 1 p.m., she came out alone and walked to her Clio on hard standing that must once have been the noble property's noble front lawn. It was a dozen paces from the door to the car. That would do for what Esther wanted from this visit. Anything would do for what Esther wanted. She could now safely and destructively certify Amy Dill *was* beautiful in the way the screen pictures had shown her to be beautiful: skin perfect, nose straight, mouth wide and friendly, hair dark and cut short, eyes of indeterminate colour at this distance through the car window, but the dossier said brown, and they were unquestionably set in the right spots. Channing must have appreciated face-to-face with such a face. Esther thought that at one moment she caught a gleam from a diamond ring on Dill's left hand. There *was* a fiancé, then? Did he share the flat with her?

Dill wore a neat, management-style dark suit and white blouse, the collar up. The dossier had her as 175 cm – five foot nine – and she looked at ease with this height: ungawky, lissom, poised even, plainly unencumbered by anyone like Gerald, so far. Life could take some of the gleam out of engagement rings, though. Driving back, Esther felt very vindicated. Oh, yes, she must ditch Amy Dill. This journey had been a good and essential journey, even, in its way, kindly: it concerned Dill's welfare and safety, didn't it? Didn't it?

She called Channing in late that afternoon and listed the objections to Dill she thought him entitled to hear, and manufactured some minor material that should stop any difficult, prolonged debate. She thought she'd, so to speak, give body to the ideas she had about Amy's engagement. Things had to be got under way quickly, and Esther saw how. 'And then, in addition to all that, there is the present love life element. I went to East Stead, you know.'

'Oh?'

'I felt I should.'

'When did that happen, ma'am? I was speaking on the phone to Bob Lette there just after lunch. He didn't mention a visit.'

'By chance I saw her with her fiancé,' Esther replied. 'Did you notice diamonds when you observed her hand movements? Oh, yes, they're there. Three nicely shaped rocks. Dill and he looked so content with each other, so happy. Well, the way engaged couples *ought* to look. The fact is, Richard, having seen them like that, I'm not sure she could take the separation, separation that might run to months. It might unsettle her, rock – rock! – her concentration. Another point, Richard – perhaps a sentimental one: I came to think it would be wrong to risk someone so obviously content and fulfilled in her life. I'd even see it as an abuse of our authority.'

'She'd have a choice. She'd still have to opt for Out-loc if we did decide on her.'

'She's the kind who would – brave, dutiful, unselfish. She'd put the job first. One can see that much in her. I don't think she should be asked. It would be improper pressure.'

'Did you talk to her – to them?'

'I fear she'd take a request as an order. Sometimes leadership must give way to human feelings,' she replied, 'even among police officers!' God, Esther knew she should avoid such feeble jokes. They showed nervousness, possibly even hinted at the lying.

'Where were you when you ran into them, ma'am? He's not police, is he? I don't imagine it would be in the East Stead nick, especially as Bob Lette didn't say anything about –'

'It was decisive, that quite brief sight of them together,' Esther replied. 'No longer than five minutes. You know how it can be, though, Richard. Sometimes a seemingly small incident or word can suddenly resolve sticky, long-lasting doubts.'

'In what sense?'

'Oh, yes.'

(ii) Dean Martlew

'This, of course, is Superintendent Channing's operation – very much so – with myself as not much more than a spectator,' Esther said, 'a thrilled and fascinated spectator, but that's all. Or perhaps I should more correctly say it is *your* and Superintendent Channing's operation, Dean. You are the one who will be Out-located and Superintendent Channing will control and liaise. I called it *his* just now to make clear that my own role – if I have a role in the true sense at all – my own role keeps me at a distance – is to do only with policy and general overseeing. That's one of rank's drawbacks. You'll experience it one day, I'm sure.

134

The fact that we are in my suite means nothing. I'm excluded – justifiably excluded – from the pattern of immediate, urgent decisions. This falls to Superintendent Channing, and I can assure you, Dean, that his are capable hands. But what I wanted to stress, and why I set up this little meeting – yes, I wanted to stress that I endorse absolutely his final choice of you for the Cormax Turton sortie. I call it his "final" choice. Clarification is needed. From the first days of preparation for this project I can say outright now that we both knew, absolutely *knew*, you would be our ultimate choice. Richard?'

'Oh, absolutely.'

'Yes, absolutely. Naturally, though, we could not at that stage, juncture, simply settle for Detective Sergeant Martlew, no matter how strongly we held that nobody else would do as well. It's why you featured early in Richard's interviews. But we had a compulsory procedure to follow. In the police, there will always be a compulsory procedure, won't there? And let's not be wholly dismissive of it. I've said Superintendent Channing and I were convinced from the start you'd be our man. Fine and simple. But it might not have worked out.

'Undercover is voluntary and, regardless of how *we* felt, what we could *not* be convinced of then was that you would take this on. It remained necessary that Superintendent Channing should build a shortlist of other possibles, in case Dean Martlew proved unavailable. You can visualize our delight, Dean, when, first, you showed during a very general and informal interview with Richard that you guessed the face-to-face to be about recruitment for Out-loc; and, second – and much more important, naturally – you repeatedly insisted the job should be yours. Because of procedure and the shortlist Richard could not offer it at that time, though he, alone, had the power to choose. In this kind of operation it's vital that the controller and detective are one, so to speak. Nobody must interfere with the selection. The due rigmarole had to be gone through, though as no more than a routine following your response so early in the search, Dean.'

'I think I sensed I would get it – but an anxious couple of weeks,' Martlew said.

'We're sorry for that, aren't we, Richard?'

'Inevitable delay.'

'Yes, inevitable,' Esther said.

'I recall some rumour – quite strong – about a woman detective in the frame,' Martlew said.

'But one additional benefit came from the irksome compulsory procedures,' Esther replied. 'It helped Superintendent Channing create a useful diversion – a smokescreen. People might have guessed at something special when he conducted a one-to-one with you, Dean. That could be dicey. It's not helpful if a detective is suddenly pulled out of standard duties and disappears after a confidential interview. People naturally speculate. Speculation brings hazard. But because Richard so wisely arranged a very wide trawl – or appeared to – nobody would see our – that is, Richard's – nobody would see Richard's interest focused specifically, exclusively, on you. Numbers helpfully confuse the scene. To that end, Superintendent Channing scheduled sessions with young detectives all over the domain. I believe he even went as far as East Stead. A feint, but useful.'

'Right,' Channing said.

'I heard of that – East Stead,' Martlew said. 'I think the rumour might have been about a girl there, as a matter of fact. It was the kind of thing to stoke my worries.'

'This had to be gone through, and gone through in credible, thorough fashion,' Esther said.

'What especially bothered me was, if Mr Channing wanted someone reasonably unknown to make Out-loc feasible, a young detective working at a remote station like East Stead might be best,' Martlew said.

'I *have* heard an argument along those lines,' Channing said.

'Say an officer fairly new to the Force,' Martlew said.

'Possibly, but what do we mean by "best"?' Esther replied. 'That's the crux. It's unlikely that anyone from East Stead would have experience of Out-location in a big urban firm, especially someone not long a detective. Yes, that could have some benefits. But aren't they outweighed by other considerations? Could Richard reasonably ask someone so untried to do it? He would hesitate at that, and I entirely sympathize with his reluctance to expose a novice. What we have in you, Dean, is a seasoned detective, gun-trained and, I heard, brilliant at it, familiar with the big city, and who, according to the records, has successfully done something akin to undercover while on secondment to another Force, so you're not known for it here. That's a grand combination. Not to be equalled.'

'It wasn't full-scale undercover,' Martlew said, 'though I made a lot of noise about it in the selection talk with Mr Channing. I can admit this now the job's in the bag!'

'We know what it was,' Esther said. 'You'd expect us to ask the people who ran that task, wouldn't you? They said you did remarkably. It's a beginning, and one very few detectives of your age have. Hilston Manor will see you're fully up to the mark, won't it, Richard?'

'Hilston's pretty good,' Channing said.

'And they'll be impressed by your shooting. I did undercover once myself, you know, Dean,' Esther said. 'I think it's given me an instinct for what will work and what won't – who's right for it, and who isn't. Though, obviously, the actual selection has to be – can only be – Superintendent Channing's. I'm the rubber stamp, and very content to be so.'

Chapter Thirteen

Out-location of DS Dean Martlew: Esther's narrative

2. Operational Method

As Esther would have expected, Richard Channing actually did look up Walter de la Mare's poem about the horseman at the door. He said he'd enjoyed it. He gave the verse three or four readings, 'from the start right through to finish, no skipping, line by line every time, a veritable experience with a capital E'. If Channing promised to do something, even in what seemed a casual aside, he'd have a real go. Esther reckoned this kind of sweet behaviour might help him move higher in the police, or not. He told her he especially liked the sentence, 'Never the least stir made the listeners.' Channing recited this in a voice full of acclaim and recognition, and gave 'Never' true, timeless boom. That was how undercover had to be, he said: the art of not unsettling anybody in a target firm – not causing them to 'stir' to any special, dangerous alertness; and then the accompanying art of quiet, concentrated listening, of hearing everything. In fact, he said he'd decided during his final thrilled reading of the poem line by line that Dean Martlew's code name while Out-located should be 'Wally', as a confidential, affectionate, in-house tribute to 'The Listeners' and its author. For security, every undercover detective had a headquarters code name throughout an operation. Only a few top officers would know his/her real details.

Channing said he'd toyed with 'de la Mare' as the code but eventually dropped this because too flowery and possibly difficult for some to remember. In any case, it *sounded* like a code based on the first two, and first three, letters of 'Dean Martlew:' possibly a give-away, by accident. Although Channing recognized that in modern British speech 'Wally' could occasionally suggest someone stupid and inept, e.g. 'the manager's a right Wally', he considered this did not matter, or, in fact, contributed an extra element to the disguise, because nobody picked by Esther for a job as deeply perilous as undercover in Cormax Turton could be stupid or inept.

'Pardon – not picked by me, not at all, Richard. Not my role. That would be interference. I simply and wholeheartedly endorsed the inevitable choice,' Esther replied.

'Yes, certainly. What I meant.'

Esther could accept 'Wally' as the Martlew cipher. Of course, within Cormax Turton, he must use another false name, his gang alias. Martlew could choose for himself on this. He said he fancied something hyphenated. The middle classes were more into crime these days and he'd come across a lot of crooked hyphens. Again, Esther remembered Officer B at Fieldfare discussing the need to get the right 'working' handle. For undercover, identity came in multi-packs.

As follow-up to another of Esther's idiotic poetry tips, Channing had also done some internet research on John Keats and his writing gospel, but couldn't fully understand the 'negative capability' she'd recalled from lessons at school and mentioned to him. However, he thought he did see how negative capability might resemble vital undercover qualities. The point was, wasn't it, that for Keats, negative equalled positive, Channing said, making Keats very different from electricity. Negative capability helped Keats create some of his best poems, and you couldn't get more positive than that, could you? Similarly, an undercover officer must try for negative capability, in the sense that he/she mustn't stand out, or get especially noticed, and this was how eventually to turn positive by piling up evidence that sent villains to jail, 'or, oddly enough, "stir", as it's sometimes called,' Channing said.

'There's a Keats sonnet called "Why did I laugh tonight?"' Esther replied at once.

'Is that really right, ma'am?'

'I'm pretty sure.'

'Well, there you are.'

'What?'

'He regrets drawing attention to himself by mirth, instead of staying void and negative and keeping an eye.'

'I've forgotten why he *did* laugh.'

'Probably not just a trip to a well-known early nineteenth-century ale-house comic. No, it could be a sort of hysteria, a break-out from self-suppression, if he's been switching his capability on to negative for a long spell for the sake of more poems. It's bound to get wearing. That's another resemblance to Out-loc: occasionally, a detective isolated, corralled, very vulnerable, in a firm will crack mentally. It's classic. Noisy, mad laughter could be part of this, the cause soon forgotten, if there *was* a cause, as such.'

'Stir crazy.'

'A tumble into mad, noticeable, dangerous behaviour by the over-stressed officer. Keats understood this scene as much as de la Mare. You were entirely right to see parallels, ma'am.'

'I believe in "Why did I laugh tonight?" he speaks to his heart and says, "Thou and I are here sad and alone." That's just Keats and his heart.'

'Exactly,' Channing said. 'This could match the beginnings of the Stockholm Syndrome in an undercover cop, couldn't it? He, or more likely *she*, gets to need friendship and perhaps love, and seeks it from the people at hand, although the only people at hand now are the criminals she/he is supposed to shop. It's an attempted escape from that sadness and loneliness.'

Well, up yours, Channing, you macho lout. Esther fumed at his assumption that women would be more likely to go over than men, but she stayed quiet. She had to: she'd quoted Stockholm Syndrome as one reason to block Amy Dill from the Cormax Turton jaunt and prefer a male.

Once Dean Martlew had been installed, the team on stand-by in case he needed to be retrieved from undercover in a crisis came to be known as 'Wally Watch', though Esther guessed they'd miss the de la Mare reference. She didn't mind the title. Dark jokiness was a tradition in the police and armed services, and the more dangerous the situation the more flippant the language, as if to reduce menace and fear. That lampoon session between her and Channing about poets and poetry had been in part a mickey-taking, joke-driven game, of course. Yes, part comedy, part frighteningly serious. But – also, of course – a rescue team would need to get beyond the 'Wally' label should things turn bad and orders come to find Martlew fast and bring him back, if possible, intact and still recognizable. A sealed package containing photographs of Martlew, plus his real name, his accepted name at the crook firm, and a full physical description, was passed between leaders of the salvage party at shift change, along with the £1000 for possible greased lightning greasing. The package would be opened only if the party were sent to intervene. It notified them, also, *where* to intervene: Cormax Turton. But CT operated from a range of locations. The information pack probably wouldn't be able to specify. And so, the absolute requirement for life-and-death speed when locating him. And so, the absolute requirement for the life-and-death, up-front, direction-finding £K.

Esther called in on the wait-around aid contingent now and then. It could not be too often or they would suspect she distrusted them for readiness and thought surprise checks necessary. They'd feel huffy about that, and Esther wanted to cause no distractions. She did trust them for readiness pretty well. But she needed the occasional contact of a visit. It could feel briefly like a kind of indirect communion with Dean Martlew himself, though her mind would correct that addled notion almost at once: Martlew remained unreachably, terrifyingly solo, except for those occasional meetings or phone links with Channing. And it was she – solo, autocratic and devious – who had placed him unreachably, terrifyingly solo. The responsibility roughed her up continually, and once in a while she'd concede to herself that she deserved it.

Esther had two hopes for Wally Watch: (a) obviously, that it would never be called on to bring Martlew out of a possibly terminal pickle; and (b) if it *were* called, that she would be visiting the group at the time and could get a place in one of the cars.

Esther wished she had someone to talk to about her anxieties, but realized she must maintain a confident show with the recovery teams and a relaxed, playful show with Channing. Didn't a high-ranking British army officer walk around with an umbrella up during some ferocious battle in the Second World War, claiming it would shelter him from German gunfire? Leadership. Gaiety. Sangfroid. This blatant craziness was meant to boost morale, a duty for all commanders. The boss had to believe in what the boss decided to do, or *seem* to believe in it, anyway.

If she had spoken at home to Gerald about her special job stresses, no question he would initially sympathize, in his half-baked, frowsty-breathed, mostly well-meant, fleeting fashion. He did not lack sensitivity or sense even now, and was sure to glimpse the risk and the gravity, and notice her chronic nervousness. He owed her some gratitude, and knew it: hadn't she gone through the bother of moving from her job with the South Wales Force to here, much nearer London, so he'd be handier for work in the capital, closer to agents and impresarios? It hadn't made much difference yet, though, and now, because of Gerald's vast, likewise chronic, ever-expanding, egomaniac worries, he would usually commandeer any serious conversation, then direct it towards (a) his career problems; and (b) his contempt for all notably successful musicians – repeat, *all* notably successful musicians, not just notably successful bassoonists – and the system, and/or Fate, and/or God, and/or diseased public taste, that favoured them.

Loyally, Esther had often been through this with him and didn't fancy a rerun now, thanks. Self-pity made a poor mix with those rancid bow-ties. And Gerald might find extra, special things in the Out-loc situation to babble about. Possibly he'd see a paradox. Gerald could more or less get off on paradoxes. If they ever asked him to give the Reith radio lecture he'd do it on paradoxes. In the present case, he'd point out that his personal, agonizing, engulfing troubles sprang from non-recognition, non-acknowledgement, enforced obscurity – each of these acute anguish for an artist. But, on the other hand, and amazingly, Esther's undercover detective would actually reverse this and calculatedly *seek* such non-recognition and non-acknowledgement – non-recognition and non-acknowledgement as a police officer. He'd cherish obscurity: lived by such obscurity. What a bizarre and unfeeling world it must be that could put cheek-by-jowl here in one small area such exactly opposed outlooks!

Gerald would probably develop this notion for a fair period, watching her non-stop. Then he'd be liable to get to the abuse point and ask in snarl register which of these two polarized cases Esther felt more womanly concern for, his or the detective's: 'mine or your sodding precious snoop's', as he might put it. Plainly, the only sane answer to that was her sodding precious snoop's. Gerald's pain came merely from slipping behind in the national and international bassoon stakes, perhaps irrecoverably, though possibly not. In any case, he could always busk. A busker in a bow-tie would be a novelty and might coin it.

But if things went wrong for the Out-loc officer, his/her pain could be real, maybe prolonged bodily pain, and bodily pain from which there might be no bodily recovery. Compared with Wally's situation, Gerald's was piffling. Plainly, Esther could not say this. Gerald would regard it as being spat on. Betrayal. Maybe he'd allege a vile, seething sexual intimacy with the undercover officer,

143

woman or man – on hold, clearly, while the Out-loc detective was Out-loc, but all the juicier and more voracious when he/she returned. Esther might mutter to him a bit about offering different types of sympathy for people in different kinds of tricky spots – for instance, the detective and himself – each type valid. Almost certainly he'd reject this and might turn weepy and more wordy, or clumsily, feebly violent. To Esther, it always seemed uncivilized to armlock Gerald, who had once been an authentic bassoon artist: like the burning of books by Goebbels, or the vandalizing of a Louvre picture. She did not want him humiliated to the point of despair. She feared the possible outcome. And if she inadvertently broke his arm it might have permanent effects on the bassoonery.

Right after one of these raucous, around-the-room fights he would always urgently need to shag *in situ*, the immediate *situ* – crucial, this – especially if one of his ludicrous punches had somehow caught Esther and possibly cut her chin or an eyebrow. Blood on her face excited him as much as paradoxes: there'd be a whole chapter on him if someone did *An Anthology of Kinks*. As things quietened down, Gerald would lick at the wound/wounds. He had a very active mouth because of woodwind skills. Sometimes, to increase the grief he felt for himself in one of these episodes, he pretended she actually had broken his humerus or dislocated his shoulder and would lie on her with one arm as if useless by his side, to suggest he knew his sex obligations despite suffering and must honour them. She put up with the slobbering ritual. He probably remembered he once had dignity. He needed to get honour from somewhere now, even though make-believe. She regarded it as only right to help restore that dignity, if this could be done.

Some members of the rescue group were available for general rapid response duties, besides their Wally commitment. The cost of keeping a full party exclusively centred on Martlew would be unacceptable to the Force accountants and the Chief Constable – to the Force accountants and *therefore* to the Chief. One advantage came from this: if some of the party answered other emergency calls, the variety would be a kind of disguise for the main assignment. But Esther had to be sure that at least a minimum core of officers was always present for this assignment, several armed, and that they included someone carrying the instantly accessible thousand bung; plus the guide material on Dean Martlew as Dean Martlew, with clear Dean Martlew photos.

So far, no alarm messages about Wally had been received, not even false ones. Some of Esther's tenseness slackened but she continued her visits to the team. She had to help keep them vigilant. Wally Watch occupied a couple of big, connected, ground-floor rooms at headquarters, no distance from the car park and their two Volvo estates and an Omega, pointed towards the gates, unmarked but with sirens and interior blue flash lamps fitted to get them through jams. Channing in early briefings of Esther recorded that, so far, meetings and phone contacts with Martlew went exactly to schedule, and remained unsuspected at Cormax Turton; or at least Martlew saw no sign of suspicion. Channing said Martlew had delivered nothing of much significance yet. That didn't matter. The priority was to get him safely settled and accepted as enlisted villain. He had to 'make his bones', or pretend to: prove his crooked competence. In early contacts, Martlew had told Channing he thought this might be happening. Naturally, he'd never feel at ease in the Guild, but he did feel easier now than at the very start. People seemed less guarded with him. These would be ordinary, run-of-the-mill members of the firm, though. There'd been no closeness for Martlew with any of the policy-making, top Turton–Crabtree family members to date. That would come. Esther and Channing had to hope that would come. A long-term hope.

Yes, long-term, gradual. But now a very short-term and ungradual situation appeared from nowhere. No, not from nowhere, from Wally, known to some as Dean Martlew and

145

to some others – in Cormax Turton and around the streets and docks – as hyphenated Terence Marshall-Perkins, or, matily, The Quiff, after his hair-do. This was the night Wally began to produce what looked like significant stuff. Significant? A damn pest in some ways. As a matter of fact, Esther had decided to go with Channing to the Wally rendezvous and so heard his information first hand. Yes, in some ways a damn pest. But, of course, they told Martlew he'd been a genius to get it. Leadership, leadership, leadership – always leadership: and leadership demanded they should butter him up. His morale must be tended – morale, morale, morale, always morale: tend his morale, so he'd get more stuff, and, with luck, stuff that might not be such a damn pest as this stuff.

His morale seemed good, anyway. 'Mrs Davidson!' Martlew said, when he first saw her with Channing. 'I didn't expect this. I *must* be important.'

'Did you doubt it?' she said.

'Doubt it?' he said.

'That you're important,' she said.

'I didn't know *how* important,' he said.

'*How* important do you think you are now, then?'

'Quite,' he replied.

'I'd say "very".'

'Didn't they teach you that at Hilston Manor?' Channing said. 'Lectures on the importance of your ego?'

'Well, yes, I suppose they did. They told us we, the Out-located, were the pinnacle of policing, but a pinnacle for ever hidden in the clouds.'

'Remember, they're biased and self-serving,' she said.

'But for an Assistant Chief to turn up like this, back-alleying to see me – sensational!' he said.

'I'm let out in the dark now and then,' she said.

'If Mrs Davidson is running an operation, she'll want to familiarize herself with it at all levels,' Channing said. 'Famed for that.'

'But I'm not running this operation,' she said. 'It's yours, Richard. I'm a tolerated observer. '

'What I meant, yes,' Channing said.

'And I'm grateful to be tolerated.'

'Valued.'

'We've explained this – about control of the operation – to . . . to Wally,' Esther said.

'It's probably senior officer flair,' Martlew said.

'In what sense?' Esther said.

'For you to choose tonight to come,' Martlew said.

'It might have been any night,' she said. 'Random.'

'It might *appear* random, but I'd still call it flair,' Martlew said. 'I'd call it mystical, inspired.'

'Tonight's special?' she asked.

'But how did you know it's special?' Martlew said. '*Feel* it was special? That's a gift, ma'am.'

'I didn't,' Esther replied.

'Are you telling us something's on the move in Cormax Turton?' Channing said. 'Something major?'

'I *think* something's on the move,' Martlew said. 'It'll need more work, but, yes, developments.'

In fact, the meeting place was no back alley. He'd exaggerated the grubbiness. Esther saw he wanted to highlight his pride that she – an Assistant Chief – would come here to talk to him. And, yes, all right it could be considered unusual for someone of Esther's rank to attend a secret debriefing session. Assistant Chiefs and Chiefs generally stayed well back, directing the show overall, but not getting into spots that might one day force them to do a witness turn in court and face cross-examination. No Assistant Chief had arrived to chat with Esther when she did undercover years ago. But now Esther found she needed to see and hear Martlew/Wally/Terence (The Quiff) for herself, not at the tactical one remove, via Channing, nor fancifully imagined from occasional contact with the rescue party. She couldn't have convincingly explained the impulse. Womanliness? Perhaps womanliness combined with a helping of guilt that she had fiddled things to favour Martlew in the job selection. She needed direct, personal reassurance that he seemed OK. Plus, there was, she knew, a touch of control hunger. She had to have it, no matter how hard she pretended the opposite. She knew she should fight it, and really might one day. 'I'd like to come with you next time,' she'd told Channing.

'Come with me?'

'To a rendezvous.'

'Oh. Is that –'

'It will be fine,' she replied.

'But in this kind of –'

'What's your procedure?'

'Procedure?'

'The way it's done.'

'A set timetable, so any failure to turn up signals trouble. Likewise for phone calls.'

'Yes, I know that. I fixed the waiting limits, didn't I? But the meetings? Where?'

'In cars.'

'Right. Whose?'

'Always mine.'

'He comes to yours and sits where?'

'Passenger. I'm in the driver's.'

'This is invariable?'

'Absolutely.'

'You go alone?'

'Yes. Nobody else knows the arrangement.'

'We hope.'

'I think it's secure.'

'What kind of location?'

'Somewhere very public and reasonably crowded with vehicles that are constantly changing.'

'Tesco's?'

'Possibly *too* public. Too big a social mix. Cormax Turton have to shop, and so do little people with big eyes who sell them info. CT have a very capable intelligence unit – and I don't mean negatively capable.'

'Under Sarah Lily Dane still?'

'She's a clever old piece. And a fine listener.'

'So, you meet Wally in a hotel car park?' Esther said. 'Right?'

'Yes, sometimes a hotel – preferably a hotel with a special, advertised public function on for the night, so there are a lot of once-only vehicles to mix with and get shrouded by. Wall-facing for the motor, if possible. Only the back of our heads visible. Varied car, of course, from the pool, which he's told the make, colour and registration of at the previous meet. Memorized, no notes. He's good on memory. The dossier's correct about that.'

'But his car's always the same?'

'Unavoidable.'

'Perhaps.'

'He's been taught anti-tail drills here and at Hilston.'

'Sometimes they work.'

'The dossier says he's competent at it.'

'I'm sure. I'd like him to be better than competent.'

'It's his shooting that's much better than competent. And his memory.'

'Well, I suppose he could be *too* competent at shedding a tail,' she said.

'In what sense, ma'am?'

'If he does a successful shake-off routine will that prove he's on something secret and doesn't want Cormax Turton chaperones, because, obviously, the something secret is unfriendly revelations about Cormax Turton?'

'Success equals disaster?'

'Does the ability to lose a tail indicate police training? And would the extra time taken on ditching the surveillance vehicle or vehicles mean the alarm is activated and our rescue unit needlessly goes in, so the whole Out-loc operation is kiboshed?'

'If he came on foot he's just as likely to be noticed. And if he hired a different vehicle each time or called a taxi that would get noticeable, too. Besides which, people in car hire firms and taxi drivers talk. OK, his car is a risk. We're into risks, though, aren't we? I try to minimize. If we want inside stuff on Cormax Turton –'

149

'Yes, we're into risk.'

'That's why I queried your ... your ... Excuse me, ma'am, but do you think it's ... it's, well, all right for you to come on a –'

'I'd better go in the back of yours,' Esther replied. 'Important to stick with the procedure. He'd get confused otherwise. I imagine he's already tensed up when you meet.'

'Excuse me, ma'am, but I don't know it's sticking with the procedure for an ACC to –'

'This is part of an operation, isn't it?' she said.

'Of course.'

'Well, I'm ACC (Operations).'

'Yes, but –'

'Which hotel?'

'The Millicent.'

'Ah, they have live music tea dances there. I've tried to get them to take on a bassoonist. It's a nice, soothing sound, fine with tea.'

The Millicent management might feel pissed off if they'd heard how Dean Martlew described their car park. Channing would never pick a back alley for such a get-together, and nor would anyone who understood even a fragment about Out-loc liaison. Back alleys looked dubious and those who loitered in them looked very dubious – drew special attention because they looked very dubious. Back alleys were for cats, knee-tremblers and old chow mein cartons tumbling and yellowed, carried by the wind. Channing could arrange things better. Outside the Millicent tonight, their two vehicles stood in bays a little distance from each other. Martlew left his Renault and joined Channing in the unmarked Rover. Martlew failed to notice Esther behind until he opened the car. Then, his surprise. 'Mrs Davidson! I didn't expect this.' It was genuine shock. It disturbed her – angered her – that it was genuine shock, and she'd wanted to tell him a capable undercover cop on a rendezvous would never get into a car without knowing exactly how many people it contained and who they were, even if the situation seemed, on the face of it, exactly as planned, and friendly.

So far, Martlew who was called Wally, and Terence (The Quiff), lacked that wise, all-round, non-stop, possibly life-preserving caution of the complete undercover cop. But Esther let it go. She didn't want to sound like a fusspot mother talking to a kid. This kid remained a kid in the undercover trade and needed to learn. And needed encouragement. Therefore, she told him how important he was. He wouldn't be if he ever got into the wrong car, though. Remember that passenger side garrotting by Clemenza in *The Godfather,* the victim's shoes bursting through the windscreen in his death throes?

A placard outside the Millicent tonight announced an evening seminar in its Xavier Suite on 'Inheritance Tax And How To Avoid It'. Esther agreed they'd be all right here. There were naturally some very classy cars of the loaded in other bays, but probably none belonging to Cormax Turton, or to people who associated with Cormax Turton. Possibly Cornelius did think pretty often about who would inherit what when he went, but he would not be asking for advice from finance wizards in the Xavier Suite, nor telling anyone what he added up to and how he came to add up to it. He would be expert in avoiding experts on Inheritance Tax And How To Avoid It. Tax? He'd have his own way of dealing with that, dead or alive. Of *not* dealing with it, more likely.

'So what's up among your new friends, Wally?' Channing said. 'Mrs Davidson and I – we're very much the listeners. Bang on our door, will you?'

'What does that mean?' Martlew said.

Chapter Fourteen

Esther decided she had better be present on Monday for the last session of the judge's summing-up in the Ambrose Tutte Turton trial. Diplomacy, humanity, ordinary decency demanded this. Occasionally they overlapped. For now, she'd drop the visits to East Stead and the Dill situation.

At home, Gerald obviously picked up the signs of big nerviness nibbling Esther and said he would come with her to the court and give his personal backing. Some grandeur thickened his voice and he brought resolve into his eyes. Often his first reactions to Esther's troubles were astonishingly warm sympathy and good support. Wreckage bits of what in the past had been a fair relationship would bob to the surface now and then, like stuff from a sunk freighter.

But a tricky one, this – a sensitive one. Obviously, she did not want him there. *Want* him there? In the court? God, some brutal joke! Admittedly – reversing things – it was probably true that, if Gerald ever managed to return to concert performing, in a principal or even backbench role, she would make sure she went with him and sat in the audience for at least one session, smiling her congratulations from a spot where he could see her. Yes, she'd attend, despite detesting most of the fly-in-a-bottle eighteenth-century works he especially liked to blow. Never mind, he needed her to be there signalling groupie-style admiration, and she'd go.

But Gerald trying to prop her morale at a trial was different. Although he had enough control not to heckle or hiss, after a short while listening to the judge he might become hurt and/or enraged – almost certainly *would* become hurt and/or enraged – by the cascade of words in public about someone, something, other than himself. He'd regard this as a filthy and calculated affront.

Naturally, in some of his calmer, saner moments, even Gerald realized that most of the world's business happened without in the least noticing him. He knew the name G. Davidson did definitely mean something, but not to very many. His complete and obvious irrelevance to what went on in the court would affect him like a sickness. Gerald was not made for spectatordom. And he would fiendishly hate this trial because, although he rated as nothing, Esther *could* claim to have real involvement here. Clearly. Flagrantly. In fact, he'd spot that what Esther had decided months ago to do with undercover actually *caused* this summing-up; actually caused the entire fucking trial. This was bound to torment Gerald with envy. He shone at envy. Exclusion brought him vast pain. He was that famous starving kid, nose pressed against the restaurant window, watching the polished clientele gorge. After not very long in court, Gerald would probably become unmanageably restless and start grunting and whispering to Esther, and twitching his body about as if it was worth looking at or giving the kiss of life to. This would insult the court and, much more important in Esther's opinion, insult Dean and the Martlew family. If Gerald were thrown out by attendants she couldn't pretend she didn't know the barmy sod.

So, she must put him off. Must. But, unless she got the timbre and phrasing right, he'd begin to overheat and start one of his riffs about her only wishing to attend solo because she had, or had had, a wondrously satisfying carnal connection with the dead undercover officer, or some of his family, or with the judge, or Channing, or one or more of the Press reporters, or Ambrose Tutte Turton, or Iles: she'd spoken to Gerald now and then about Iles and his quirks and dandyism, and mentioned that, for his particular reasons, he attended some sessions of the trial.

On this key day, she felt it would be bad to appear at court showing sucked wounds. It could seem self-indulgent, and lacking decorum. Nor would she have time, let alone wish, to fuck following a full donnybrook rough-house, as Gerald would undoubtedly demand under established *après scrap* custom and practice.

'It's so kind of you to offer to come with me, Gerald, my love!'

'Darling, what else could I do? I mean, if you have trouble don't I also have trouble – share that trouble?'

'What else could you do? What else!' She smiled, a lingering, soulmate to soulmate construction. 'But you see, it's only because you are you that you ask that question! I can tell you, Gerald – and I probably *need* to tell you, since, in your kindliness, you'd never suspect this yourself – but I can tell you some men would feel not the least obligation. Zilch obligation.' She thought this would probably get to him – the word 'obligation', and used twice tickled up by the slangy 'zilch'. He was an artist and didn't do obligations, despised obligations, would want no truck with obligations, in the usual social-fabric, family sense. Ultimately, his only obligation was to his art, his bassoon, his work, although he didn't have any just now. He might ask, 'Did Picasso let "obligations" stop him painting women with eyes where their tits should be?' Esther said: 'People there will admire you so much for knowing your duty.'

'People where?'

'At the court. And generally. Television news pictures of you arriving with me – me as recognizable in this context, of course.'

'Duty? I see it as a natural, spousely impulse to be with you at this time, only that,' he said.

'Yes, and I'm sure it is. But then, *I* know your character. To them, *not* knowing it, you would appear to have accepted a mere satellite role – very much a second-string role as compared with mine on this occasion – and they'll esteem you for that willing and willed self-effacement. This

will put you into a lowly, yet not utterly insignificant, position, say like Thatcher's husband, or footballers' wives.'

'I've played solo in many a fucking concerto, you know,
including at the Drapers' Hall,' he replied. '"Unmatch-
able", my Mozart Rondo K.191 was called by a reviewer.'

'Yes, yes, I do know. And perhaps some of them will
know also, and feel it truly humble of you to step down
from K.191, and recognize that this might be the life-stage
when you take on instead – ungrudgingly and devotedly
– the sidekick identity, as if subsumed by me. Mind, they
will not suppose the bassoon, or the thrill of performance,
are completely forgotten, but they'll assume you have
decided these are no longer supreme priorities.'

'They fucking *are*,' he replied.

'*We* realize this, not them.'

'I hate people like that.'

'Like what?'

'Trite, formula minds.'

'Not many of them would have any real hope of understanding someone of your temperament, Gerald.'

'Always the bassoon will call me, call me, call me, the
way a battlefield flag called to troops in old wars.'

'And you are the greater man for that, though it is too
much for them to take in. They will see at this point a self-
sacrificial, gifted, contentedly bypassed, former celebrity.'

He didn't go with her. 'Have you been messing me about
– all that worthy aide-de-camp wool, Esther?' He said he
didn't know why *she* had to go to the summing-up again,
with him or alone. 'You can't affect anything.'

No, she couldn't. More zilch. But it was what Gerald
would call an impulse. She did have impulses. She got out
of the house before he could turn imaginative, dirty and
physical. Maybe Iles would show. Dean's father certainly
would: a main reason for Esther to be there. She didn't
want him to think her indifferent. He might in his mind
reasonably accuse her of all sorts, but not indifference.
Now and then she wished she *could* manage a spell of
indifference, of numbness.

155

She'd missed a few hours of the summing-up here and there, including while she was at East Stead on Friday morning, and thought that if necessary she could read the missing bits in transcript sometime. Probably it *wasn't* necessary. Things would go as they were going, regardless. Gerald had that right. She might come to the transcript as more or less an historical document, weeks on, months on. But Esther wanted the closing words of the judge's performance live. They should be heard raw, not read for retrospect. Why? They should, that's all. On the chief issues that would figure today, Esther needed to savour the seeming reasonableness of the judge's manner, and the mild, precise way she presented logical options for the jury to think about. The tone would be crucial – not necessarily favourable or comforting but crucial. Tone you couldn't always get from a transcript.

Although Esther had considered giving the court another miss and returning to the Dill situation at East Stead, she sensed that people working on the case there found her a persistent, interfering nuisance during her Friday, Saturday and Sunday visits; the Saturday and Sunday ones quite long, as there was no sitting court or office meeting to compete. Actually, she'd realized from the start they would regard her as an interfering nuisance, and decided she could ignore this: Esther felt impelled to be there, and rank saw her all right, entitled her. Rank was beautiful sometimes. This morning, though, the pull of the trial grew strong again. The judge had already been talking for more than a day and a half when she adjourned on Friday lunchtime for the weekend, as judges tended to. She must be near the wrap.

'Members of the jury, I come now to the evidence of the witnesses, Mr Charles Edenbridge Rowan and Mr Frank Claud Bates. Both told the court that they had seen the accused with Detective Sergeant Dean Martlew and another man on 8 June, the day the Prosecution say Dean Martlew was killed. This, of course, is totally at variance with the claim of the accused and others that Martlew had left the Cormax Turton companies and been paid off on 27 May, and that neither he – the accused – nor, as far as he knew, anybody in the companies, had seen Martlew or been in contact with him since then. The evidence of Mr Rowan and Mr Bates is therefore fundamental to the Prosecution case, and it will be for you to decide how you regard that evidence.'

As Esther had half expected, Desmond Iles *was* present for this final session, sitting near the front of the public gallery a few places from Mr Martlew. Just before the judge began, Iles and he shook hands standing, and talked together for a few moments. It seemed amiable. Perhaps Iles had done what he promised and won him and the family over.

The judge said: 'There are some resemblances between Mr Rowan's and Mr Bates's testimony and some differences. This is to be expected. Let us take the resemblances first. Both say they saw Detective Sergeant Martlew with the accused and another man in the Dunkley Wharf area of the docks on 8 June. As you will recall, the court made a visit to the wharf during the trial so that you could be familiar at first hand with the locale. It is not in dispute that some of Cormax Turton's waterfront business takes place at Dunkley Wharf, nor that the accused is from time to time involved in that side of Cormax Turton's work. Both witnesses put their sightings between 7 p.m. and 8 p.m. Mr Rowan says about 7.10 p.m., Mr Bates, around 7.35 p.m. Neither of them checked the time on their watches. They had no reason to. They were not witnessing anything exceptional. It would be entirely usual to see the accused and other members of the Cormax Turton companies at the wharf, particularly when a vessel was discharging, as on the evening of 8 June. These are approximate times, then, but in the same general segment of the day. Mr Rowan and Mr Bates work at the docks and knew the accused by sight and his name. They also knew Dean Martlew by sight and name, having several times previously seen him at Dunkley Wharf in connection with

Cormax Turton business; though the name by which they knew him was not Dean Martlew but Terence Marshall-Perkins, or, familiarly, The Quiff. They both also thought they recognized the third man, though neither felt totally certain about this, and they had no name for him. "Third Men" do tend to be touched by mystery, don't they, as we know from Greene's famous film and novel, *The Third Man*? Mr Rowan runs a mobile snack bar near Dunkley Wharf, which we saw during our visit. Mr Bates is a member of the Docks Manager's staff responsible for allocating berths at various wharves, including Dunkley.'

Esther felt marginally strengthened by Iles's presence. She realized this could have been otherwise: he'd failed in a comparable case and might have now seemed to her a nomadic jinx. *I sympathize, Esther, with your impending disaster because I've had one myself. It's why I come. Let's mourn dead undercover men together.*

The judge said: 'It is not disputed by the accused that he and two colleagues were at the wharf between 7 p.m. and 8.30 p.m. on 8 June. The accused told the court they were present to identify and examine certain items in the ship cargo, which had been ordered and imported for several Cormax Turton customers. The accused described this as a routine matter because inspections were always made, in case items had been damaged in transit and, if so, to record that the damage occurred before Cormax Turton became responsible for them. The three men arrived at the wharves in the accused's silver-coloured Lexus car, which was seen and recognized by Mr Bates and Mr Rowan. None of this is in doubt, but, of course, ladies and gentlemen of the jury, what *is* in doubt is whether one of the three men at the wharf on the evening of 8 June was Terence Marshall-Perkins – Detective Sergeant Dean Martlew. The accused says he at no point knew or suspected that Terence Marshall-Perkins might be a false name and that Marshall-Perkins had left the Cormax Turton in unexceptional circumstances on 27 May.'

Esther could watch Iles in profile. He stared at the judge,

his head utterly still, in that gundog pose once more. But now it was as though, even so late in proceedings, he meant to help her, browbeat her, hypnotize her, towards a right understanding of what had happened to Dean Martlew; this right understanding being based, naturally, on the Prosecution's and Esther's version of events, and forget the Ambrose Tutte Turton eyewash and his lawyer's twists.

The judge said: 'Mr Rowan and Mr Bates were in basic agreement about the appearance of the man they took to be Terence Marshall-Perkins. Mr Rowan said the man was dark-haired, between twenty-four and twenty-eight years old, just over six feet in height and about 170 pounds, athletically built. Mr Bates gave the age as twenty-seven, height 185 centimetres, around 175 pounds, "strongly made", hair dark, with the tuft above his forehead that earned his nickname, "The Quiff". We heard from Dean Martlew's official police dossier that he was twenty-six, 187 centimetres, 173 pounds, hair brown.

'The clothes as described by the two witnesses are similar: a dark double-breasted suit, light-coloured shirt, possibly white according to Mr Bates, a tie, dark like the suit but too far away for any decoration or pattern to be seen, no hat. Mr Rowan said that Terence Marshall-Perkins had bought refreshments at his snack bar several times in the past and that they passed the time of day on these occasions. Mr Bates said he had met Terence Marshall-Perkins once some months ago when Ambrose Tutte Turton introduced him on Dunkley Wharf. Both Mr Rowan and Mr Bates said that the man they saw on the evening of 8 June in the company of the accused and another man was, in their opinion, certainly Terence Marshall-Perkins, whom they knew from earlier close contact. It was evening, but the evening of a sunny summer day and the light excellent.'

Esther wondered if somebody had once called Iles 'iconic' in his hearing, and he'd decided this to be so brilliantly correct that he should act up to it. Or he might have read the word somewhere – about, say, Mandela or

Castro – and at once seen a clear similarity to himself as deserving homage, though they were damned old and quite unBritish. Always Iles's clothes looked chosen to excite worship. She recalled that magnificent suit Officer A sported at Fieldfare, and her idea then that the cloth held his shoulders the way a midwife might present a newborn child to its mother. Looking at Iles's single-breasted grey job now, she felt this still a pretty good comparison, though not quite magnificent enough. This jacket, too, cosseted the shoulders brilliantly, but with the kind of joyous, delicate reverence a member of the Japanese royal family might show the long-awaited male baby heir to media cameras.

The judge said: 'The evidence of Mr Rowan and Mr Bates gives the court, and specifically you, members of the jury, two considerable problems. First, have they got things right, and this man was Detective Sergeant Dean Martlew, known to them as Terence Marshall-Perkins? Against the evidence of Mr Rowan and Mr Bates we have to take what we heard from Ian Lysaght Brain, Maurice Cadenne and the accused. Of these, it is, of course, Ian Lysaght Brain who is the most significant. The Defence claim that the man Mr Rowan and Mr Bates took to be Terence Marshall-Perkins was, in fact, Ian Lysaght Brain. You have seen Mr Brain in the witness box and you have seen photographs of Dean Martlew and been given the police dossier account of his height, weight, build, age, hair colour. You have to decide whether there is a likeness and a likeness strong enough to have deceived Mr Rowan and Mr Bates from distances of 100 metres and 140 metres respectively in perfect light.

'You may wish to give some weight to the fact that both Mr Rowan and Mr Bates were used to seeing Terence Marshall-Perkins on the wharf with the accused and that this might have influenced the identifications: sometimes if we are expecting to see something or somebody and we, in fact, see something or somebody approximately the same, we decide we are seeing what we anticipated seeing. The Defence say this was the first time Mr Ian Lysaght Brain had worked at the wharf with the accused, and that an error could easily have been made by Mr Rowan and Mr Bates. Mr Brain in his evidence says that he was with the accused and Mr Maurice Cadenne inspecting cargo from the vessel, *Astrolabe III,* at Dunkley Wharf on the evening of 8 June. He says Terence Marshall-Perkins was not present, and that in fact he had never met Marshall-Perkins, who left Cormax Turton before Brain joined. In their evidence, Mr Maurice Cadenne and the accused say Marshall-Perkins was not present, and that Mr Ian Lysaght Brain was the third member of the party at Dunkley Wharf on 8 June. Having seen Mr Ian Lysaght Brain in court Mr Rowan and Mr Bates agree he could have been the third man.'

Esther felt it would be short-changing Iles to regard his distinction as only a matter of garments. He could actually *sit* iconically, as now. Esther fantasized: on a Hollywood set where the chair-backs of some crew members were labelled – 'Director', for instance or 'Continuity' – Iles's would carry the simple word, 'Icon'. It amazed Esther that the judge seemed able to trundle on imperturbably while Iles from no real distance gave her his dogged, stupendously unmatey glare. Anyone coming into this courtroom and knowing nothing about the proceedings would soon feel where dominance lay: not with the methodically gabbing judge but with Iles, although entirely quiet and motionless today.

The judge said: 'I come to the second problem associated with this part of the evidence. We are here trying a case in which Ambrose Tutte Turton is accused of the murder of Detective Sergeant Dean Martlew. No evidence has been shown to us as to where, how and exactly when this murder took place. The Prosecution's case rests on the assertion that Ambrose Tutte Turton was, allegedly, one of the last people to see Martlew alive, and that Turton would have a motive for the murder if he had discovered the supposed member of staff, Terence Marshall-Perkins, to be, in fact, a police undercover detective. This has not been proved, and, as I've already mentioned, the accused denies that knowledge.'

Although Iles maintained such stillness now, at other times, when on his feet and moving about, he had what seemed to Esther amazing lightness, grace and confidence. She'd noticed it even on that memorial visit to the stony beach at Pastel Head. Esther had the feeling Iles could gracefully snake up behind someone he'd lost patience with on some account or another and break their skull open with one blow from a cosh, or garrotte them, in what would seem to anybody observing a single, easy, fluid, textbook sequence. He was only of middle height and slight – not traditional male police build at all – yet he conveyed somehow a sense of brisk physical power, and famously once with a single butt broke the nose of a colleague at an otherwise almost civilized Force function.* Although many said he had driven one of his former Chief Constables into breakdown by open, affectionate contempt and laughing disregard for his orders, he showed almost pathological loyalty to subordinates. This might help explain why he had never got over the death of his Outloc officer, and why he felt compelled to attend this vaguely similar trial.

The judge said: 'The Prosecution maintains Dean Martlew was put to death in an unknown location sometime shortly after the wharf visit. The difficulty here is not only the accused's denial he ever knew Terence Marshall-Perkins to be the police. In addition, you might not think it sufficient for the Prosecution to try to demonstrate, through witnesses Rowan and Bates, that Dean Martlew was one of the three men at Dunkley Wharf. This, even if true, cannot of itself prove the accused killed Dean Martlew. The Prosecution asks you to make the following deductions: if you believe it to have been established that Dean Martlew *was* one of the three, then you will ask yourselves why would Ambrose Tutte Turton claim – backed by

* See *Protection*

162

two Cormax Turton witnesses – that Mr Rowan and Mr Bates were mistaken, and have mixed up Terence Marshall-Perkins with Ian Lysaght Brain? The Prosecution argues that there can only be one answer to this: the accused wishes to refute any report that he was seen with Terence Marshall-Perkins on 8 June, the likely date of the murder. Why?

'The Prosecution says the logical inference is that Ambrose Tutte Turton murdered Dean Martlew on or about that date. The Prosecution maintains that all the circumstances of the occasion, including the possible discovery by Cormax Turton of Marshall-Perkins' real identity, point to Ambrose Tutte Turton as responsible for the death. I have just referred to "the circumstances of the occasion": this kind of evidence is, in fact, called "circumstantial". It is not the same as what is termed "direct evidence", when a witness describes a crime that he/she actually saw being committed. Circumstantial evidence can only go so far and requires us – requires a jury – to fill in certain gaps. Obviously, this must not be done by casual guesswork.

'Members of the jury, you have to look at those events you have decided to be true, and then ask yourselves whether they indicate beyond reasonable doubt that some other event or events would inevitably follow. In this case, it means you would come to the conclusion that Terence Marshall-Perkins did not leave Cormax Turton on 27 May, and was with Ambrose Tutte Turton at Dunkley Wharf on 8 June; and that the false evidence given by Cormax Turton indicates there is something to be hidden, namely, the murder of Dean Martlew by Ambrose Tutte Turton. Nobody else is charged with the murder, though Mr Maurice Cadenne appears also to have been present at Dunkley on 8 June. No explanation was given by the Prosecution for this omission, and it is for you to consider why this might be. Is it because the police have long been set on targeting a major figure in Cormax Turton, rather than an employee, and did not wish to widen the focus of their case, perhaps weakening it in some particulars? Or might there be some other hidden reason?'

Iles said: 'May I ask, Esther, is there someone who wears a bow-tie associated with you at all?'

'What?' she replied.

'Or perhaps a stalker.'

'Where?' She glanced about. They were on the steps outside the court: an adjournment.

'A musician, possibly,' Iles said.

'Well, yes.'

'Or machine-gun hit-man.'

'But where?'

'Carrying an instrument in a case – woodwind, I think, if not a Kalashnikov. Bassoon?'

'Where?'

'Was watching you very intently from under the Central Market sign across the road.'

'No, I don't see anyone like that.' God, she ought to be able to recognize Gerald.

'You had your back to him. He seemed to realize I'd noticed his vigil and at once went out of sight into the market.'

'My husband.'

'Oh? A yellow bow-tie, red spots, worn loosely.'

'Yes, my husband, Gerald. There can be complications. I expect you know how it is. You're married?'

'He really watched you,' Iles replied.

'He has an interest in trials – that kind of thing. Trials as trials.'

'Especially when you are personally concerned, I expect.'

'And court architecture – as symbolic of a particular law-and-order system, but in the broadest sense. He'd be much taken with the façade here.'

'Fascinating.'

'A professional bassoonist,' she replied.

The judge had broken for lunch. She said she would need a couple more hours afterwards before sending the jury home with instructions to come in tomorrow morning

164

and start discussing their verdict. Iles had Mr Martlew with him.

'Will he join you?' Iles said.

'My husband? I don't know.' But she doubted it and high-speed prayed he wouldn't. There'd be something especially untoward about a disturbance in the street here, near the courthouse. He'd seen her with two men and would probably think he understood now why she'd discouraged him from coming to the trial. Perhaps he'd guess Iles to be Iles: Esther had mentioned the great tailoring, and it would be apparent to Gerald although 100 metres off.

'I've suggested to Mr Martlew that we look for a pie and a pint somewhere,' Iles said. 'Perhaps if Gerald's not coming back from his market visit you'll eat with us?'

Oh, God. 'If he was carrying his bassoon he might be on his way to some work. They'll phone for him in emergencies – when an orchestra or group is short, because of illness and so on. He's mainly bassoon but oboe and clarinet also, if pushed.' Maybe the Millicent had at last heard her hints and wanted him to do a rehearsal run-through for the tea dance this afternoon. Of course, she had never spoken of the possible Millicent work to him, fearing he would feel degraded and go into one of his all-out diva fits, bawling about crappy music for the ancient, limping, waltzing, early-home bourgeoisie. But if the offer had come seemingly direct and unsolicited . . . well, an offer was an offer in a bleak calendar. The hotel stood near. He might have wanted to announce his triumph to her. A call on the mobile could have seemed inadequate. It would be important for him to come to her damn prestige milieu, the court, and confront Esther in those surrounds with his proud, unique, earned news.

And then, what happens? He sees her with Iles and Martlew. Gerald's disappointment and rage would not get soothed by the comfy, local-produce aroma of Central Market. She wondered whether she should go at once and look for him among the traders. But, of course, if Esther found him he would ask – and ask at artistic-temperament volume, full shindig volume – how she could possibly know he was in the market. He'd disturb business, and pull a ready audience. An ACC mustn't be associated with that kind of froth-flecked public strife among stalls selling cold meats or sisal matting. Police might be called. Gerald would have noted Esther had her back to him at first, and it was bound to make him even more embittered if he thought that one or other of the men had spotted him staring and alerted Esther. This he would consider cheeky and intrusive, and regard Esther's acceptance of the tip-off as treachery, especially as it had been completely right.

'I expect he mentioned the fucking bow-tie, did he, did he?' She could imagine Gerald screaming something like that at her in the market. Occasionally, he could reveal painful, disarming self-awareness, though he still kept on with the fucking bow-ties. 'This seemed distinctive and comic to him, did it, did it?' Naturally, Esther would not admit the bow-tie had singled him out, and certainly not the 'worn loosely' aspect. She'd have said it was the bassoon made him noticeable. That might work. But it could also go wrong. The bassoon represented his victory, his recall to life, and earnings, and he had wanted her alone to share this with him today. Instead, the bassoon's role had been hijacked and changed. It had become something that simply labelled him 'musician', just as carrying a broom said 'road sweeper'. This, too, would wound and inflame him. On balance then, Esther decided it would be best not to seek him in the market. Besides, if he was on his way to a rehearsal at the Millicent he might have left the building via the rear doors, which would take him closer to the hotel.

Martlew said: 'I hope this doesn't sound far-fetched and precious, but there's something terrible, almost disorientating, about the way my son, Dean Martlew, became Terence Marshall-Perkins, or The Quiff or Wally, and then ceases even to be any of these, according to some voices, and turns into Ian Lysaght Brain. This struck me so before, of course, when hearing the actual evidence. But it seemed worse in the sum-up words of the judge. She sounds so reasonable and measured. It's like my son had, as it were, disappeared, had been dissipated into so many forms, had lost his essence, even before he died.'

To Esther it seemed a worthwhile chance for her finally to get some rapport with him. She said: 'Yes, I've had the same thought, Mr Martlew, and –'

'"Far-fetched"? "Precious"?' Iles replied, thoughtfully.

'I wouldn't want my reactions to appear either,' Martlew said.

'Not in the least,' Esther said. 'These bewildering shifts of –'

'Martlew, yes, you're right, it *does* sound far-fetched and precious,' Iles said. 'Exactly the words for such chic twattishness. *Fucking* far-fetched and precious. I can't stand "as it were" shit. Leave that to the writerly. Nothing of his essence was dissipated. He got shot from close and dumped in water. That's not the same as dissipated essence. It's slaughter and disposal. Bad, bad, bad. We're here today because we're mourning a real lad – your lad, Detective Sergeant Dean Martlew – so don't pollute the genuine catastrophe with sale-price sodding pseudery about cliché crises of identity, OK? Many wish *I'd* have an identity crisis. They want me to decide I don't exist and they'd landslide vote for it.'

Quickly, Esther said: 'This shuffling off of names and assumption of other names, perhaps it tells us something about the nature of –'

'It tells us nothing about the nature of anything except about the shuffling off of names and assumption of other names briefly,' Iles said. 'That's simply basic undercover equipment – no mysticism or psychobabble bubbles. Half the driving tests in London are passed by people mas-querading for someone else. The substitute driver assumes a string of Learner new names every day. The one who takes the tests doesn't go home to Camden Town all twitchy and confused about loss of identity – the "Who really am I?" blather. He knows who he is, and hopes the police don't, he meaning she as well here, of course. He's the guy with the money, that's who he is. He's got hundreds of quid in his pocket and more to come from the same charades tomorrow. It belongs to the one-and-only Camden Town him. That is, the original Mr Wheels him; the cash-heavy, undissipated essence of him; the himness of him. His advertising says, "*Your* name, *my* driving." The judge obviously believes it really was Ian Lysaght Brain at Dunkley Wharf, anyway, the retarded old bitch, so she'd dismiss the last name change.'

They began their walk to a pub. Esther resisted looking behind. It would be pathetic to seem scared Gerald might tail her. 'I think it's all right,' Iles said.

'What?' Esther said.

'He's not there,' Iles said.

'I don't have to worry about that either way,' Esther said. 'Good.'

She hadn't noticed Iles make checks to see if they were followed. 'How do you know he's not there?' she said.

'It's the sort of thing I *do* know,' he said. 'At Staff College I was called Ungumshoeable Iles, hard to shorten.'

'Those two did see my son at Dunkley on 8 June,' Martlew said. He was between Iles and Esther as they walked.

'I don't have anything against people who run snack bars,' Iles replied.

'They described my son. Unmistakable,' Martlew said, 'when they gave their evidence and today, in the judge's version.'

'Rowan and Bates?' Iles said. 'Disastrous witnesses. Couldn't they have been enhanced a bit?'

'How enhanced a bit?' Esther said.

'Their testimony smartened up, given better focus,' Iles said.

'Someone else suggested a similar ploy to me,' Esther said, 'about the campaign against Cormax Turton generally.'

'Who suggested it?' Iles said.

'A fine detective here. Bernard Stonevale. He was retiring. At his leave party.'

'It's good he should be out of the service if he can make disgraceful suggestions like that,' Iles said.

'But *you* just did,' Esther said.

'The ineptness of talking to you about it,' Iles said. 'And when he's no longer active.'

'You mean he should just have got on with it privately, done it?' Esther said.

'"A fine detective", as you call him, would be able to get the feel of a situation,' Iles said.

'You told me to keep everything straight,' Esther said.

'I told you to keep everything straight and win,' Iles said.

'I did keep everything straight, to win,' Esther said.

'But what *is* win?' Martlew said. 'A conviction won't bring back my –'

'Not more fucking flim-flam, for God's sake,' Iles replied. 'A win is Ambrose Tutte Turton locked up for ever as cold murderer of your boy, and the firm imploding soon after. Doesn't that sound like victory? One villain inside and a villain network expunged. They might be scared of Cormax Turton,' Iles said.

'Who?' Esther said.

'Rowan and Bates.'

'We'd have given them witness protection if necessary,' Esther said. 'They'd been told.'

'Yes, but they might be scared of Cormax Turton, just the same,' Iles replied.

'Do *you* believe he was there on 8 June, Mr Iles?' Martlew said.

'Who?' Iles said.

'Dean,' Martlew said.

'For instance, to improve their value in the box, Bates and Rowan could have been briefed with special distinctive features about his shoes, say, or hand-jewellery, things they'd swear they'd noticed before,' Iles said. 'It was all there, I gather, on the body.'

'What do *you* think, Mr Iles? *Was* Dean on the wharf?' Martlew said. 'If not, where was he during those days in late May, early June?'

'And tonight, when you get home and he gets home, will it be all right?' Iles said.

'He's intensely taken up with music,' Esther replied. 'It possesses him.'

'Will it be all right, when you and he get home tonight?' Iles said. 'Some music makes them tetchy and cruel. César Franck.'

They reached the pub and Iles bought ploughman's lunches and beer for the three. In a while she saw Gerald look in at a window behind Iles and Martlew. Yes, like the starving kid in the restaurant picture, but less easy to sympathize with: she'd applaud a restaurant owner who went out, handed him a couple of old monkfish bits and told him to piss off. She smiled a quick, confidential smile at Gerald while the others were preoccupied with their food, and tried also to make it a smile that pleaded with him not to come in with his teeming lunacies and piffling resentments, while yet thanking him unstintingly for his husbandly closeness to her in a time of true tension. *Off to the fucking Millicent you bilious roving soul.* Esther didn't mention that Gerald was there, because she thought Iles would be mortified at getting successfully gumshoed in daylight on a main street by someone with a lurid, loosely worn bow-tie on and carrying a bassoon.

Gerald did not enter the pub and disappeared again. Probably he'd be thinking up some nicely structured malice for when he and she were next alone, if he had time for such ideas before the Millicent, or wherever the work was – malice not necessarily to do with César Franck. There'd been a time when she kept an excellent masonry hammer handy, but this had come to seem crude and unfair and she'd given it to a charity as very suitable for development work in the Third World. On the way back to the court, Iles said: 'He showed again, did he, your clever music man? I thought the "Get lost, sweetheart" smile a masterpiece, and I've seen a lot of them from women.'

Chapter Fifteen

Out-location of DS Dean Martlew: Esther's narrative

3. On the Waterfront

Near the start of that Millicent car park evening conference in Channing's pool Rover, Dean Martlew had said: 'Of course, I've been trying to get in on the dockside operations.'

'Don't rush them,' Esther said.

'I don't know what that means,' Dean said.

'Don't rush them. You make yourself noticeable. Too eager. Let things develop.'

'They might not,' Dean said.

'No, they might not. But it's safer like that.'

'I'd have been wasting my time there.'

'Patience – it's one of the chief requirements in undercover. I know. I've done it,' Esther said, and thought, Oh, God, so weighty, so historical!

'Their docks operation is a sure route for me to Ambrose,' Dean said. 'I don't see a route to Cornelius or Palliative at all. But Ambrose seems to control all their waterfront activity. Look, ma'am, so far I do some street-level, chickenfeed dealing with H and Charlie and this is about it. One up from a courier.'

'How *I* began,' Esther said, 'though not so much Charlie about then. How most undercover starts.'

'I'll never get to the management that way. We've got to know the scale of things, haven't we, if the prosecution's to be worthwhile – how Cormax Turton is organized, the turnover, their substances suppliers, the pay Cornelius, Palliative, Ambrose draw? All right, I know we have *something* on their business structure, but no detail in depth. And I'm nowhere near discovering any of that.'

'The Pope didn't start in the Vatican,' Esther said. 'Slowly. They're watching you. All of them. I expect you can feel that. You're someone with no checkable past.'

'Well, I hope so,' Dean said.

'They're fond of checkable pasts, like a prince picking a bride. They're *used* to checkable pasts. Your sort makes them uncertain. They're always on guard, but now they'll be very, very on guard. I'd bet they've heard the long-time investigation's a likely write-off. They won't assume that's the end, though. The thing about true, career crooks is they know from a kind of modesty/arrogance that this is what they are, crooks, and that they have to be hounded. Somehow. It's a kind of social imperative. And if they're *not* hounded and hunted, they think it's because they've become negligible and must be missing something good: a kind of slight on their work. So, now, they'll be watchful for a different ploy. You're it. They don't know, and won't know – mustn't know – until you're out of there, but they'll wonder. Possibly, they've even heard I've been to Fieldfare. CT have a good Intelligence Unit. Although they'll try for a trace on you, the biog we built has several sweetly placed brick walls and go-nowhere mazes,' Esther said. 'You've spread the tale?'

'Sure,' Dean said. 'Liverpool, France, Italy, Ruislip, Preston. I've told them.'

'Not all at once.'

'I eked it, as rehearsed. Anecdotal. Like, "The police in Milan – too bloody tough and efficient, so I decided to quit Italy." That kind of thing. And they might say, "How, too bloody tough and efficient, Terry?"'

'And what do you answer?' Esther said.

'Well, obviously, I'd had that briefing on Milan before I

172

went into CT – a briefing on all the spots in my supposed past – Marseilles, Preston, Liverpool, Ruislip.'

'Stick exactly to what you were told,' Esther said.

'I do.'

'Nothing too damn graphic or specific,' Esther said. 'They can check these things, you know. CT will have connections in Italy, especially a wealth centre like Milan.'

'I wasn't given street names to quote or even districts – not for any of these places. Just "Milan" or "Ruislip".'

'That's all right,' Esther said. 'They'll notice the vagueness, maybe, but villains don't like talking over-thick details about their past, even to other villains. '

'I just say, "I was lucky to get out. I went to lie low, very fucking low, in Liverpool for months, and then a move to Preston, all under extremely changeable names, naturally. I'm not Terry in any of those places. Well, you wouldn't fucking expect it, would you!"'

'You and Superintendent Channing agreed some fine alternative names, didn't you – additional to Terry and our own coverall, Wally?' Esther said.

'"Klaus Nightingale", "Lance Vesty", "Hugo Maine-Sillett". I would have quite liked being a Lance, in, say, Marseilles. It's got something – glamour and barminess. I see Lance in very dark three-piece real wool suits, despite the Mediterranean heat, and a nose stud. Lance is one up on Wally, for sure.'

'Do they ask?' Esther said.

'What?'

'Which name you used where?' Esther said. 'Such as, "So, were you Lance Vesty when operating in Marseilles, Terry, and Hugo Maine-Sillett in Ruislip?" This could be awkward, if they go for a trace and can't get any confirmation that Lance Vesty ever villainized in Marseilles.'

'Not yet,' Dean said.

'Not yet what?' Esther said.

'As far as I know,' Dean replied.

'What as far as you know?' Esther said.

173

'As far as I know, they haven't attempted to tie one of the extra names to one of the places,' Dean said.

'What does that mean?' Esther said.

'What?' he said.

'"As far as I know." How *would* you know?' Esther said.

'Nobody's mentioned it,' Dean said.

'Nobody would, surely?' Esther replied.

'I sort of *feel* they haven't,' Dean said.

'"Sort of feel" it why?' Esther said.

'Yes, sort of feel it,' Dean said.

'I'm not sure I like this, the lack of curiosity about your background,' Esther said.

'When I say "not yet", my feeling is they would certainly do these CV checks abroad and in Preston and so on if they came to think I might be phoney, but at present they believe I'm all right,' Dean answered.

'Do they repeat things, or even write them down?' Esther said.

'Which things?'

'When you say you were Lance in Marseilles and Hugo Maine-Sillett in Ruislip –'

'Hugo Maine-Sillett in Preston. Klaus Nightingale in Ruislip,' Dean replied.

'When you tell them which you were where, do they act as if they want to keep the right name for the right place, so they can do their inquiries?' Esther said. 'This is what I was getting at – do they say each name and place several times, as if to get the pairings into their memory? Or possibly make a note?'

'I can see they might do that if they wondered about me,' Dean said. ' But my instinct is they don't.'

'Or someone getting you on to a hidden recorder?' Esther said.

'I do listen for any hints of that – whirring, clicking,' Dean said.

'Why? Did something make you think they might be recording?' Esther said.

'Just basic alertness,' Dean said.

'Devices these days don't whirr and click. There've been improvements, or we couldn't bug people ourselves,' Esther said.

'I'm pretty sure it's not happening,' Dean said.

She decided to move to other topics. She might unnerve him, otherwise. 'So, they let you loose on rag-tag-and-bobtail assignments first, and note how you do. Yes, the way I started.' Did she quote her own Out-loc chapter too loud and often? Maybe it signalled fear at committing Dean Martlew. Perhaps she had to keep reassuring him and herself that she knew undercover all through from both sides, wasn't shit-scared of it, and would get things right. Or as near right as undercover could be: not always *very* right at all. She *was* shit-scared of it. That's of late. Not as a practitioner back then, but as an impresario, now.

'You followed all the counter-tail drills on your way here, did you?' Esther said. She realized she might have changed the topic, but not the nervy tone. 'But of course you did. It will come automatically after Hilston.'

'Every second roundabout I did a double-back on,' Dean said. 'Nothing behind me. And I almost cracked the mirrors, staring so hard.'

'They'll know the roundabout trick, I expect,' Esther said.

'I expect they know *all* our tricks,' Dean said. 'I suppose the tricks themselves could be a giveaway. They're police tricks.'

'If you can think of some better ones use them,' Channing said. Dean had left his Renault on the other side of the hotel car park and then come on foot to the Rover.

'They do regular visits to the wharves,' he said. 'Ambrose and sidekicks.'

'Oh, yes. We monitor these trips,' Channing said at once. 'That was part of the running investigation. On the face of it, they check arrival state of cargo for clients. Authentic business. Cormax Turton are genuine factors, import-export agents. *Inter alia.* It's smart. An impeccable frontage.'

'Down twice or three times a week to Great Stanton, the Dunkley, Laker's Quay,' Dean said. 'It's always Ambrose – he's the constant – plus one or two mid-rank people, in his Lexus. I've got some names or nicknames: usually from Maurice Cadenne, Glen somebody, an Ivor Brain, and one known as Tertiary. Ivor Brain – spoken as "I've a brain," so maybe a joke alias. These assistants to Ambrose change about. I might get an opening. Something special's happening.'

'Glen Coupland,' Channing said. '"Tertiary" is Roderick Nile Layton, conceived on a package tour to Egypt. Cadenne used to be in shipping – knows a lot about cargo and the container game. Brain I've not heard of. New?'

'What special is happening?' Esther said.

'Yes, special,' Dean replied.

'To do with the docks?' Esther said.

'I'm trying to sort it out,' Dean said.

'What *kind* of special, then?' Esther said.

'It being to do with ships, you could call it a sea-change!' Dean said and had a big, comfortable laugh. He seemed cocky, in command, obviously a natural for three-way confidential briefings in car parks. Next stop, chair of a board meeting. She thought she might have been right to pick him, after all. He liked stringing out whatever it was he brought. Understandable, in Esther's view: he'd enjoy a spell of relaxed talk. Dean wouldn't have had much of that lately. She could recall the same kind of wind-down relief when she did undercover and occasionally reported back.

'Oh, yes, a sea-change!' he said. Esther's father, also, used to like repetitive gags. He thought a joke should do a full day's work, like waitresses or trawlermen.

'Get fucking on with it, would you, Sergeant?' Channing replied.

'Minor symptoms so far,' Dean said.

'Being?' Channing said.

'They're expecting trouble,' Dean said.

'In what sense?' Esther said.

'Arming in defence,' Dean said. 'But I suppose they're

176

always expecting trouble, to some degree. The trips to the wharves – they're not just sightseeing.'

'And not just legit business,' Channing said.

'A touch of sharp crisis now, though. Apparently.'

'In what sense, Dean?' Esther said.

'These minor symptoms. Pointers. Nothing clear.'

'That's how undercover works,' Esther said. Hell, there it was again – the drab, Oracle voice, Old Mother Knowall: *Been there, done that, got the commendation.*

'They're carrying handguns,' Dean said.

'To the wharves? Is that unusual?' Esther said.

'For the last couple of weeks,' Dean said. 'It's new.'

'How do you know?' Channing asked.

'Which?' Dean replied.

'Which what?' Channing said.

'Are you asking how do I know they're armed, sir, or, if they are, how do I know it's new?'

'Both,' Channing said.

'They've all got Glock 17, nine millimetre self-loaders,' Dean replied. 'Same as our armed response people.'

'You've seen these?' Channing said.

'It's been made standard,' Dean said. 'Anyone on this wharf duty with Ambrose draws a weapon and shoulder holster for as long as the job lasts. And Ambrose himself, naturally. A departure: policy at Cormax Turton is nobody carries a piece unless a specific job absolutely requires it. People have to get authorization.'

'Yes,' Channing said.

'Definitely no casual or routine packing. It's always a management decision.'

'Yes. But Ambrose *is* management,' Channing said. 'He OKs himself?'

'Ambrose would have to refer up to Cornelius Max in person, most likely,' Dean said. 'If he approves – and he obviously does or there'd have been no change . . . if he approves, it shows how worried they are. As far as it's con-venient and safe, Cornelius wants to take the firm out of gunplay. He reckons it's counter-productive. And maybe he's trying to move CT towards respectability.'

'But not very fast,' Channing said.

'What I mean is, Ambrose wouldn't want to go to Cornelius Max on guns unless it's serious,' Dean replied. 'Cornelius grows old, has his eyes and bad knees and knuckles to humour, and most probably can do without routine admin decisions, thank you – though, actually, this one isn't. Not routine, I mean. The opposite. And then Ambrose probably dislikes touting for permission to gun up. *I* would if I were Ambrose.'

'You're not,' Channing said.

'Humiliating – like a kid asking parents can he sleep over. "Please, *please*, Uncle Corn, may I stash a Glock?" Creepy. And, look, all main people at Cormax Turton are deep into self-image protection and projection now. They have to be ready for the leadership fray once Cornelius quits. Begging for a gun pass wouldn't do much for Ambrose's claims as next Guild emperor, if the word got around. Words do get around.' Dean nodded a couple of times, wowed by his own logic. Esther loved the confidence, as long as it didn't kill him.

'So, anyway,' he said, 'as I see things, what it adds up to, this fact – Ambrose wearing a weapon at the wharves, and having to clear this with Cornelius Max . . . what it adds up to is the dockside has suddenly turned perilous, *more* perilous.'

'This "fact" – is it in fact fact?' Channing said.

Esther was leaning forward from her seat in the back. The other two had slewed a bit to face her and each other. This obviously intense conversation might look strange from outside, but Esther still thought they were all right here. Plenty of vehicles cloistered them. They had a multi-coat, dark green Bentley worth about £200,000 on their immediate left and an Aston Martin next but one to the right. Most likely, their elderly owners had been arse-kicked by loving family into the seminar, 'Inheritance Tax – how to see your heirs all right while there's still time, you loaded bastard.' But, no, Cornelius wouldn't be here, though he might have a £200,000 Bentley. He probably didn't empathize with tax, any sort of tax. Esther tried to recall who said, 'Behind every great fortune is a great crime.' Conrad? Machiavelli? Hosea? The Lord Chief Justice? It would be a plural – crimes – for Cornelius. And he'd definitely decline to have them and/or the great fortune poked into by whippersnapper moolah gurus at the Millicent.

'I talk a bit off and on with the Cormax Turton armourer,' Dean said. 'He's pally. I think he accepts me as a colleague.'

'Felix?' Channing said. 'Felix Mortimer Bernard Glass.'

'"Moonscape", they call him, on account of his face skin. *We* call him.'

'You've got an understanding with the armourer?' Esther said.

'He's some sort of remote relation to one of the top people,' Dean replied.

'I don't have any note of that,' Channing said.

'On the Turton side,' Dean said.

'And he's willing to talk to you about Ambrose and a Glock?' Channing said.

'It's dicey for Ambrose and the others,' Dean replied. 'Bad if they're stopped and searched when carrying. It could happen. Three armed men together, like some violent job ahead. These are Glock 17s, i.e. seventeen rounds apiece. A threesome is big firepower. We – that's the police "we" – wouldn't care for it, would we? It could look like a conspiracy. Grave. And these days, and nights, at the wharves, they've got plentiful anti-terrorist precautions: patrols, round-ups, searches, random detaining. All wharves, everywhere, since 9/11. Yes, especially New York: on the waterfront is tough, but not as tough as a smuggled-in dirty bomb would be – what they call a "low-probability, high-consequence event". Very high-consequence, so do everything to make it low-probability.

'And here, too. Docks police are around Dunkley and the others, no let-up. Possibly MI5. There was a *Newsnight* feature about how easy it is to get into Britain by small boat from the Continent, and the precautions have been stepped up even more since. And who knows what's arriving in those interesting, sealed boxes brought by the bigger vessels? So, yes, security, security, around the wharves. Moonscape reckons Ambrose would never risk taking a gun there, unless the firm had some really bothersome intelligence that makes it unavoidable. I don't mean there's any terrorist link with Ambrose or Cormax Turton, but he and the other two might get caught by, like, accident in a protective sweep. Not intended but just as bad.'

'Tell us how you built this connection with the armourer,' Esther said. 'Sounds great, doesn't it, Richard?'

'Great,' Channing said.

'An armourer would see a lot,' Esther said.

'Very core,' Channing said.

'You think I'm being set up?' Dean replied.

He still sounded cocky, aggressive, not scared, and he moved slightly so he could give Esther face-to-face square on. He was plump-cheeked, blue-eyed, almost cherubic. Did he really look like a villainy career already spread over Liverpool, France, Ruislip, Preston, and dodging Milan's *polizia*? But, then, wasn't some big-wheel US crook called 'Baby Face Nelson'? That's what she'd told herself when picking Martlew ahead of Dill. 'Set up?' she said. 'Not necessarily, or even probably. But tell us how it happened, step by step.'

'Yes, step by step. Nothing pressured or forced,' Dean said. 'No rushing.'

'Good,' Esther said.

'Well, would I, would I? Am I dim? Suicidal?' He was shouting. Channing glanced about the car park. 'You're not going to pull me out because of this, are you? Are you? I think of it as true progress. Look, it's happened very ... like very normally ... like an ordinary bit of workplace comradeship: he admires my shooting, that's the start,' Dean said. '"Life-threatening", he describes it as. This is praise – equivalent to calling good surgery "life-saving".'

He brought his voice down. Perhaps he realized the yelling made him sound touchy, uncertain, as though he suddenly had some doubts about Moonscape's friendship himself. He needed to underline the easy, credible closeness of the buddydom.

Dean said: 'Moonscape will relax and reminisce. He used to be a soldier – recalls how a corporal instructor asked him and other recruits at the start of their firearms course, "What is the object of all weapon training?" They scratched about, muttering, trying for a sensible response, but the corporal cut across them. He recited the only answer allowed: "The object of all weapon training is to kill the enemy and not get killed." Moonscape's inherited philosophy. We go to the range together now and then. Actually, I fuck up a bit occasionally or he might think I'm police gun-trained. Not too many perfect scores.'

'And he gossips?' Esther said.

'He'll talk weapons. Only weapons, the way some people talk only food or sex. He's a technician. He enjoys that sort of professional chinwag. I can more or less keep up. He says Ambrose prefers this or that handgun, because of ... because of this or that. They had some debate before choosing the Glock. Felix recommended it. Ambrose thought too much plastic. But Moonscape said the police use them, so they've been well tested and proved OK. He bought six, new, of course. I sensed something strange here, but I couldn't spot what. So, I raised no questions, let him go on. We'll chew over all sorts of guns. He's an historian. I put in my pennyworth from what I know about pistols. I think I sound credible. This is general, not always to do with the immediate situation, but it helps things along.'

'Step by step,' Esther said.

'Right,' Dean said. 'Coming at what I'm really interested in from him, but coming at it out of what to him will seem just experts' gun gossip. Like, he's read an FBI paper on what's called "the myth of the one-shot-drop". Know it, ma'am? Moonscape and I chewed that over a few days ago. Its message – no single shot will put a man down, out

181

and harmless unless the brain is disrupted or the upper spinal column severed. So, it's bullet placement not calibre that's important. Size definitely doesn't matter here. And other fallacies are hammered – the "myth of the *proper* handgun" and "*proper* ammo". That Clint Eastwood/ Harry Callaghan reverence for the Magnum would be crap on this reckoning. I'd seen the paper a long time back, argued over it in a group, but, obviously, I didn't say so, because it was at Hilston. From the FBI National Academy, I think: tells officers how to survive these listed, stupid myths – rather vital if someone's coming at you and you're trying to stop him. We chatted about it – head as target, accuracy/distance ratios, two-handed, stiff-armed stance obligatory, when there's time. That kind of general, happy, urban battle prattle.'

'Excellent,' Esther said.

'But then, out of this, you see, we *do* reach something with a crucial bearing on now,' Dean replied. 'He thinks I'd be brill at "placement", and therefore the "one-shot-drop", whatever I was firing. A Moonscape laurel. I'm a talented warrior, a priceless, murderous find, and he found me.'

'So did Mr Channing,' Esther said.

'Absolutely,' Channing replied.

Dean said: 'Cormax Turton might be against guns as routine equipment, but they also know guns can be deeply necessary now and then, and, when they are, CT want them used with max effectivness, Cornelius Max effectiveness.'

'It figures,' Channing replied.

'And then yesterday,' Dean said, 'after some blasting away on the range, we're having a coffee in his little office – he's clean, of course, no drink or substances – and he says . . . well, it came out as more or less an aside, really . . . he switches back to those special-purchase Glocks, and mentions that Ambrose might be looking for someone like me – someone like me being someone who knows guns and can do a nice job with them – yes, Ambrose might be looking for someone like me because there's been a CT

Cabinet-level rethink on kit for the wharves. That's the phrase, "a rethink on kit for the wharves". He's not in the Cabinet, of course, but he'd hear about gun matters because . . . well, because it's his area and he has to arrange supplies.

'Again, I perk up, super-alert. But, again, I don't get what he means. I say, "What rethink, what kit, Felix?" I don't call him Moonscape to his face, though some will. Management do, but not Cornelius himself. He's very civil and old-style polite, unless things turn bad. "What kit?" Moonscape says. "Gun kit, the only kind I'd know about." "Rethink how?" I ask. "They'll carry," he says. "Don't they always?" I ask. "Terry, you know the CT rules. Guns for named jobs only," he says. "Aren't the wharves a named job?" I ask: I need to float the questions but not seem too daft and ignorant. "Yes, they are – now. That's what I'm saying. This is new," he tells me. "Why?" I ask. "Why?" he says. He sounds totally bamboozled. Lost. Defeated. Even insulted. The query's beyond the technical, you see. We'd be into strategy. He doesn't make guesses outside his expert, cordite corner. He despises what he'd regard as gab.'

'That's Felix,' Channing said.

'Well, we get back to his expert, cordite corner, and he's fine again,' Dean replied. 'He says next time we're on the range he'll help me correct a bit of what he calls "right side yaw". This will make my shot "placement" even better. He reckons a job with Ambrose would be good for me, and for Ambrose, because after the yaw's been therapied I could unquestionably see off anyone looking unhelpful and remain unhurt myself: the object of all weapon training. Maybe he's been asked by Ambrose to look out for someone capable. Confidentially, Moonscape thinks Cadenne and Tertiary are not gun naturals and although Coupland can do it all right, his heart's not there. It hasn't mattered previously. The wharf work wasn't about guns. But Ambrose has decided it might be from now on. Moonscape doesn't speak of Ivor Brain.' Dean had another laugh: 'I'd cultivated the "right side yaw", of course, so as not to look suspiciously perfect.'

'Yes, it all could be promising,' Channing said.

'Came out like an aside, you say – the suggestion about work for Ambrose?' Esther asked. 'That the word – "aside"? As if off the top of his head?'

It was dark in the car but she saw Dean frown. The executive pitch laughter seemed gone for good. He didn't start shouting again, though. Perhaps she'd done what she feared and begun to unsettle him with her wariness, her jumpiness. Some of that cocky confidence might have drifted away, momentarily. Maybe this was for the good. 'You think it's an act?' he said. 'You believe "as if" off the top of his head is *only* as if, but not really? I'm being led? You believe we should abandon undercover because I'm rumbled?'

Channing said: 'We've always assumed the cargo inspection rigmarole was a mask while they identified other desirable cargo. Cartons go missing. You mentioned *On the Waterfront*, Dean. Right. It's not New York, but we have our rackets. Some boxed freight items are damn valuable. Perfume in bulk. Electronic equipment. Vintage claret. Art. We and the docks police get convictions. We've never been able to tie any thefts to Cormax Turton, though.'

'Why I'm there – to make the link,' Dean said. He'd half recovered his bullishness?

'But take it gently,' Esther said. She disliked the film reference – a dark, ruthless, mawkish movie.

'Here's a possible, probable, scenario,' Martlew said. 'Ambrose and party identify cartons they want – not their clients' goods – no, not those pretext goods – but others they spot as juicy. This doesn't happen every time or it would be stupidly blatant. Now and then. Manifests stuck on these boxes are often vague, traditionally vague. They need interpreting. Maybe Cadenne is fly at that. So, occasionally, they move on a container or more than one – perhaps especially when they've had a sharp, bought whisper from abroad about what's inside some of the woodwork. They've most likely got dockside people paid to guide selected units to a wrong collection point. Wrong for the owners, not for Ambrose and CT. They're waiting. They come by car, but they've got a van on call. Two in the van, plus driver, one in the Lexus, chaperoning.'

'Could be,' Channing said.

'But maybe another firm – other firms – has/have cottoned on to what happens,' Dean replied. 'Wouldn't we expect that? They'd fancy the prospect. All the real work's been done, hasn't it: maybe costly foreign information, bribed dockers, then identifying, misdirecting, misdelivering? They decide to waylay Ambrose and his support, van and Lexus. Easy-peasy.'

'Classic hijack,' Esther said. 'Pinching what's been pinched. Nobody's going to complain to the police or supply the evidence, because the evidence would convict the complainant.'

'If *I* can see that sort of plot, the professionals can, can't they?' Dean said. 'And, on top of this, there are the normal hatreds of Ambrose and CT around for all sorts of old grievances. Think of Claud Seraph Bayfield. He's still a power, and no way a seraph, which is probably a let-down for his parents. Ambrose puts himself into very predictable spots at very predictable moments, and to date is accompanied by people who might know a bit about cargo, but not much about guns and minding. All an enemy has to do is discover berthing times at Laker or Dunkley or Great Stanton. Two gorgeous pluses at once could be on. Eliminate Ambrose and friends, and collect the prize load, whatever it is: they'd trust Ambrose's nice taste for that. The Seraph owes one to Ambrose and Palliative after their very capable combined op against him. Ambrose would do as openers.'

'It's possible,' Channing said.

'But now there's been a hint to Ambrose of possible ambush, or to someone in Cormax Turton,' Dean said. 'Yes, CT have an Intelligence Unit. It's headed by a clever old wig-wearing, garlic-chewing piece called, I think, Dane –'

'Sarah Lily Dane,' Channing said.

'What's the answer to a hint like that?'

'Consult Moonscape, you think?' Esther said.

'Then get Glocks,' Dean said. 'And possibly bring in someone who can offer one-shot-drops as the norm. *Moi.*'

'Sarah Lily Dane will be the one testing Dean's biog, will she, Richard – the Klaus, Lance, Hugo trail?' Esther said.

'It's probably watertight,' Dean said.

'We worked hard on it,' Esther said.

'I'm not going to shift straight away from right side yawing to constant bull's-eyes,' Dean replied.

'No, don't,' Esther said. 'Humbly take instruction.'

Channing said: 'We've been here long enough, ma'am.'

'Yes,' Esther said.

'I'll drive you to your car, Dean,' Channing said. 'Less exposed than a walk.'

'Why would they want to set me up, Mrs Davidson?' Dean said.

'I haven't said they do.'

'No, but –'

'Things are happening fast,' Esther replied.

'*Too* fast, you mean?' Dean said.

'Fast.'

'Maybe the eight months of nothing from the investigation makes us think that's normal pace,' Dean said.

He said 'us', out of tact, but must mean her. 'Perhaps,' Esther said. Or even, yes. Had she become ACC Plod?

'*You* think that *they* think I'm more likely to give myself away in a major job with them than as a small package pusher?' he said.

'I believe they very much want you to be OK – that is, through-and-through gifted crook, not two-timing, invasive cop,' Esther said. 'They'd like to think you a true one-shot-drop acquisition whose PhD thesis on "The Object of All Weapon Training" will be rewarded by Cambridge with acclaim, and which when applied in gang fights will put CT brilliantly ahead.'

'And I try to behave like that,' Dean said. 'Perhaps it's working. I'm on the way up.'

'Possibly. I don't question it,' Esther said.

'Excuse me, ma'am, but I think you do,' Dean said.

'Cormax Turton know that anyone infiltrating would aim to get to one of the top figures – Ambrose, Palliative, Cornelius himself. Maybe they'll wait to see if you really agitate for the Ambrose job now you've had a helping of bait from Moonscape.'

'You believe that's what it is, all it is – bait?' he said. 'You don't accept I've really got to Moonscape?' He sounded sad and hurt. He'd reject – struggle to reject – the idea that Moonscape might be fooling him. No, no, it was Dean had to fool Moonscape.

'Not every genuine villain would rush for a role where there's a bad ambush risk – plus the chance of getting stopped, searched and who knows what by security at the wharves,' Esther replied.

'Oh? I think most villains with any guts and appetite would,' Dean said. 'They're in a danger trade, anyway, and looking above all else for loot. There'd be more of that alongside Ambrose than in low-level substance dealing. And prospects would come with the new spot in the organization. It's bound to be a major career move – with still more loot.'

Esther was being told, was she, that she had chosen someone for his guts and appetite, among other goodies, and shouldn't go crumbly when these showed themselves in action? Fair? Probably. 'Crooked firms are not like the Brigade of Guards where people volunteer for sticky duties because that's what the Brigade of Guards and its sense of honour are about,' Esther said.

'I've got to take this sticky duty if it's put my way,' Dean said.

'But, to repeat, wait for it to be put your way,' Esther said. 'Don't shove yourself forward. Over-eagerness can betray. It smells.'

'And if Ambrose does opt for me?' Dean said.

'He's not someone you can turn down, anyway, not when you're working inside Cormax Turton,' Channing said. He drove over to the Renault. Dean transferred fast. Esther, watching him go, felt more fearful than ever. She could immaculately tabulate her pain. She liked tabulating:

1. Dean plainly had to take the Ambrose job if it came, or why was he undercover at all? A refusal – suppose Dean *could* refuse – would be like a boxer too frightened to get off his stool for the next round. But, of course, a boxer's corner and management could decide to throw the towel in, surrender *for* him, regardless of what he wanted. Should she close down this Out-location?

2. The job might be part of a test or trap, something contrived by Sarah Lily Dane because she couldn't get a clear biog of Terry Marshall-Perkins from Liverpool, France, Italy, Ruislip, Preston, where, so Terry Marshall-Perkins claimed, he wasn't Terry Marshall-Perkins, anyway. Despite what Moonscape said, Cadenne, Coupland and Tertiary could be quite competent with a Glock, as well as Ambrose personally: competent enough to do Terence Marshall-Perkins if they stopped believing this cover, suppose they ever *had* believed it. Did they want him at the wharves and near the sea, so they could lose his body: a sea-change, yes, and considerable – from life to death? That was not something she could suggest to Dean as warning, but she did wonder, and she wondered, too, whether he had thought of it. Perhaps the appetite and guts let him blank off the idea. It was called audacity, and might often be admirable. She didn't think she could afford very much of it, though. Of course, if Dean got washed up somewhere and it came to a trial, Ambrose and the others would never admit they went to the wharves armed. But they'd make sure, for extra flagrant innocence, that the bullet, bullets, in Dean did not come from a Glock 17. They'd assume he'd reported back to his managers with Moonscape's planted account of selecting the armament, and they'd think, Forensic.

3. Or, the job with Ambrose might, indeed, be genuine, and the risk of a hijack plot, therefore, also genuine, meaning:

(a) Dean could get killed in an ambush, and Esther up to her hairline in blame.

(b) Dean would *not* get killed but drop-shoot one or more attackers, making himself chargeable for the death(s) and Esther up to her hairline in blame. Judge and jury would not care for that kind of gang fight gunnery from a police officer, even though meant in a good cause; the good cause being concealment of his status as a police officer, and confirmation of his identity as Terry, the gang fighter.

(c) Or, there would, in fact, be *no* hijack attack because rival firms chickened when they heard Ambrose had a one-drop-shot marksman aboard who'd been taught the object of all weapon training, and had survived in Liverpool, France, Italy, Ruislip, Preston. Dean would then be implicated in a successful, possibly massive container theft, and Esther up to her hairline in blame.

4. Or, forget most of this. The wharves and cargo business might be of only marginal, incidental relevance or none. Possibly Ambrose was amassing an army of all the talents for The War Of Cormax Turton Succession when Cornelius at last gave in to his eyes, knees and knuckles. Dean said Moonscape came from the Turton branch of the family. Perhaps he'd be keen to help Ambrose with additional, dedicated personnel, especially someone skilled at the one-shot-drop, and who knew and endorsed the object of all weapon training.

Yes, she liked tabulating. Clearly, it seemed to put a system on things, even if there wasn't one, or only one about to break up. But some tabulating could terrify her. Did the sweet paragraphs and sub-paragraphs add up to an injunction to lift Dean Martlew out of Cormax Turton now and, also now, extinguish Terry Marshall-Perkins, The Quiff, Wally, Klaus Nightingale, Lance Vesty and Hugo Maine-Sillett, of Liverpool, France, Italy, Ruislip, Preston, not necessarily in that order? Driving to headquarters, Channing said over his shoulder to Esther in the back: 'It looks as if you were right, ma'am. Remarkable.'

'In what respect?'

'To prefer him. He reports tremendous advances – the well-founded chumminess with the armourer, if it's all right. Yes, if it's all right. Martlew's astonishingly gifted. He's made for undercover. Brilliant of you to deduce this when all you had was paperwork and an interview.'

'Not at all like that. We chose him together,' Esther said.

'Well, yes, absolutely, ma'am. I forgot.'

She let the sarcasm go. He probably needed to have a bite back occasionally. It would help his morale.

Channing said: 'Suppose the armourer is genuine. We've got three men on the docks now and then with guns and the possibility of a shoot-out next time a vessel brings in something especially desirable to one of the wharves. Well, obviously, ma'am, I'm wondering about our response.'

'In which respect?' Esther replied. Of course, she saw in which fucking respect, respects, but didn't want to dictate too blatantly how he had to play things, though she *would* certainly tell him how he had to play things. On the face of it, he ran the Dean Martlew operation. She had appointed him. He must be allowed to do the deciding, some of the deciding, some of the simpler deciding; and, if possible, made to think he did some of the major deciding, too. He deserved that much. He was a very good man. He was a very good man or she wouldn't have appointed him to this operation above Tesler. And if she'd appointed him, he must be allowed to do the deciding, some of the decid- ing . . . The logic of the sequence coerced her, almost.

'I could have Ambrose and his companions stopped and searched, apparently as part of routine security around the docks,' he said. 'That needn't point to Martlew as our

190

tipster. We're only doing to those three what's done to all sorts down there under anti-terrorism ways.'

'And if they're carrying?'

'If they're carrying we've got them on a gun possession charge, as starters,' Channing said.

'And if they're *not* carrying?'

'If they're not, we make our apologies and say times are exceptional and we hope they understand,' Channing said. 'We do that every day and night.'

'But if they're not carrying it means Moonscape was lying about the policy change, doesn't it?' Esther said.

'Well, yes, it *could* mean that.'

'What else could it mean?' Esther said. 'Why would he do it?'

'You think to snare Martlew?'

'Possible? Probable?'

'I'm to allow three men with about fifty rounds between them to behave as they want around the wharves?' Channing said.

'*Perhaps* with fifty-one rounds between them. There might be no rounds and no guns at all.'

'We *want* the three to be illegally carrying, do we, because that means Martlew is safe?'

'Undercover brings very tricky choices,' Esther replied.

'And we'd also like a full, firearms battle about swag, eventually, with deaths, would we, possibly including Martlew's, even if he *is* a one-shot-drop?'

'Undercover brings very tricky choices.'

'So we leave the situation as now?' Channing said.

'We're looking for a really big outcome here, Richard – the permanent wipe-out of Cormax Turton. It has to be more than just a nab for firearms possession. As retaliation goes, this is on the fireballing of Sodom and Gomorrah scale, not merely Job's boils. As I told Dean, we mustn't rush, mustn't move too early.'

'And it's too early?' Channing replied.

191

Chapter Sixteen

'Ladies and gentlemen of the jury, I will complete my summing-up this afternoon, then send you home and ask you to return and begin to discuss your verdict tomorrow morning. I have one or two important matters still to address. First, I would like to say something about the general topic of undercover policing, or Out-location, as it is officially known. This mode of detection – for that's what it is – can entail special difficulties and special dangers, but you should be clear that it is a wholly legitimate and, indeed, lawful practice, as long as the Out-located officer is able to keep a proper division between his police role on the one hand and, on the other, the alleged criminal activities of the group or gang he/she has been able to infiltrate. I feel it necessary to say this because the decep-tion necessarily involved in undercover work might strike some of you as shady and distasteful, and that could colour your views in this case. It must not be so. The trial is a murder trial and you are called upon to decide only whether Ambrose Tutte Turton is guilty of the murder of Dean Martlew. Your opinion of the kind of work being done by Detective Sergeant Martlew is not relevant one way or the other.

'You have heard police evidence that Out-location of Dean Martlew could be regarded as a last resort. What we might call conventional methods of detection had failed to establish any criminal element in the business activities of the Cormax Turton group. Nor has any criminal element been discovered subsequently. Until I ruled their argument not admissible, the Prosecution had begun to maintain that the death of Detective Sergeant Martlew was of a pattern with other cases where an Out-located officer had been murdered because of the eternal, powerful hatred and fear of undercover intrusion by a detective on a criminal gang. I should explain that I stopped the Prosecution from developing this point because it was merely general, not of proven application to this case; and, more importantly, because the argument rested on a presumption for which absolutely no evidence has been provided – I mean that Cormax Turton at any time conducted criminal operations.'

The judge giveth, the judge taketh away. During the few opening sentences in her words to the jury after lunch it had looked as though things might be turning favourable. That clear instruction to ditch any contempt for undercover work and simply decide the case for or against Ambrose Tutte Turton seemed to Esther magnificently, blatantly, intelligently helpful. Then, though, right after, came the stupid, bolshy insistence that, as far as the court knew, Cormax Turton was spotless, and, therefore, none of its management would have a reason to adopt the traditional violence of crook to spy. The phrase 'merely general' would glue itself into a jury's mind. 'Merely' had a nasty, dismissive, raw 'ee', foully lingering squeak to it. And, perhaps liable to stick even stronger, came what the judge called the presumption of criminality 'for which absolutely no evidence has been provided': so damn blunt and sweeping and categorical, you ugly sag-tits scrubber. That fucking 'absolutely'! Wholly intemperate. These jury members lived through the Iraq invasion and aftermath and would have become very wised up and unforgiving about presumptions for which absolutely no evidence was provided. Esther, Iles and Mr Martlew sat together in the public space after their pub visit, and when Esther glanced at Iles's face she saw he once more had his gaze on the judge, still trying by eye force to lean on her and make *her* lean the way he wanted. Perhaps, during those initial, strangely enlightened words about the validity of undercover, he thought his influence had clicked. But then, bang! – the let-down.

The judge turned to what she described as the 'painful detail of Detective Sergeant Martlew's death'. Medical evidence said that the detective had been killed by two gunshot wounds to the head from very close range, either of which would have been fatal. 'The Prosecution argued that this closeness suggested Detective Sergeant Martlew knew the murderer through social contact or work, possibly someone within the Cormax Turton organization, and therefore, perhaps – or in their view, probably – the accused. The Defence says that such point-blank use of a gun is typical of criminal executions and could have happened to Dean Martlew wherever he went after leaving Cormax Turton on 27 May.

'We have, of course, two opposed versions of Detective Sergeant Martlew's whereabouts between that date and 8 June. The Prosecution says he remained with Cormax Turton and was seen at Dunkley Wharf after 27 May. The Defence says he left for some undisclosed setting, among new people, and was murdered there: this would mean he did not, for his own reasons, wish to return to his police managers and colleagues. You will need to consider these contradictory speculations. They are central. Firearms experts whom we heard agreed that the two bullets came from the same weapon. They also agreed that the weapon was a nine millimetre Browning automatic pistol. This has never been found.

'You heard from police witnesses that a rescue party raided several Cormax Turton buildings when Detective Sergeant Martlew failed to keep to pre-planned communication arrangements. They were unable to find him. It is not disputed that all Cormax Turton personnel cooperated fully, even though police would not disclose the object of their search, in case, by their reckoning, this pinpointed the undercover officer and increased the danger to him at a location they had not discovered. Presumably, if police *had* mentioned whom they were looking for it would have been explained to officers that Marshall-Perkins, as Dean Martlew was known at CT, had left more than a week previously and therefore no longer worked at any of the group's sites. On the instructions of Mr Cornelius Max Turton, chairman, the companies waived their right to demand that police obtain a warrant before continuing the investigation. This cooperation you may decide is of some significance.

'A room-by-room search took place, seeking not only Detective Sergeant Martlew, but anything indicative of criminal activity. Many Cormax Turton members, including (a) the accused, (b) Mr Cornelius Max Turton, (c) Mr Nathan Garnet Ivan Crabtree, a director, and (d) other company heads, were also searched, with their consent. Again you will note this willingness to cooperate and judge its significance, if any. Nothing incriminating was found and no firearms. These searches occurred, of course, before the discovery of Detective Sergeant Martlew's body, so the police could not have been specifically looking for the Browning automatic. But the fact is that they found no firearms at all. There is, therefore, not a proven link between the death by gunshots of Detective Sergeant Martlew and the accused, or any other Cormax Turton director or employee.

'Such evidence as exists to do with the death of Detective Sergeant Martlew is what I have described earlier as "circumstantial". I defined such evidence for you at that point in my summing-up. I will now say only that circumstantial evidence may certainly be acceptable and valid, but rests to some degree upon deduction and inference, rather than on an eyewitness – or earwitness! – account of something that allegedly took place actually in the presence of that witness. It is for you, members of the jury, to decide what weight you give to any evidence put before you, but perhaps your combined opinion is especially valuable when dealing with circumstantial evidence.'

Esther glanced at the jury, got her eyes to inventory the faces, as much as it was possible to inventory twelve at that speed. No, she couldn't read a lot there: some showed symptoms of confusion; some of boredom; one of agonizing for a piss; two transmitted a sunny, brain-dead pretence at recognizing the gulf between various types of evidence. She saw nothing admirable and shrewd on the chops of any of them that she could interpret as, 'This fucker in the dock is guilty as charged, so let's cut the crap and finish.' No jury member gave her a comforting, inspired wink.

The judge spoke for another hour and a half about recovery of the body from the beach at Pastel Head. She recalled the conflicting evidence of two oceanographers on local currents, and their differing views of where Dean Martlew's corpse might have entered the water. *Sort that one out for us, would you, please, ladies and gentlemen of the jury, by the toss of a coin, or cutting a deck of cards, most probably?* Carefully, the judge went over the detailed medical evidence and dealt with the possibility of torture marks on the torso. Then she released the jury until next day.

Esther, Iles and Mr Martlew stood outside on the court steps again. Esther wondered whether such a repetition was stupidly provocative, rubbing Gerald's nose in it. She looked over James Martlew's shoulder towards Central Market but did not see Gerald. If he had a job at the Millicent it should be under way by now, perhaps. A bassoon would more than likely be a real novelty in tea dance numbers, bringing what Esther thought to be very appropriate mellowness to that kind of old folks' do. She hoped they'd give him plenty of blow bits because this would keep his mouth engaged and he'd have less time to slag off the music, the people around him – either dancing or playing – and the hotel for running such pathetic, wilfully quaint, foxtrot-and-dandruff sessions.

'I think I was rather surly to you previously, Mrs Davidson,' James Martlew said. 'I apologize.'

'I understood,' Esther said. 'I helped put your son in danger. I might be seen as part responsible for his death.'

'Surly. Hostile. I'd describe my attitude so. Unnecessary. Unhelpful to either of us. Unpardonable.'

'Don't feel bad,' she said.

'I admit I did feel resentment towards you. And then I read in the Press about the woman officer at East Stead,' he said. 'This was bound to change my perspective on things.'

'At East Stead? Amy Dill,' Esther said.

'Killed in that . . . well, almost casual way, ' he said. 'A seemingly small-scale incident. It made me realize that death can hit anyone from anywhere, and perhaps, especially, it can hit police officers. I shouldn't chuck blame around.'

'Too fucking right,' Iles replied.

'I think the report explained: she was called to a violent husband–wife row,' Esther said. 'Neighbours had phoned us.'

'Yes,' Martlew said.

'So sad that these frenzied fights between couples will happen, Mr Martlew,' she said.

'Sad, indeed.'

'And any police officer will tell you such situations can be bad – among the most dangerous we ever meet,' Esther said. 'Both parties are liable to turn on the supposed peacemaker. They see him/her as an intruder on a private battle. That's what seems to have happened here. Dill wasn't in uniform. We don't know whether this made things worse. She had picked up the call on her car radio while nearby. Sometimes the uniform will quieten people, scare them. Sometimes inflame them.'

'Awful,' Martlew said. He was solid-looking, of middle height. His long, clean, grey hair went to a pony-tail held in what seemed to be a red Post Office rubber band, and most likely changed at least weekly in case it perished and broke. He had a wide nose that looked just right for healthy breathing and unlively brown eyes behind rimless Himmler glasses: Esther had been reading a couple of illustrated books about the end of the Second World War recently. She felt massively grateful for Martlew's switch to friendliness.

But what would he make of it if she admitted that Amy Dill might have done the Cormax Turton Out-location, if Superintendent Channing had made the selection? That is, if he had been permitted to make the selection? If, if, if: if – infinitely recurring, as they said in maths. And, of course, he *should* have been permitted to make the selection, because in some respects, or even many, he ran the job. She had picked him to run it, in some respects, or even many. Dean Martlew would be alive if she hadn't overruled Channing.

Amy Dill, who became Mrs Patterson, might also have been alive if Esther hadn't overruled Channing. Possibly, Dill couldn't have responded to that domestic fracas call because she'd still have been Out-located with Cormax Turton. Yes, perhaps she would have handled the under-cover role better, more cleverly, more carefully, less pushily. Had Channing diagnosed early on during the selection period such qualities in her? His approval had not been simply a managerial lust matter, then? Would she have been shrewder and safer and more cautious than Dean Martlew in CT? From the first mention of Moonscape in the Millicent car park, Esther had wondered about that fucking chatty armourer. Did he see Terry Marshall-Perkins as a sucker, as well as a snoop? Had Moonscape from his experience somehow spotted Terry's police training in the way he handled a gun, despite Dean's clever-clever, delib-erate right-hand yaw on the range? He'd been picked by her mainly because he wasn't Amy Dill, but also because he could shoot. Had that skill killed him? Oh, God, God, the chaos built in to choices! Did they ever fully answer to reason? The unstoppable ifs could always clobber you, in retrospect. But Esther would certainly not offer James Martlew these thoughts, nor Iles. She longed to think her silence about the choice of Dean was meant to spare Mr Martlew any more pain. Of course, though, she realized it was to spare herself.

'And only recently married,' Martlew said.

'Dill? Yes,' Esther said.

'Tragic,' Martlew said.

'Immortality and weddings are different,' Iles said.

'Did either of you know her, I wonder?' Martlew said.

'That judge,' Iles replied, 'menopausally unhinged, poor judicial baggage? Do Lord Chancellors consider these things properly when they appoint?'

'Yet she's up to scratch enough to know the Americans call an unmarked police car a pastel, as in Pastel Head,' Esther said.

'Judges swot up underworld slang books to try to sound with it,' Iles said.

'The jury will convict,' Martlew said. 'I'm sure. I sense it.'

'Sense?' Iles said.

'Yes, like . . . well, like sense it,' Martlew said.

'They shoot judges, don't they,' Iles said, 'in Iraq? Why do we try to impose our blurred, civilized ways on that country?'

Mr Martlew said: 'Sense it in the sense that I sense –'

'I certainly think it was worth bringing the case,' Iles said. 'Well, obviously. The Crown Prosecution Service, incomprehensible as it might be, still wouldn't have let things go forward if there'd been no chance at all of doing Ambrose.'

'Three women are at the top now,' Esther said.

'Where?' Iles said.

'The CPS,' Esther said.

'There you are, then,' Iles said.

'What?' Esther said.

'Oh, yes,' Iles said.

Mr Martlew said: 'As I stated before lunch, the conviction of Ambrose Turton . . . the necessary, deserved, triumphant conviction of him that I sort of . . . sort of, well . . . sort of, yes, *sense* is coming to us will not bring my son, Dean, back, but nonetheless I –'

'Yes, you did state that,' Iles said. 'Stuff it now, as before, will you? So, then, he's not around.'

'Who?' Esther said.

'Your husband,' Iles said.

'Oh, Gerald?' Esther replied. 'No, I imagine it was just chance that he should have appeared at lunchtime.'

'And then at the pub window?' Iles said.

'Does he take an interest in your work, Mrs Davidson?' James Martlew asked.

'Well, yes,' Esther said. 'Supportive.'

'He loathes it, I expect,' Iles said, 'and is half demented through envy. More than half? It's understandable enough. Think of the crap he's been told to treat as worthwhile and wholesome throughout his life, the cajoled mutt. Not just César Franck. Brahms. Elgar. Copland. My God, though! It's bound to fray someone's poise. I never believed in the *male* menopause, menopoise, but then along comes Gerald.'

'Music encompasses him,' Esther said. 'Inhabits him. Possesses him. It's so wonderful to see his spiritual yet also workaday response to this or that piece.'

'Will the poisonous bastard behave properly later?' Iles replied. 'Shall I come home with you?'

Oh, the splendid possible double message here! *Shall I come home with you?* meaning, come home with her to take care that Gerald, in a pip-squeakish rage, didn't get brutal – another dangerous domestic fracas. Or, *Shall I come home with you? . . .* meaning . . . well, meaning what *Shall I come home with you?* would generally mean – Shall I come home with you, Esther, and we'll make our own kind of sweet music, not his, to compensate for Gerald's sad, accelerating slide into total self-pity, panic and prize oafishness? Of course, she thought for a while this sounded fine, and more than fine, much more – that is, the second interpretation, the 'own kind of sweet music' interpretation. She felt willing to gamble that Gerald would be involved at the Millicent for several hours yet, if that was where he'd been going. Not long ago his name amounted to something, and the hotel would surely want to get as much as they could from his very available bassoon now.

Esther found something grossly fanciable in Iles, though not to do with any of those personal features he'd probably think irresistible himself – say his haircut or lips or finery or legs: the only times she'd noted him break his stare at the judge in court was when he looked down to check on his legs, not simply refreshing his memory, but refreshing *himself* at once by enjoying new sight of them although trousered; and, yes, of course, subsequently stocking these in his memory, like a squirrel with winter nuts. But she loved the combination in Iles of majestic pride, wise offensiveness and devotion to the cause – the cause, now, being the police cause, and specifically the Dean Martlew undercover cause, and therefore her. True, as a sort of artist, Gerald also naturally had very notable pride and offensiveness, but it could not always be called *wise* offensiveness. True, also, Gerald showed devotion to a cause, but that cause was music, and, although this certainly added up to something worthwhile, for Gerald it did ultimately only come down to wind in a hollow stick, and this never entirely grabbed Esther.

Iles could surprise. For instance, she had noticed in the pub that he went at food with remarkable refinement, almost squeamishness, as if marooned for ages on a barren spit of the Madagascar coast and ultimately forced to eat shipmates or lemurs. Iles possessed admirable, attractive delicacy, often part disguised by a degree of brassiness in his public behaviour and words, or entirely disguised.

'I won't come back with you to Mrs Davidson's home,' James Martlew said.

'Oh, dear,' Iles replied.

'No,' Martlew said.

'Oh, dear,' Esther replied.

'You'll have private police matters to discuss,' Martlew said.

'Very likely,' Iles said.

'Yes,' Esther said.

'Will justice be seen to be done, do you think, Mrs Davidson?' Martlew said.

'That depends who's seeing it,' Iles replied.

'I believe in the British jury system,' Martlew said.

'I've met quite a few like you,' Iles said.

Esther's mobile phone rang. 'Davidson,' she replied. 'Oh.'

'Gerald?' she said.

'I thought it would be switched off,' Gerald said. 'In the court. I wanted to leave a message on voicemail.'

'The court's adjourned. What message?'

'Where are you then – on those damnable steps again, with them, flaunting it?' Gerald said.

'Flaunting what?' she said.

'In that disgusting way of yours,' he said.

'Are you calling from the Millicent?' she replied.

'Fuck the Millicent,' he said.

'Some hitch, dear?'

'Fuck the fucking Millicent,' he said.

'Are there people around where you're calling from? They'll overhear, dear.'

'Fuck them.'

'Did you play at the dance?'

'They don't want me,' he said.

'You played – did a rehearsal?'

'They said, graciously, "No thanks, old son," which being interpreted means, "You and your bloody bassoon, get lost. You don't suit the Millicent."'

'Suit in what respect?' Esther said.

'Suit.'

'It's not important, Gerald,' she replied. 'To some extent that kind of work is beneath you.'

'To which extent?'

'Yes, well beneath you,' Esther said.

'Exactly how far beneath?' Gerald said.

'There'll be other calls with work offers,' Esther said. 'Major orchestras. They probably don't realize you're available.'

'The assistant manager – no interest in me at all,' Gerald said.

'They're fools,' she said.

'All he can talk about is celebrities who've been to the hotel.'

'*You're* a celebrity,' Esther said.

'And "the prestige" of the damn place.'

'*You've* got prestige,' Esther said.

'Film people, TV people, that big-time local business guy, Cabinet ministers.'

'Which big-time local business guy?' Esther said.

'You know – Cornelius Max Turton.'

'Cornelius Turton was at a tea dance?'

'No, no, at some Inheritance Tax thing, with his team not long ago.'

'He's a crook,' Esther said.

'They don't care about that. He's a celeb. He's an important name. He's risqué but legal so far. As you know. The assistant manager says I'm a goner, a bit of yesterday. I don't fit into the image they want for the Millicent.'

'Tea dances are a bit of yesterday,' Esther said. 'The people who go to them are a bit of yesterday, or the day before.'

'I think they'll cut the tea dances, anyway. But, whatever, I'm out,' Gerald said. 'O. U. T. I'm ignored. Discarded. Treated lightly. And now you – *you'll* get a victory and professional *gloire* at the court, but what about me? Have you thought of that? Do you ever think of it? Am I marginal to the whole way of the world?'

'Has he got a dark green Bentley?' Esther replied.

'What? Who?'

'Cornelius Max Turton.'

'Would I know?' he said.

'Where are you?' she said.

'I suppose you're with those people, male, the ones on the steps, in the pub, filling your damn faces, you smiling your For fuck's sake, Gerald, fuck off smile. God, the heartlessness, the selfishness, the casual cruelty.'

'Are you at home?'

'Why would I be at home?' he said.

'After the Millicent.'

'After the disgrace of the Millicent? After gross scorn at the Millicent? What's at home for me?' he said. 'What companionship? What comfort? I'd be like that child in the old movie, home alone.' He cough-sobbed.

'Where, then?'

'I suppose you want to bring one of the fuckers back there, do you – thinking I'm busy at the Millicent? Or more than one. Yes, fuckers.'

'Say where you are, Gerald, please.'

'Where d'you think, for God's sake?'

'No, I can't tell. How would I?'

'Somewhere meaningful,' Gerald said.

'Well, yes, I expect so. Where?'

'Don't mess about,' he said. 'You must know.'

'I don't honestly.'

'Meaningful,' he replied.

'But where? Why did you want to leave voicemail?'

'Just to tidy things,' he said. 'I hope I'm always considerate, kindly.'

'Well, yes, definitely. What things?'

'I wished to do the decencies,' he said. 'A proper dignified, necessary goodbye.'

'Goodbye?'

'Listen,' he said.

'What?'

'Just listen,' he said.

She had the idea he held his cell phone away from his ear to pick up background noise. She heard waves breaking, probably on pebbles. 'Christ, he's at what we were talking about,' she said to Iles and James Martlew.

'Which?' Iles said.

'Pastel Head.'

'He's going to top himself?' Iles said. He began to descend the steps fast and went out of sight.

'Get it?' Gerald said.

'The sea?' she said.

'Of course the sodding sea,' Gerald said. 'It's all that concerns you, isn't it? His body on the beach. Your

204

obsession. You can't ever stop asking yourself if you were responsible. You don't care about anything else, such as me. Well, now you'll have another body on the beach to worry yourself over, won't you? This is my only way to reach out to you, Esther. Gone, gone are the moments when I might lick your significant wounds.'

'No,' she replied, strongly. 'No, Gerald.' At the foot of the steps, a Volvo appeared, Iles driving. Two blue lights flashed above the dashboard. He opened the pavement side rear door and the front passenger door.

'I'm coming to you, Gerald,' Esther yelled into the phone. 'Please wait.'

'Give my bassoon to a charity of your choice after cleaning,' he replied.

Esther and Mr Martlew ran down the steps. 'You here, Esther,' Iles said, pointing to the seat alongside him. 'It's bad form for me to emergency flash on someone else's ground, but they'll all recognize you and I'll look like the chauffeur.' Mr Martlew got into the back. The car pulled away.

'Can he swim?' Martlew said.

'It will be all right,' Iles said.

'There's a kind of . . . well, nobility . . . yes, nobility to it,' Martlew said.

'Bollocks,' Iles replied.

'He seeks status, even in death,' Martlew said.

'The arch jerk wanted to voicemail, so that when the terrible, end-it-all message was heard it would seem too late,' Iles said. 'Then, after a while, he'd turn up, all safe and grieved over, and the relief and reconciliation would be extra sweet, extra sexy. He's an artist. He stages things.'

When they reached the beach, they saw Gerald sitting there in his suit facing away, towards the breakers. He had scooped out a good little dent among the pebbles for comfort. His body was hunched forward, his arms folded. Even from the back, he looked like detritus. His bassoon, cased, lay near him. 'You are loved, Mr Davidson,' Iles shouted with big volume as they approached. 'Oh, so much loved.'

'These are the two, Esther,' Gerald said, turning his head. 'I saw them with you.'

'But you had to get off to something urgent in the Central Market, always a magnet,' Iles said.

'Mr Iles and Mr Martlew,' Esther said. 'This is my husband, Gerald Davidson, the musician. You've probably heard of him. Woodwind.'

'Martlew?' Gerald said. 'Related to the dead officer?'

'His father,' Martlew said.

Gerald bent his head forward further and, unfolding his arms, put up a hand to each side of his face. He seemed to cough-sob again. 'Oh, God, God, I'm so sorry. Forgive my fucking flippant carry-on, can you?' He kept his head bent.

'It's all right,' Mr Martlew said.

'Me, trivializing this beach,' Gerald said.

'This beach is a focus for all of us,' Martlew said.

'Yes,' Esther replied.

'Your wife – so devastated, so committed to you, Mr Davidson,' Iles said. 'An example to many. She *would* come to you at once, regardless.'

'Regardless of what?' Gerald replied.

Mr Martlew helped him to his feet and picked up the bassoon. He handed it to him. 'That unfeeling, philistine Millicent hotel,' Gerald said.

'I only got one side of the conversation but I imagine they have failed to value you properly,' Iles said. 'However, does that matter a fish's tit when your wife regards you with such lasting, unlimited esteem?'

'I don't hold it against you,' Gerald replied.

'What?' Iles said.

'On the steps. And the pub meal,' Gerald said. 'It's in the nature of things. I see that now.'

'Your wife hurried out of the pub to press you to join us, but you'd gone, unfortunately,' Iles said. 'We were all disappointed.'

'Considerably,' Mr Martlew said.

Iles drove them back to near the courthouse so they could pick up their own parked cars. On the way, Esther

206

asked: 'Cornelius Max Turton at the hotel with a team, you said, did you, Gerald?'

'Family, minders,' Gerald said. 'All that bodyguard stuff really excited this pathetic assistant manager – continually checking the building and the car park. "Power." "Dark glamour", he called it, essential for the Millicent's "changing profile". That's why they'll most likely kill the tea dances.'

Esther tried to remember if she'd noticed people moving about the Millicent car park that evening – not just walking to or from their vehicle, but checking who might be lurking there, or who might be holding a three-way meeting. Maybe she should have had a full squint to make sure nobody was lying low and watching in the Bentley. Or the Aston Martin. Or . . . you name it.

'I think a really quiet evening now, Gerald,' Iles said. 'Rest. You've had a bellyful of stress, though you come out of it looking wholly unruffled, bow-tie brilliantly stable, your complexion almost normalized by sea air. Yes, I do recommend a period of quietness and rest. It would trouble me badly if I ever heard you'd been bully-boying, you dismal fucking freak.'

Chapter Seventeen

But, of course, when the rescue group had finally gone into Cormax Turton for Dean Martlew, Esther did not – could not – accompany them at once, though she'd longed to: high rank disqualified again. Assistant Chiefs had to stand back. Assistant Chiefs did not do raids, only organized the people, method and apparatus for raids. Overview. On screen Esther monitored things from a proper, executive distance in her suite: the Control Room relayed running, search-team reports to her, and she followed the operation's progress via data-bank pictures and detailed architectural drawings, inside and out, of Cormax Turton's main sites. Progress? Non-progress.

The reports were graphic, thorough, regular, and hopelessly, sickeningly, devoid of Dean Martlew, or traces of Dean Martlew, so far. Although the stand-by teams had known him only as Wally until the call to move came, this unit would have by now opened the sealed orders and found pictures of him, his true name, and cover identity, Terence Marshall-Perkins. But, naturally, they would not disclose at Cormax Turton who it was they wanted – not under any of his tags: or not disclose it until desperation point, and probably then accompanied by the thousand pounds.

If the failure to find him, or pointers to him, continued till the end despite the bribe, Esther recognized that a lot of damned harsh publicity might follow. Would Cormax Turton turn awkward? The Guild could reasonably complain they had been subjected to wrongful, unexplained rough treatment by thug police of both sexes. God, it might look nearly as absurd as that massive, futile, anti-terrorist invasion by the Met of a house in North London; though, at least, nobody at CT had been shot, as *did* happen in London. Or nobody at CT had been shot *yet*. Esther decided it would be OK for her to go to one of the main sites under search after, say, an hour, and wait somewhere near, observe events, but not actually enter any CT building or ground. Overview.

Perhaps she'd order the mobile Incident Room there and use it as a base. She'd go uniformed. Top brass had to show it backed the onslaught, even if she couldn't take part, and even if it went nowhere and produced nothing. Maybe especially if it went nowhere and produced nothing. Somebody must carry the can. No, not somebody – *she* must. ACC: Arsehole, Carry the Can. The media would swarm. You couldn't run a blitz programme like this without word getting about. It was unreasonable to expect the unit inspector to, first, lead the pry, then, as a no-win extra, take hostile Press questions and talk safe platitudes to television and radio news. Anyway, the inspector could have only a limited idea of why he/she was scouring Cormax Turton with a thousand pounds in reserve. Naturally, reporters would spot the likely resemblance to that fabulous Met shambles. They loved recording gargantuan police flops. It showed journalists weren't muzzled, cowed, or slaves to official spin. They'd squeeze the laptop thesaurus for equals to 'bungled', 'heavy-handed', 'unprovoked', so they could rave on without repeats. 'Hard-hitting' – how their training manuals categorized this style.

And, unless Dean Martlew were successfully salvaged, Esther might agree that 'bungled' and 'heavy-handed' could be about right, and some hard-hitting justified, hard-hitting of her: ACC. But 'unprovoked'? The Out-location itself had definitely been provoked – brought on by Cormax Turton's disgustingly long-time, brilliant, nauseating, masterful, insolent skill at appearing through-and-through innocent. And the attempted rescue of Martlew had also been provoked. Esther, in that way she liked, could tabulate how:

1. her certainty that Cormax Turton was profoundly and utterly crooked;
2. her fear Cormax Turton would slaughter an undercover cop, because
3. the undercover cop might have collected evidence to prove – and prove solidly enough for a court – prove that Cormax Turton was, yes, in fact, profoundly and utterly crooked and not through-and-through innocent at all.

The Chief came in. Esther pointed on the screen to the picture of a Cormax Turton warehouse used in the sea cargo business, where the latest search report came from. 'Dud?' he said.

'It's going well so far. They've got quite a bit to look at yet, sir,' she said.

'Dud?' he replied.

The Control Room spoke on the intercom. Esther changed the screen image and pointed again. 'Where do they come from?' the Chief said.

'What?'

'All these photographs and drawings.'

'We've amassed them over a period,' Esther said.

'Secretly amassed them?'

'It's important to keep an eye on how the Guild spreads.'

'Are we all right with the data protection legalities?'

'Façades are in the public domain for photographing, sir. Think of Buckingham Palace.'

'These aren't just façades.'

'The internal visuals help give a fuller idea of the buildings,' Esther replied. 'Necessary for a search.'

'But obtained how?'

'Yes, it took a while,' Esther said.

'What do *they* say about him?' the Chief asked.

'Cormax Turton? What do Cormax Turton say about

where Martlew is? Oh, we can't tell them the search object. He might be still around on any of a dozen bits of CT property, his cover intact, and this would blow him, finish him. For the same reason we can't yet try the thousand bribe.'

'You still hope he's all right?'

'We've found nothing to say he's not.'

'Right. But *if* for dark reasons he's not they'll know who the search object is, won't they?'

'Probably, yes.'

'And they'll have got rid.'

'That's on the cards. We can't risk telling them at this point, though, why we're there.'

'Which point?'

'While he might still be on CT premises, in his role, OK, and accepted as Terence Marshall-Perkins, marksman.'

'Wouldn't he have been in touch, if that were so? He failed to meet his timetable, didn't he? Why we went in.'

'There might be some snag – something not dangerous but a nuisance, stopping him.'

'Did your alarm system allow for that?'

'For some delay, yes. But limited.'

'It's all so vague, so chancy.'

'As far as is possible I try to make it neither of those, sir.'

'Yes, I'm sure, but how far is that?'

'How far is what, sir?'

'How far is it possible?'

'We have the timetable, plus rehearsed procedures for all potential developments.'

'So what do you do if you find him, and he's all right, and still accepted as Marshall-Perkins?'

'That's for the search leader's operational judgement.'

'How?'

'If everything looks fine, and if Martlew gives no signs of special anxiety, the search unit pretend they're looking for something else and move on.'

'Cormax Turton will believe that?' he asked.

'They might.'

'What something else?' the Chief said.

'We don't have to disclose what. But there've been inter-firm fights with injuries and deaths – at the end of 2004. We still have active files on them. So, possibly something to do with those.'

'And you'd leave him there?'

'If that looks safe to the search leader. Martlew wouldn't want to be pulled unless he saw real trouble. He's by nature determined and calm. It's taken a long time to implant him. And he's done excellently at establishing himself there. A shame to put it all at hazard if there's no need.' She knew the Chief liked 'at hazard' as a phrase. She'd heard him several times warn against putting achievements at hazard.

'So, what's your feeling, Esther?'

'In which respect?'

'Could he be already finished?'

Yes, of course he could be already fucking finished, but the bluntness of the question knocked her hard. She gestured towards the screen: 'The search is very careful, very skilled, very systematic. I have to wait on that, sir.'

'The search confidently aims to find him alive?'

'Aims to find him alive, yes,' Esther replied. 'That's its *raison d'être*.'

'And bring him out?'

'If appropriate.'

'What would make it appropriate?'

'If he appears to be in danger. This would mean that, in any case, the undercover operation's no longer viable.'

'He's always in danger, isn't he? It's the nature of under-cover. You'll know. You've done it.'

'If the danger seems exceptional and immediate,' Esther said. 'Actually meeting our search people he'd be able to signal somehow whether that's so.'

'And CT cooperate with us on this wholly unprovoked rummage?' The Chief went in for all kinds of phrases, some given continual use, some seemingly spontaneous and requiring odd vocabulary.

'I don't think I'd say "unprovoked", sir.'

'No, I suppose you wouldn't.'

'I'd say unavoidable.'

'Yes, I suppose you would. Anyway, they cooperate?'

'Yes,' Esther said.

'Entirely?'

'Apparently, sir.'

'God. Does it mean they were expecting us, and made sure we find nothing shady? They come out of it cleaner than clean, and therefore stronger? The cost of error?'

'We don't know what it means, sir.'

'No, we don't, do we?'

'Sir?'

'Perhaps matters are genuinely as they appear,' the Chief said. 'All right, Cornelius has done time, yes, was unquestionably a serious villain. But it's conceivable he's turned legit, isn't it? Isn't it, Esther? Crooks do. The firms might now be what they've always successfully pretended – lawful.'

'I wouldn't say so.'

'No, *you* wouldn't.'

'The firms are rotten – clever rotten, but rotten, and their cleverness makes them more rotten.'

'I remember Cornelius's rage when Brent Holywell Crabtree got his quarter-page obit in *The Times* – told his people to buy up and destroy all the copies locally. What do you make of that, Esther?'

'Mad envy. He was afraid he might not rate for the same treatment himself. So, by suppressing that issue here he pretends Brent Holywell Crabtree didn't get the treatment, either. But all the rest of the country would see the paper and so would early birds to shops in this area. Why I say mad. Ineffectual.'

'Yes, exactly, envy. He sees that kind of coverage in a major paper as giving social repute, Esther. Perhaps Cornelius had begun to crave that, and craves it even more now – he's ancient, isn't he? An indicator of what drives him these days? He's changed? Deathbed conversion?'

'The obituary referred to Crabtree as a tireless, cold villain. It was the scale and glow of his evil that interested the paper, sir. Yes, social repute, but not the sort anyone sane would want.'

'Just the same, to Cornelius *Times* coverage might show Brent Crabtree had moved, half moved, into respectability, and this had been recognized.'

'Cornelius is –'

'I'm saying only that we have to treat him respectfully. We have nothing criminal against him.'

The Control Room interrupted. She and the Chief listened. Then, Esther brought plans of an office block on to the screen. 'This could be a likely spot.'

The Chief didn't give it much attention, though. He said: 'Do you know, not long ago I went to a meeting at the Millicent on ways to avoid Inheritance Tax, entirely legal ways, of course. One has to consider these things in good time. Perhaps you and Gerald have already done so. There's the value of one's house, one's retirement lump sum, and, in your case, Gerald possibly into star earnings as a performer. I gather he's wonderfully gifted. Well, that's by the way. But who was there, do you think?'

'Not Cornelius Max Turton?'

'Cornelius Max Turton, plus family members, and heavies patrolling inside and out,' the Chief said. 'As a matter of fact, I saw him arrive – two cars, one a new, green Bentley, the other a people carrier with his muscle. He looks very dodgy on his legs, but still in charge, and, admittedly, still with mobster protection around him. It doesn't cancel the fact, though, that this is the head of Cormax Turton behaving like any right and proper member of the bourgeoisie might behave – myself, for instance. Possibly *your*self and Gerald. The implication of the Millicent trip is that Cornelius acknowledges the right and – maybe more important – admits the *ability* of the State to tax him and his, but will seek above-board means to reduce that levy after his death. This is a notable development. It's beyond what we might call acceptance of his duty as a citizen; rather the wish to establish on a legal basis those coming after him.

'The thinking possibly touches not just Cornelius but Ambrose, Palliative, the whole crew. In response, I feel we have to show Cornelius decent and due regard. Perhaps his firms *were* bent previously. But has he somehow achieved a makeover? Almost always in villains we see a yearning for the good. I don't think I'd wish to be a police officer if I didn't believe in this worthwhile impulse, an impulse admittedly often concealed, even suppressed, Our work would be dismally negative.'

'He might have had one of our people tortured, slaughtered and dumped in the sea.'

'Might. We're without anything like proof.'

'To date.'

'To date is where we're at, Esther. You say yourself that Martlew is possibly still all right, his role in CT as good as ever.'

'Cornelius runs immensely valuable freight theft, and county networks hard and soft drugs, a turnover up with ICI's,' she replied. 'The Guild kills people when necessary – when considered necessary by them.'

'Again, unproven.'

'To date. We work at it.'

'Work tactfully, then. All right, we're in there now and searching so my concerns are too late, but I trust it's done . . . done . . . well . . . decorously.'

'Decorous above all was what I told them to be, sir. Decorousness figured as theme of many briefings. Any who didn't know the word, I offered to tutor.'

The Chief said: 'Do you know that on its functions board the Millicent advertised tea dances, with live music? A pleasant, rather comforting, reminder of more *decorous* old ways?'

'The Millicent is very go-ahead. I think I'd heard about the Inheritance Tax pow-wow. But tea dances? Wow!' Esther replied.

The Control Room gave another search location. It was the Cormax Turton firearms range. Esther brought up the picture. 'Shooting's one of the leisure activities CT offer personnel,' Esther said. 'To be expected.'

It was an indoor range, at the rear of the main office block, wide enough for three target lanes. The Control Room said: 'Nobody about there except for Felix Glass who coaches people on the use of handguns. Likes Glocks, apparently. Conversational. Inspector i/c the search group wonders if this might be the one to try the bribe on, if it comes to that.'

'A reasonable idea,' Esther said to the Chief. 'I know Dean Martlew has talked to the armourer, developed a kind of friendship, even.'

'And trustworthy?'

'That's something else, of course.'

'Do we have any notion of what might have given our man away, assuming he has been?' the Chief said.

'Dean's very cautious in all his work with CT.'

'Cautious how?'

'Yes, exceptionally cautious.'

'I don't get how someone undercover *can* be cautious,' the Chief said. 'Obviously, he/she has to act the part, but cautious?'

'He saw the need, without Channing or myself having to preach.'

'Might *over*-caution be noticeable?'

'Sometimes you get impulsive people volunteering for Out-location,' Esther replied.

'But you'd say Martlew was the best choice for the role?' the Chief asked. 'You and Channing agreed?'

'Certainly.'

'Why Channing, not Simon Telser?'

'A feeling.'

'What feeling?'

'Yes, a feeling. Channing was hostile to the project, considered it too dangerous. I knew he'd expect problems, and be ready for them.'

'I think you were right.'

'Possibly I was, but perhaps the problems are beyond him, and beyond me.'

The Chief left. Esther sat for another half-hour following the search through Control Room's reports and the visuals. Then she drove down to the last-mentioned site. It was yet another of those grey-stone, spacious Victorian buildings which, say, a hundred and thirty years ago had been someone's private mansion, possibly, like Fieldfare, with its own park, but then built around and adapted to offices. CT had added the range in excellently matching stone at the rear. Esther abandoned her plan of asking for the mobile Incident Room to be sent. It would have a driver and staff. She decided she wanted to watch alone. Watch what? Not much. Probably less. She'd prefer to be without Incident Room people while she witnessed this – the nothingness.

In fact, though, it was not totally nothing. After she'd been sitting there for three-quarters of an hour, Cornelius Max Turton came out from the main entrance and walked slowly towards her, not asking too much from his knees, yet using no stick. He wore a dark double-breasted, pin-striped suit, a red and white baseball cap and red and white training shoes. He put on a very authentic smile. She thought it signalled welcome and confidence in their equal status, hers and his. His eyes were blue, lively but cheerless, the kind that might see through Out-loc cover, especially if someone like that sod Moonscape had given him a hint. She knew Cornelius had had trouble with his eyes lately, but they looked healthy enough now, just intimidating and unjumpy. He actually spoke about them. Ambrose and Palliative were with him, though a little way behind and to his left. Dossier pictures of all three needed updating. Ambrose had put on a few kilos.

Cornelius said: 'I told them it was you, Mrs Davidson, but these colleagues wouldn't have it, despite their younger peepers. However, however . . . I suppose that in a way I was cheating – using a special advantage. Yes, I knew from deducing over many months, even, possibly, years, the kind of person you must be. True, I've seen pictures of you, in the Press and on television, but it's not that. After all, Ambrose and Palliative might also have seen them. No, I've had the time and, I might say, the wish to guess from your actions as ACC what you must be like as a person. Some might say it's easy to deduce this because you are an Assistant Chief and therefore fit the eternal Assistant Chief pattern. I don't go along with that. Of course, these boys are too busy with work and their social lives to give much effort to wondering about you. It's a fault in them, disrespectful to you, perhaps, but understandable. Maturity of outlook can't be rushed.

'Myself, I know you are of a type, Mrs Davidson, who will see things through – I mean *personally* see them through to the end. Under the bludgeonings of fate your head is bloody but unbowed. For instance, this visit by your people today: you are not one to leave subordinates to get on with it and give no presence yourself. It is creditable that you wish to be on the as it were spot. Do you know, a celebrated picture comes into my mind. It is of Mr Winston Churchill in 1911, and then Home Secretary, actually standing with armed police taking part in the London, Sidney Street siege. Now, I don't suggest that the visit to our establishments is anything like as exciting or, indeed, dangerous as that episode involving Peter the Painter and his criminal gunmen all those years ago. And, of course, our companies are entirely lawful and in no way resemble that wild gang. No, it is the need you feel, the obligation you feel, to get to what would be called, I suppose, the nitty-gritty of the situation – this is what puts me in mind of Churchill. And, because I would be *expecting* someone of your "hands-on" character to appear, it's perhaps natural that I should spot you, though Ambrose and Palliative failed – not merely failed, but laughed at me, told me I was mistaken.

'They'll be rather ashamed of themselves now, believe me. I tell them it's Assistant Chief Constable Davidson and they say something like, "Why would she come here in

person to witness in person a fiasco she in person produced?" – meaning the barren search for whatever,
whomever, it might be: nobody has informed us. And I tell
them it is *because* it is such a fiasco that you will insist on
coming here. "It is *her* fiasco," I point out, "enirely hers,
and the ACC is not one to let others take the mockery and
condemnation for this absurd mess-up," as it will surely
turn out to be. We cooperate – willingly, even enthusiastically cooperate – though given no indication of what we
are cooperating *with*. Naturally we note that, as in the
Churchill picture, many of your people are armed – a real
Glock festival – so we can hardly regard the visit as casual
or friendly. If only we had some clue as to the purpose we
might be able to assist even better.'

'They're very programmed, seem to know all the buildings and surrounds well,' Ambrose said.

'This I would have forecast,' Cornelius replied. 'It would
be in line with those deductions about Mrs Davidson's
psychology that I mentioned earlier. Excellent preparation
will be a feature of any project she has charge of.'

'There must be a lot of info about the CT properties,
internal and ex, stored somewhere,' Ambrose said.

Esther had opened the passenger window of her car and
Ambrose and Cornelius were crouched there, talking to
her. Nathan Garnet Ivan Crabtree – Palliative – stood
behind them on the pavement, apparently listening to
what passed, but not bending to talk. He was thin, a bit
hatchet-faced and very nimble-looking. Ambrose did carry
the spare weight, and had rounded, softer features and a
rosy, smooth complexion, though he'd be into his forties,
a few years older than Palliative.

'We wondered if you'd like to come in and wait for them
to finish, Mrs Davidson,' Cornelius said. 'A cup of tea. That
wouldn't rate as accepting favours, would it? This isn't an
ideal way of talking. I don't suppose you're used to car-
based discussions.'

'Well, thanks,' Esther said, 'but I'm due back at the office
now. This was only a routine trip, you know.'

'For their morale,' Cornelius replied. 'You'd be very concerned about that, I'm sure. I mean, when they find nothing – and I say again, not that we know what they're trying to find anyway.'

No? No? *I don't suppose you're used to car-based discussions.* Where did that come from? A Millicent echo? 'Cheers, then,' Esther said. She wound up the window and joined the traffic. When she looked in the mirror, she saw the three of them waving, Palliative the most ardently, as if afraid he might be thought churlish for not talking, or because Cornelius had told him he might be. One of the things about Cornelius was he obviously went in for manners. She wished she'd had a camera with her to do a current photograph of Cornelius and Ambrose framed like that by the open car window. The baseball cap gave Cornelius quite a touch of trendiness.

Chapter Eighteen

Esther, sitting at the breakfast table, worked through the main section of *The Times* to the right page. Gerald came in, glanced at it for a few minutes over her shoulder before taking his place opposite and pouring himself some tomato juice. He reached across for the newspaper's separate Travel Supplement.

Esther read:

CORNELIUS MAX TURTON

Cornelius Turton, who has died aged eighty-four, was once the uncontrollably powerful and autocratic head of a group of companies eventually proved to be the biggest British criminal organization outside London. 'The Guild', as the group was sometimes known, ran drug trafficking on an enormous scale and dockyard freight theft. From 1986 until 2007, the Guild was able successfully to masquerade as a reputable commercial enterprise based, apparently, on legitimate trading as shipping and cargo agents, and as couriers, and on property development. It was said that, at the height of its crooked success, Mafia chiefs came deferentially to visit Cornelius Turton in his stately Victorian office headquarters for tips on how to create credible lawful 'fronts' on out-and-out criminal firms. Turton was a learned devotee of Georgian and Victorian architecture and an active conservationist except, as one associate said, of enemies.

Local police found it impossible to investigate the Cormax Turton Guild effectively by conventional methods of detection and finally decided to put in an officer under cover to gain incriminating evidence. It was as a result of this tactic that Cormax Turton became for a while of nationwide interest. Ambrose Tutte Turton, a nephew of Cornelius and one of the Guild's directors, was accused of the murder of the undercover officer, Detective Sergeant Dean Martlew, after discovering his real identity. But juries twice failed to reach a verdict and Ambrose was formally acquitted. A suggestion of police perjury was not substantiated.

When Ambrose returned to the companies, Cornelius, who had been suffering from knee and other health problems, began to withdraw from Guild leadership. This led directly to a conflict between Ambrose and Nathan Crabtree (ironic nickname, Palliative), a relation of Cornelius through marriage, and also a Guild director. They jointly ran many activities of the Guild from late 2004. But each sought the full leadership role and each saw himself as Cornelius's proper successor. This antagonism was aggravated by Palliative's claim that Ambrose had deliberately left him exposed during a gang battle in 2004, hoping in this way to clear the route to the top of the Guild. Rumour about how Cornelius proposed disposing of his fortune after death following specialist financial advice increased antagonisms between Ambrose and Palliative Crabtree.

Late last year, Ambrose deliberately shot and killed Palliative while the two practised with handguns on the Cormax Turton private firearms range. Eighteen months after his acquittal in the Dean Martlew case, Ambrose was convicted of Palliative's murder and jailed for a minimum of twenty years. Cornelius never altogether recovered from the shock of these events and his already poor health grew worse. At the trial of Ambrose for the Palliative murder, Felix Glass, an armourer from the Guild, accused of providing the murder weapon, turned Queen's evidence and said that, in fact, Palliative had murdered Detective Sergeant Dean Martlew because Palliative thought Ambrose was gathering a private band to help him take over Cormax Turton and had recruited Martlew, a noted

marksman, to this cabal under the pretext that cargo con-
signments needed special protection.

    In his later months, following the loss of Ambrose and
Palliative to the companies, Cornelius had to watch the
Guild disintegrate. For some time before his death, it was
no longer a force, commercially or criminally. He had cer-
tain lifelong interests to occupy him in his later months and
years. He loved to read nineteenth- and twentieth-century
history, and was an expert on the life of Winston Churchill.
He also studied minor Victorian poets such as W. E.
Henley. Cornelius Turton was well known for magnifi-
cently polished manners, except when business matters
required viciousness. During the Guild's most prosperous
years he could exercise his taste in cars and would drive
only state-of-the-art Bentleys. It became one of his most
keenly held ambitions to earn an obituary in The Times,
and he would have been pleased to know he was considered
significant enough to merit these words, regardless of what
they say about his arrant gangsterism. He married Jane
Closse in 1946. She and two daughters survive him.

Esther put the newspaper down. 'Do you think we
should do something about avoidance of Inheritance Tax,
darling?' she said. 'Even though we benefit from the new
exemption level, there's the value of the house and
my retirement lump sum. Plus, when you get back to
orchestral starring work you'll pile up capital. I have nieces
to think of, and you, your cousin. The Millicent puts on
advisory seminars.'

    'I told *you* that, an age ago,' Gerald snarled. 'Do you
think I'd go back to that shit-hole after the way they
treated me?'

    'That wasn't you as a man of potential wealth. That was
you as a bassoonist.'

    'I *am* a bassoonist, you dim prat.'

    He stood and she thought he might move around the
table to her. 'Gerald, love, I don't want any violence or

wound sucking, not exactly now. I have to look all right for this conference in Hull.'

'Do I care what you want?'

'Yes, ultimately I really think you do.'

'How ultimately? I think you love attending such damn orgies alone.' But he sat down again. 'Well, I think *I'll* go somewhere solo. I've been reading about Kashmir. And Tasmania.'

'This trip of mine is only work – the way *you* used to go off on orchestral tours, and will again.'

'My God, a complete week at Hull on "What next for multiculturalism: a police strategy". That's what you said it is, didn't you? Who cooks up that kind of thing?'

'You'll be fine, Gerald. The fridge is full. Stay away from Pastel Head, won't you? Please. So corny.'

'And will *you* be fine? Of course you will. What do you mean, you have to look all right? Is that sly slob Iles there? You'll be able to celebrate your triumph, won't you?' He nodded towards the account of deaths and jail in *The Times*. 'Damn disgusting rapport with him. Did you notice his Adam's apple? How couldn't you?'

'Some conferences Iles is absent from,' she replied.

1